The Cha-cha Affair

Lynne E. Marino

ALL RIGHTS RESERVED

Publisher's Note:

This is a work of fiction. All names, characters, places, and events are the work of the author's imagination.

Any resemblance to real persons, places, or events is coincidental.

Solstice Publishing - www.solsticepublishing.com

The Cha-cha Affair

Lynne E. Marino

This novel is dedicated to my grandmother Meta Englehardt Jungmann, and to Daniel R. Marino, the most patient man on the planet.

Chapter One

Stephanie Ledger was on her twentieth sit-up when her best friend, Peg O'Malley, waltzed through the front door without knocking. Stephanie knew the lecture that would inevitably proceed.

"You really should keep that door locked," Peg said, her voice lightly dipped in sternness. "It's not like Max is around anymore, and you canceled the alarm system, which I know you did to save money, but I think it's a stupid move."

Stephanie pursed her lips and spoke with a degree of bristling pride she no longer felt about much. "First off, if I locked the door, how could you walk in unannounced? And second, Max being gone is worth being broke."

"Yeah, okay, I get it. But you still need to stay safe." Peg flipped the deadbolt in place and plopped down on the couch.

"And to what do I owe this visit?" she asked, between sit-ups twenty-three and twenty-four.

"I have a plan."

As usual, Peg's plan involved Stephanie, and although she'd never tell Peg, this one sounded sort of fun. Unfortunately, it also cost money.

"I don't want to learn how to dance," she lied to Peg.

"Oh, come on. You might actually like it. It beats those stupid sit-ups you're doing."

Stephanie took note of the fact that Peg ratcheted up the pleading tone in her voice by half a notch. Her friend could be merciless when it came to guilt-induced cajoling.

"It's another one of your meet-Mr.-Right schemes, and you know it. I am done with men. If Patrick ever has kids, they'd better be girls."

"You just contradicted yourself. Your son is a fourteen-year-old male, so you're not done. Ever."

Peg had her on a technicality, but she would use it to her advantage. Defending herself was a completely legitimate excuse to take a break from doing sit-ups.

"Okay, okay. I acknowledge there's an exception to every rule, and Patrick is my exception. My only exception. After I get my half of this house and college tuition for Patrick, I am on my own. Forever."

Peg leaned forward on the couch until her head was at Stephanie's level. "You owe me."

"What for?" Stephanie asked. She sat up and turned around to face her.

"Remember when I changed your *F* in French to an *A* on your report card?"

"It only bought me two weeks, and then Mom and Dad found out about it at the parent-teacher conference, and I was grounded for a month. Remember?"

"Oh yeah," Peg's expression went from defiant to sheepish. "At least I bought you some time to get your affairs in order."

Stephanie tried hard not to smile. "Come up with something better, and maybe I'll reconsider."

She loved this back and forth. It harkened to a time when she and Peg had been young and all of life had been ahead of them. Every day had been an adventure. They would never grow old, and if they did, they would never look like their mothers. Houses would magically clean themselves, fantastic careers would land in their laps, and husbands would never cheat on you with your look-alike first cousin.

"Remember when we were freshmen and I pulled you out of the front seat of that drunk guy's car?" Peg's eyes lit up as she said it.

"No." Of course she remembered, but if she admitted it she'd never win another argument.

"Look, the first lesson is free."

Stephanie's ears perked up.

"It's only a one-hour class, with an optional practice session afterward. If you don't want to stay for dance practice, we'll go. Promise." The fingers on Peg's right hand formed the Girl Scout salute, but that didn't mean that the ones on her left weren't crossed behind her back.

"Let me see your other hand."

Peg rolled her eyes and pulled her left hand out from behind her, wiggling all five fingers in the air.

She did say the first lesson was free, and Stephanie had come to love the word *free*. Unfortunately, it was seldom used. "I need to check with Patrick."

"I already did. He told me he's at Max's tonight, and he won't be home until after school tomorrow."

"Oh yeah, I forgot," Stephanie lied. "He's starting to see his father more."

Max had been spending more time with Patrick because, at the last mediation meeting, her lawyer had hinted that increased child support was needed since he spent so little time with his son. She'd known her soon-to-be ex had been caught off guard because his nose had begun to twitch, and his foot had tapped nervously against the conference room chair. Sixteen years of marriage to the guy had taught her a few things. Most of them she wanted to forget. She sighed and started her sit-ups.

"You'll have a good time dancing," Peg said again. "And you need to get out and stop stewing over everything."

Peg had her the minute she'd burst through her front door, simply because Peg was Peg. While most people had flitted in and out of Stephanie's life, the two of them had stuck together like burrs on bobby socks since the third grade. When Max split twelve months ago, Stephanie had quickly discovered she could count her real friends on less than one hand. "I'm considering it, okay?"

"Wonderful." Peg clapped her hands together and plopped back against the couch, which was the only piece of furniture remaining in the living room. And tomorrow, it was good riddance to that overtooled brown leather monstrosity, too. The couch was going out the door along with the furniture in the fourth and fifth bedrooms.

Their conversation kept Stephanie so occupied that she finished ten more sit-ups without realizing it. Amazing the exercise you could do on your own that cost absolutely nothing. All those years Max had been after her to stay in shape, paying for gyms and personal trainers so she'd look the part of a plastic surgeon's wife. She could have done it on her own and pocketed all that money for a rainy day. And if anyone was asking, her life right now was more like a category-five hurricane.

Peg pursed her lips. "You know, I'd give anything to look like you."

Stephanie Webloski Ledger was long and lean in every place that mattered, except her chest and butt. In those two areas, her genes had been generous in dumping the right amount of fatty tissue.

"Would you really want to be me right now?"

She watched the struggle going on in Peg's head, which always played itself out on her friend's face. Peg couldn't lie if she tried. "I didn't say I wanted to be you. I said I wouldn't mind looking like you."

Mary Margaret O'Malley, Peg for short, was a large-boned woman with shiny, rusty-red hair and a generous sprinkling of freckles across her high-boned cheeks and nose. Her maple-brown eyes never ceased to twinkle, unless she was angry, and if she was angry, a wise person would exit the stage. Quickly.

Before Stephanie could organize a retort, Peg launched in again. "All the more reason to go to dance class with me. Have some fun. Learn to dance the right way instead of how we did it when we were teenagers, just making it up and jiggling around."

"You said lesson, not lessons, and stop, okay? I'll go." She got up off the floor, grabbed her towel, and shot Peg a dubious look.

"Fantastic." Peg slapped her hands together and beamed.

Stephanie wiped off her forehead with her towel as she walked into the kitchen for a glass of tap water. The bottled and delivered stuff had been the first thing she'd canceled twelve months ago. "But I'm only going because it's free. And I hope it's better than that meet-and-greet thing you dragged me to last month. That was horrible."

Peg walked into the kitchen to join her, her eyes lit from behind. "Hey, if you're worried about fending off advances—"

"I didn't say that," Stephanie cut in. "If some guy hits on me, I'll simply kick him in the nuts. Really hard."

"Oh." She frowned slightly and continued. "Anyway, to avoid a nuts-kicking lawsuit, put your wedding rings back on. Those diamonds are so big nobody could ignore them even if they wanted to." Peg's eyes narrowed. "You didn't sell them, did you?"

"Funny you mention that, because I was thinking about it."

When Max had left, her first thought had been to eventually take the diamonds out of their setting and put them in earrings. Now, when she looked at them, all she could see was the lie they represented and the money she might get if she sold them. An extra four or five thousand would come in handy right about now. She knew she'd never come close to their original cost, but they had to be worth something on the resale market.

"Where's this class?" Stephanie asked, digging herself out of thoughts she'd rather not have to think about in the first place.

"It's right here in Scottsdale on Indian School Road. Ten minutes at the most," Peg said, and then she corrected herself. "Maybe fifteen. You'll have a good time."

A good time? She'd become allergic to the entire concept. Good times usually required money, and the more she thought about dance class, the more uncomfortable she became. What if she made a doofus out of herself? Well, it wouldn't be the first time.

"I'm not getting all cleaned up to go. I'm wearing these sweatpants and this shirt."

"Maybe comb your hair?" Peg suggested. "It looks a little messed up."

Lately, Stephanie had taken to cutting her own shoulder-length, naturally blond hair. She was getting better at it, although pulling it back in a ponytail hid a lot of the uneven whacks she'd perpetrated on her back layers.

"I'm not even putting on more deodorant," she told Peg. "And I'm not wearing any makeup, either. Not even lip gloss." She walked over to Peg and put her arm around her shoulder. "And by the way, this act of charity goes under the, Stephanie-is-saving-Peg's-butt category, so I'm one up. Okay?"

"Deal. I'll drive." Peg paused for a moment and then said, "You might really want to rethink the deodorant thing."

***

Peg swung the door open to the Let's Dance studio with anticipated gusto, while Stephanie trudged ten feet behind.

"Come on." Peg turned around and motioned for Stephanie to hurry. "We're late already. There's always more women than men. We might end up with each other."

"Ah, the tragedy." Stephanie fingered her wedding rings and walked into the studio as though she were headed for traffic school. After so many months of not wearing them, they felt awkward to touch.

The interior of Let's Dance screamed George and Jane Jetson were here. The mid-fifties entryway, light fixtures, and check-in desk had never been remodeled, as was the case with the stone exterior of the building.

Like much of Central Phoenix, and the older neighborhoods of Scottsdale, midcentury modern design reigned supreme. Much of the city took its hint from the architect Frank Lloyd Wright. No part of Phoenix boasted colonial architecture, and Greek columns were an anathema. It was almost as if Phoenix and its slightly fuller of itself sister city, Scottsdale, put up a sign at the entrance that said, "Get lost, Scarlett O'Hara."

There was one home off Central Avenue with big white columns that wanted you to believe all that back-east, prominent-family baloney existed out west too, but Stephanie shut that house out of her mind. The inhabitants, her cousin Christie and her soon-to-be-ex-husband Max, weren't worthy of a single thought, much less a thought in the form of a complete sentence.

While she and Peg had arrived for the class slightly late, they were not as late as the two men who flew in after them and got into the men's line across from where Stephanie and Peg stood.

Stephanie scrutinized the duo. The one directly opposite Peg was definitely some kind of Latin. He was dark, short, and slightly pudgy, but with the same mirthful look in his eyes that Peg often had. And he looked smart. Despite his height and shape, there was a determined and alert look about his carriage that sent out a don't-mess-with-me message.

The other guy was an entirely different matter. His genes had hung around the Mediterranean, but he wasn't Latin looking in a Spanish sense. His eyes were as blue as Sinatra's. Whatever he was, it resulted in him being far too handsome for his own good.

Look at the way he holds himself, Stephanie thought as she took in another fleeting eyeful. And that smirk on his face. Arrogant down to the last molecule. She knew the type. She'd married the type. Why did she have to be standing across from the type? With her ring hand, she made a point of scratching her forehead. He had to see them. Like Peg said, you'd have to be blind to miss those rings.

Although she'd never admitted it to anyone but herself, the size of those diamonds embarrassed her. They bordered on garish. Scratch that. They'd crossed the border and were well into the territory of tasteless. Even Marie Antoinette would have thought twice before wearing them. Max had taken her mother with him to pick the rings out, and they'd thought they were wonderful, so that was what she'd gotten. The two of them hadn't even bothered to ask her opinion. The rings had been wonderful because they'd thought they were, and whatever they'd thought had been the truth.

"We'll start with a simple waltz," the instructor called out, walking between the two lines. She wore a pair of two-inch black heels, toes and back enclosed, with a strap that went across her feet and fastened below the ankle. Stephanie scanned the other women. The more serious female dance students, the ones who looked like they wanted to be there, all wore similar shoes with a Mary Jane strap. Even Peg had a pair on. She, on the other hand, was wearing track shoes, and with those she would beat everyone out the front door in – she glanced at the clock –

fifty-five minutes. No way were they staying for the practice session, free or not.

"The beginning box step, nothing could be easier." The instructor walked quickly down the aisle to the end, the French roll of her dyed jet-black hair as tightly sculpted as her calves. "Let's start with you two." She motioned to Stephanie and Mr. Disgustingly Handsome.

Let's not. Stephanie heard Peg chortle, and turned to give her a dirty look.

The instructor looked at Stephanie and said, "Please, don't be shy."

"I'm not." Defiance was her middle name. With stained sweatpants, she jumped into the middle of the dance floor and turned to Mr. Handsome. "I don't bite," she said.

He gave her a dubious look and took two steps forward. Nervous laughter could be heard from both the men's and women's lines.

"Let's have some introductions." The instructor smiled and looked at Stephanie first.

"Stephanie Ledger. And you are?" she asked, looking directly at the instructor.

"Me?" The woman looked incredulous.

"Uh-huh."

"You weren't at class last week?"

Sarcasm dripped from Stephanie's voice like syrup off pancakes. "I'm afraid I missed it."

"For those of you who weren't here last week, I'll repeat the introductions. Again. I'm Rita Murphy. You may call me Ms. Rita."

Ms. Rita turned to Mr. Handsome, using a nicer voice than the one she'd used with Stephanie. "Please introduce yourself to your partner."

Stephanie watched as he nudged his chin her way and held out his hand. "I'm Joseph Schmidt. Joe."

Not the last name she'd been expecting. She held out her hand, shook his lightly, but not so lightly that it screamed prissy.

"Now." Ms. Rita clapped her hands together. "The waltz. Very simple. You are making a box with your feet. A simple, graceful box. Leads, here is your part. Followers, you do the exact opposite. One, two, three, one, two, three."

Miss Rita modeled the dance steps with an imaginary partner several times before she walked back over and stood next to the two of them. "There is one more important part of the waltz. It is the frame. How you hold your partner, and how you let your partner hold you, is essential. In all the smooth ballroom dances, you do not look at your partner. You think of a window over your partner's shoulder and look out of it. In all dances, smooth or Latin, you never look down. Looking down is looking like a fool. You feel your feet – you do not stare at them."

Thank god for the window, Stephanie thought. Tonight, she would become the expert at staring out of it. Anything but look at Joe – what was his last name, Schmidt? From the looks of him it should be Corleone or Sinatra or something Greek, like Onassis or Oikos.

Ms. Rita spent a few moments demonstrating how Joe and Stephanie made a dance frame with their arms and posture, and then she walked over to the side of the studio and pressed the player. "Begin." She nodded to Joe and Stephanie.

They joined their hands as though they were both holding tacks, while his other arm went around her back so lightly she could barely feel it. Each of them looked down and focused on their feet, as Stephanie heard him count the steps under his breath. Unfortunately, he smelled wonderful, like crisp, fresh, shaving cream. She tried not to breathe it in.

Ms. Rita called out. "Do not look at your feet. It makes your frame look clunky, and it makes you look like an amateur."

"I *am* an amateur," Stephanie whispered. She felt Joe's chest stifle a laugh.

"This is the waltz," Ms. Rita continued. "You should extend your back and be looking over your partner's shoulder. Remember the window, the window that sits on their shoulder." She motioned for the rest of the class to begin.

Joe looked at Stephanie and asked, with a ruler straight face, "What did you say your name was?"

"Stephanie. And you're not supposed to look at me," she said, looking at him.

"I meant your last name."

"Ledger." She wanted to add, and if I'm lucky it'll be that for about three more weeks, but she stopped herself. In this class, she was happily married and had the rings to prove it.

"You know, Ledger, like an account book." She'd used that line so many times, but it did describe Max to a tee. Money should have been his middle name, Maxwell Money Ledger. Unfortunately, it was Oscar.

"So you're Mrs. Ledger?"

"That would be correct. Yes, I have a husband. I'm happily married, and I'm just here to support my friend." She pointed with her chin to Peg, who, it happened, looked amazing in the Latin guy's arms.

"And your husband?" he asked.

Stephanie turned her gaze back to Joe. "What about him?"

She watched him swallow hard before he spoke. "He wouldn't be a surgeon, would he?"

"Um, yes." Was this any of his business?

"A plastic surgeon?"

She cringed inside before she answered. "Yes. Why? Do you need a facelift?"

He looked at her cross-eyed. "So you're Mrs. Dr. Ledger?"

Window or no window, Stephanie turned and looked him straight in the eyes. "Yes, but no one goes by Mrs. Dr. anything. Are you trying to be funny?"

"Not really."

"Good. Because you've gotten an F in the humor department, and since we're being extremely nosey here, what do you do for a living? Wait. Don't tell me. You're a proctologist."

"I'm … a tax attorney."

"How nice for you." She said it with a Georgia drawl, but judging from the blank look on his face, the guy had no clue as to what the hidden meaning of that Southern phrase was.

Joe silently continued to focus on his feet, like he wasn't supposed to. She thought about telling him to look up but decided that he didn't deserve her help in the first place. Instead, she turned her focus back to the imaginary window over his shoulder, wishing like crazy she could jump out of it and run to the car.

Peg and the Latin guy waltzed by again. The two of them looked like they were having the time of their lives, and they already had the box step mastered. She watched them laughing as he led her in an elegant turn.

When the music ended, Ms. Rita announced, "Let's take a five-minute break. We have the box turn and the twinkle step to learn."

Joe Schmidt let go of her hand and walked away without another word.

"Nice to meet you, too," she whispered after him, wishing she could sniff her arm pits to see if she should have heeded Peg's deodorant advice. Joe Schmidt kept on walking until he reached Peg and her partner. Peg glanced over at Stephanie, wide-eyed, and then turned away quickly. This was not a night she had to worry about fending off anyone's attention, wedding rings or no wedding rings. Her last name was enough.

She sat on the bench at the far side of the room and tried hard not to look over to where the three of them stood. Peg was chatting on and on with the short guy about something. Even at this distance, Stephanie could see the color begin to rise in her friend's face. It started at the neck and crept upward, which meant Peg was excited and embarrassed. In this situation that could mean only one thing. Peg liked her dance partner. A lot.

Leaning back, she closed her eyes and tried not to think about people liking each other or the fact that there was at least thirty minutes left until she could run to her friend's car and go home.

Finally, after what seemed like an eternity, the dance class ended. When Peg pulled into Stephanie's driveway a short time later, she put her Mini Cooper in park but kept the engine running. She turned to Stephanie and said for the second time on their ride home, "So he knows Max. So what?"

"So what? Would you want to be associated with him?"

"I tried to tell you that for the last fifteen years, and you pick tonight to realize it?"

It was true. Peg had done everything she could to talk Stephanie out of marrying Max, while her mother had done everything to talk her into it. Her wedding was the last time her mother and Peg had ever spoken. When she had Patrick, Peg had never come over when her mother was around. Once, Stephanie had seen Peg drive past the house when Peg had spied Stephanie's mother's car in the driveway. As for her mother, it was as though Peg had never existed.

"Why do you care what that Joe guy thinks? You told me you thought he was a jerk the second we got in the car."

"He is a jerk." She folded her arms across her chest. "Absolutely the worst kind."

"He's certainly good looking."

"That's why he's the worst kind."

Peg shrugged. "I could tell Jorge you're separated from Max, when he calls."

"Ah, don't bother. You're right. Why should I care what Joe what's-his-hiney thinks?" Her eyes widened as Peg's words sunk in. "You gave that guy your number?"

"He asked." Peg turned the rearview mirror toward her, to look at the top of her hair.

"He's four inches shorter than you."

"No, he's not. Maybe three. Probably two, and if we're talking about things that shouldn't matter, that most certainly shouldn't."

Stephanie shifted her entire body Peg's way. "Why in the hell at our age do you want to get involved with a man?" She cussed more with Peg than any other person alive. It was a hangover from high school and their early years in college.

"It's not like we're headed for assisted living."

"No, but you've got a full life, and you make lots of money. You're a successful real estate agent, and the market is rebounding. Go on a cruise. Get a boy toy."

Peg stared at her but said nothing.

Stephanie felt the need to press her point. "Why keep looking for that certain someone? That kind of love doesn't really exist."

Peg frowned and looked out the front window of her car. "Maybe, because I've never been married, and I'd still like to give it a whirl."

Stephanie rolled her eyes. "Living vicariously through my separation and pending divorce isn't enough?"

"I'd like to think I'd get it right."

"You always were smarter than me, Pegster. You know, sometimes I wish I were you."

Peg laughed. "Maybe I can put my mind in your body, and we can be one person."

Stephanie stared at her in disbelief. "Not that it matters, but you really have no idea how attractive you are. So you're ample. So what? Some guys like that. Besides, once you smile, that's all anyone looks at."

Peg's smile told the world that she was kind and that she had a sense of humor. It also told anyone who was paying attention not to think they could put anything past her. Funny, Stephanie realized she'd thought the same thing about Jorge what's-his-name earlier this evening.

Peg ignored Stephanie's compliment. "Look, it was a bad joke. You don't need my brain. You're plenty smart already. You just took a vacation from your brain when you married Max, that's all. If you don't want me to tell Jorge that you're separated, I won't. Otherwise, I can slip it in at the next dance class. I'm good at that kind of stuff."

She winced at the thought of her friend trying to keep a secret. Peg was the worst secret keeper around. "I just told his buddy I was happily married."

Stephanie got out of the car and then remembered the other words Peg had said. "Hey! Did you say next class?"

Peg put the car in reverse and said nothing.

"You said one," Stephanie said through the still open car door. "And I only said yes because it was free."

"I paid for twelve sessions for both of us, and there's no refund."

"Peg, you told me it was free."

"It was for you, because I paid for it."

"See if you can get your money back."

"I told you. It's nonrefundable." Peg started to say something else, then stopped, and shook her head. "You need this. Love you." Peg backed out of the driveway before Stephanie could say another word.

She watched as her friend's headlights disappeared around the corner, then waltzed with a pretend partner—one who liked her—into the garage, where she turned the knob on the door that led to the kitchen.

"Hey, Mom."

Stephanie stopped short and stifled a scream. "Jeez, Patrick, you scared me. I thought you were at your father's tonight."

"Yeah, well, I had him drive me over here because I forgot a book, and I thought I'd stay instead of going back. It was okay with Dad."

Patrick often came up with an excuse to end up back here. She didn't blame him.

"I'm glad you're back," she said.

"How was dance class? Aunt Peg told me she was taking you."

"I learned the waltz." She forced an upbeat note in her voice.

"That'll come in handy."

Stephanie laughed. "Yeah, it's the new job requirement."

"Uh-huh."

Uh-huh was one of her son's six basic responses. The other five were *no, no duh, way cool, maybe,* and *do I have to.* Other than these few utterances, the house that was always too big for a family of three remained eerily quiet. She couldn't wait until the divorce was final and she and Patrick could find something smaller with a cozier utility bill and no pool to maintain.

"So did you eat at your father's?"

"Yep."

Okay, add *yep* to his other one-word responses and you had seven.

"What did you have?" Ah, she had him. Answering this would require a complete sentence.

"Macaroni."

"And cheese?" she asked.

"No duh." He snorted.

She walked over to the refrigerator and pulled out the pitcher of water. Chilling it dampened the tap water taste. "Do you have homework?"

"Yep."

He shut his book and walked down the hallway to his bedroom. She heard the door slam harder than usual, its sound reverberating up the hallway, through the family room, and into the kitchen. Something was going on, and Patrick wasn't ready to talk. The whole split with Max had been hard on him, especially with the cousin Christie angle thrown in. As if early adolescence wasn't hard enough to begin with.

The good thing about her current situation was that it couldn't last long. The bad thing was that it could get worse before it got better. Going up against Maxwell Oscar Ledger was a full-time job, and with Christie in his camp, that made two against one. Well, one and a half. Christie might be big on boobs these days, but she wasn't big on brains, and no injection was going to make that any better.

A year ago, Stephanie had a heck of a time finding a lawyer. No one wanted to represent her once they heard who she was divorcing and who Max's lawyer was. Finally, her father called an old friend who was semiretired but rumored to be quite the pit bull in his day. She liked the man. He knew divorce law, but he was still up against Max and Christie and their endless source of money that never seemed to show up on an assets declaration. The deal her lawyer worked out was for a monthly dollar amount that spoke more of the years before the man had been semiretired. She suspected he hadn't looked at the cost of milk, bread, and butter in the last ten years.

Max's strategy was to starve her out like Caesar had done to the Gauls. Cordon her off and wait until she gave up or starved. Max dragged his heels every time he was supposed to pay for something, and he was habitually late with her temporary-support payments but never late enough to justify going back to court. He loved watching her twist. She wished she could figure out a way to make some money without getting a paycheck that Max's lawyer could trace. Cash was her new deity.

"Mom?"

She hadn't heard Patrick walk back into the kitchen until he was standing in the archway.

"What Patty-Pie?"

"You said you wouldn't call me that anymore."

"Sorry. Old habits die hard."

"Could you at least not say it in front of my friends?"

"Deal."

"Grandpa called."

"Oh. What did he want?" she asked.

"He wanted to talk to you about some Valentine's Day dance at Leisure World coming up." Patrick sighed. It was a preparatory sigh that usually accompanied the admission of a bad grade in some subject. Either that or something expensive had been broken or lost, and he was working up to telling her. She braced herself for the news and realized to her horror that for once she'd almost prefer a bad grade over something lost or broken.

He walked over and gave her a stiff hug, which for a boy of his age was a huge admission of affection, and then reached into his pocket and handed her an already-opened envelope. "I brought this home from the office."

"Patrick, you're too smart to be flunking tests."

He flashed her as much of a dirty look as a budding teenager dared to risk with his mother. "It's not my grades."

Stephanie unfolded the envelope and pulled out the letter. It was to both Max and her, detailing the bill for a graphing calculator, a tablet, new gym clothes, the required deposit for the lacrosse team, and a list of the equipment needed to play. Being able to continue with lacrosse was the salve on the wound of switching him from Paradise Valley Country Day School to Scottsdale Vista Mesa Middle School. She'd assumed that by sending him to public school she could say goodbye to the endless trickle of incidental fees, but she'd been wrong. Public school wasn't free either.

"I gave it to Dad. He said to give it to you."

Damn that Max. It was one thing to drag his feet financially where she was concerned, but to directly involve Patrick in his sign-the-papers-or-starve strategy was unforgivable. Then again, it was so like Max and her sweet cousin to be cheap with everyone but themselves. The two of them together made each of them exponentially worse.

"Don't worry," she said, forcing a smile. "It'll be taken care of by next Monday, and I'll call your school tomorrow so you won't get another letter like this. Worry about algebra and biology, okay? And English. Worry about English, too. And Spanish."

"I'm not taking Spanish."

"Oh. I thought you were."

"That's next year." He turned and went back into his bedroom, closing the door behind him.

By the time the light went out in Patrick's room, it was ten-thirty. That meant she would more than likely be waking Christie and Max out of their much-needed beauty sleep. Good. She sat alone in the middle of her king-sized bed with the door shut tight and dialed the number of Christie's landline. She could hear the pink princess phone, her cousin's precious possession since she'd been a kid, starting to ring. It rang twice before Christie picked up.

"Put Max on the phone," Stephanie said, her tone flat and blunted.

She could hear Christie hiss, "It's her."

"Do you know what time it is?" Max asked, his voice both groggy and crabby. "This could be construed as harassment."

"Oh, bite me, Max. You want to know what time it is? It's time for you to pay for your son's school supplies."

"Let's go back to court. Or you can sign the papers and this will all be over."

"Don't take what's between you and me out on Patrick." While he was momentarily silent, Stephanie took the advantage. "In fact, it's because of him that I'm holding out, and you know it."

"Steph, I find it insulting that you would think I wouldn't pay for Patrick's college education unless it's written into the divorce decree." He spoke with a degree of condescension that made her want to reach through the princess phone and slap him.

"Okay, let's get this straight. I'm calling to ask you to please pay for his necessary school supplies, and you're trying to make me feel guilty because I don't trust you to pay for his tuition when he goes to college? Do you see the irony there? And don't call me Steph ever again. You don't get to call me that."

She could hear Max and Christie's combined breath on the receiver. "Besides, Maxie, I've known you too long to buy your moral-indignation bullshit. I'm not one of your dimwit patients who really thinks you can make them look fifteen years younger with a set of upright boobs. Nor am I like Christie, who thinks you can look like a Barbie when you're really Midge." She smiled as she heard Christie snort.

"Who's Midge?" Max asked.

Obviously, he'd never played with dolls, although the overly endowed chest on Barbie would have been right up his alley. "Forget it, okay?" She wasn't about to be derailed. "When it comes to money, it's very much like you to leave everyone else except yourself in the lurch. I hope Christie figures that out and quick. And you must have morals to get indignant about them, which you do not."

"Sign the papers, Steph."

"It's Stephanie, Maxie." She slammed the phone down and tiptoed to the door of her bedroom, looking down the hallway to see if Patrick's light had gone back on. Thankfully, darkness loomed.

Turning back into the bedroom, she caught her reflection in the oval-shaped, beveled mirror mounted over the dresser and stopped short. The beginnings of faint vertical lines down her cheeks were visible. On her forehead, thicker horizontal ones had dug in for the long haul. And the dark circles around her eyes? She wasn't even going to address those. The past year had taken its toll, but so what? Why did she even care? What did being attractive ever get her but trouble and a good excuse never to try very hard at anything?

Soon, one way or another, she wouldn't have to fight with Max anymore. After the divorce was final and Patrick was in college, years would go by, and they wouldn't have a reason to nod at each other from across a restaurant. Besides, she wouldn't be eating at the ones Max could afford anyway. Patrick's graduations and maybe his wedding would probably be all she'd ever see of Max again. A girl could only hope.

She breathed in, sighed, and then whispered to her reflection, "Welcome to your life. Buck up, Princess."

Ten forty-five the next morning, Stephanie was exactly three thousand forty-five dollars and ninety-two cents richer. She felt sick to her stomach when she realized what price the living room couch and the furniture from the fourth and fifth bedrooms had gone out the door for, but the truth was she'd never liked the stuff anyway. In the summer, her backside had always stuck to the leather couch, leaving her with a feeling that she'd lost a layer of skin every time she got up. And as for the bedroom furniture, it was large, heavy, and bulky. No way was she taking it to the next yet-to-be-determined destination. So why not get some money for it now before Max realized it was missing and had a hissy fit about it?

Smiling, she surveyed the now completely empty living room and decided it looked better like this. To her, it spoke of possibilities.

She had managed to sweet-talk the guys who worked for the resale store into moving one of the big-screen televisions out of the third bedroom and into the living room. It wasn't as big as the one she'd sold off last month, but Patrick could still set his game system up in the empty space. Today, after she drove down to school to pay Patrick's fees, she would make a beeline for Big Lots to buy some oversized pillows and a beanbag chair. What boy wouldn't want a room full of pillows, a big television, and his games? Money troubles didn't mean they couldn't have fun.

She heard a key in the front door turn, and as the door opened, Marta Del Valle, a short, trim, muscular woman with the face of a pixie, stood in the entry hall, broom in hand. "Where is your couch?" Marta asked after a glance into the living room.

"I sold it with all the stuff in the fourth and fifth bedrooms."

"Now what will I have to clean? Did Mr. Max get stingy again?" Marta asked. One of the many things Stephanie liked about Marta was that she detested Max almost as much as Stephanie did, but Stephanie never investigated what the source of Marta's antipathy toward Max was all about. Sometimes the less you knew, the better.

"Yes," Stephanie answered Marta's question. "I owed Patrick's school some money."

The two of them stood in the entry hall and surveyed the emptiness together. "I think I'll sell the dining room off, too. I always hated that Tuscan look. Too big and bulky."

Marta put her free hand on her hip and regarded Stephanie with a look of disappointment. "I thought you were smarter than that."

"What?"

"I said, I thought you were smarter than that. And more creative." Marta shook her head and looked at Stephanie like she had bricks for brains. She pointed to the top of her head with her index finger. "Think. What motivates Mr. Max?"

Stephanie thought for a moment. What did make the guy tick? "Money."

"Yes, and he won't give it up unless you push on something that matters as much as his money."

What mattered to Max besides money? She thought about it. Sex? Big boobs? Big redone boobs? Butt lifts? No, not as much as the money he got from doing them. What then? "Status?"

"Now you're thinking. What else?"

"Appearances?"

Marta pointed out the window to the house across the street. "Who is your neighbor in that ugly bubble-gum-colored house across the street?"

"She calls it *desert rose.*"

"I know what that silly woman calls it." She repeated her question. "Who is your neighbor?"

"Gloria Burnwater." Now she was completely puzzled.

"Yes, the wife of your husband's partner."

Stephanie nodded in acknowledgment. She hated living by the Burnwaters, but Max had insisted on buying this monstrosity of a house right across from them ten years ago. A really good deal, he'd told her.

"What can you do that would get Gloria Burnwater to call your husband and complain?"

"Run a prostitution ring out of the house? I've got enough bedrooms for it, although after today I'm missing some beds."

Marta smiled the smile of the Sphinx. "If you did that, Mr. Max would move back in. I have a better plan."

After they strung two clotheslines from palm tree to palm tree in the front yard, Stephanie and Marta brought out three laundry baskets full of freshly-washed clothes and towels.

"Okay," Marta said. "We have thirty minutes to get this done before Mrs. B. comes home. I don't want her to see me. She is a screaming madwoman."

Until six months ago, Marta had used to clean house for both Gloria and Stephanie, but when Gloria had criticized her towel-folding techniques and made her refold every one of them, Marta fired Gloria. Over the years Marta had built up her clientele base to the point where she could pick and choose who she worked for. Either you paid Marta a lot of additional money to compensate for your attitude or you learned to say thank you and got charged the going rate. Otherwise, and always to the shock and surprise of everyone it happened to, Marta gave you the heave-ho.

"Gloria isn't home?" Stephanie asked.

"No." Marta took out a clothespin and finished hanging up one of Patrick's boxers. "She goes to Pilates every Monday, Wednesday, and Friday. She's more faithful about it than my mother is about Mass."

"Oh. Gloria's a bit on the OCD side, huh?" She may have been Gloria Burnwater's neighbor for a decade, but that didn't mean she knew anything about her. Even though their husbands covered each other's practices, she and Gloria had done everything they could to ignore each other.

"What's OCD?" Marta asked.

"Obsessive compulsive disorder. It means you have to do things in a certain way and in a certain order every time you do them, or you get very upset."

"On the west side of town, we call that being a tight ass."

"That works too."

Stephanie smiled as she observed Marta's clothes-hanging technique. The last thing she wanted her to know was that she'd never hung up wash in her entire life. Everything in her world went into the dryer. All this natural sun and heat twelve months a year and no one in Phoenix ever took advantage of it. At least no one she knew. Stephanie grabbed a pillowcase and folded it over the makeshift clothesline.

"No, not like that," Marta said, scrunching up her nose. "You hang it from the tips with a clothespin on each end. When you fold it over, it takes twice as long to dry. You only do that if you're short on pins, which we are not, because, lucky for you, I had my laundry basket in my car." She handed Stephanie two pins. "Yes, across the street there is a little more than ODC going on. Mrs. B. thinks her body would jiggle like Jell-O if she missed a single Pilate's session, and I don't think she can have liposuction anymore. She's done it too many times already."

"Really?"

"Yes, that and a lot of other stuff." Marta nodded. "You know after I told her I wouldn't work for her anymore, she said she was calling INS. I said, 'Listen, lady, my ancestors have been in Arizona longer than yours were in Europe. Some of my family were in this area long before Mexico was even called Mexico, that's how long.' After that she started throwing things, expensive, heavy things at my head. I ran out the door."

Marta bent down and grabbed another pair of Patrick's boxer shorts. Stephanie prayed this would all be over before her son came home from school and she had to explain why his underwear were flying like flags in the front yard.

"Then she sent me a bill for the vase she threw at my head and broke. I told her I would not be giving her money, and that I could sue her for threat to bodily harm. Mrs. B. does not like hearing the word no," Marta said, continuing to talk. "Do you have a special word for that? Because on my side of town we call that being a big, spoiled brat."

Stephanie looked at Marta and laughed, loud and hard. It felt wonderful. "Well, in Scottsdale we use the word *bitch*, but big spoiled brat hits the nail on the head probably better." She grabbed a wet shirt. "You know, I've totally blown my ultimatum to Patrick. I told him two days ago that if he didn't clean his room, he was going to do all his own wash this weekend."

"Tell him I did it by mistake."

"I think you two are in cahoots with each other, that's what I think."

Stephanie watched Marta pick up her burgundy bra and put it on the side closest to Gloria's house. "Hey, do we have to use those?" she asked.

"Ask yourself, do you want money from Mr. Max sooner or later?"

"Sooner."

"Okay, then." Marta put the clothespin on the bra strap, allowing the rest of it to swing in the breeze, and then pinned up the bright-red one and the leopard-skin bra with the rhinestone-trimmed straps right next to it. "You got any other strange colored ones?"

"No," she lied.

The truth? She had several in various shades of orange, hot pink and an iridescent purple, with underwear to match. And then there were the ones with tassels. Max was always bringing home something for her to dress up in from every conference he went to. Sometimes the tags were off. Stephanie never asked. Who in their right mind wanted to think about Max, much less Max and his sexual peccadilloes?

She'd stopped thinking about a lot of things when she got married, like the fact that a degree in art history with a minor in interior design translated into next to nothing when it came to hauling in a paycheck.

Marta narrowed her eyes. "Are you sure you don't have any more?"

"Well, maybe a couple." Stephanie went inside to get the hot-pink and purple ones. No way was she pulling out the tassels.

Five minutes later, Marta stood back to admire their handiwork. "Nice." She looked at her watch and then at Stephanie. "This should do it. We've got ten minutes before she turns the corner in that black Mercedes of hers."

Stephanie crossed her arms and looked. Three loads of wash swung gently on the lines in the front yard. There was a pleasant peacefulness to it, like wind chimes without the tinkle.

"Now we wait," Stephanie said.

The two of them went inside for a quick cup of coffee and settled down cross-legged on the floor of the living room, ready for the pending show. Sure enough, as Marta promised, Gloria cruised down the street right on time.

Marta took a sip from her cup and beamed. "What did I tell you?"

Stephanie shook her head. "How come I never noticed?"

"You went to different gyms, and you came home fifteen minutes later than she did."

"Man, you've got some real underused skills there, my friend. I'm glad you're not a robber. You could clean out the whole neighborhood."

Gloria's car came to a quick halt, and the smoky-gray window on her Mercedes came rolling down. She stuck her creaseless, plumped-up face out the window and pulled her sunglasses two inches down her nose to stare, open-mouthed. After she pulled into her driveway, she slammed the car door hard as she got out.

Marta and Stephanie rolled on the floor in hysterics.

"Hey," Stephanie said, whispering for no good reason. "I think it's working."

"She's coming," Marta said, with a mix of trepidation and excitement. "Do you remember what to say?"

"Yeah. I won't blow it."

Marta crawled on her stomach into the kitchen to avoid the possibility of being seen through the windows.

Stephanie pulled her fingers through her hair and took a deep breath before opening the door. "Gloria," she said with a saccharine lilt to her voice. "How long has it been? We never see each other anymore."

Gloria pointed her long, skinny index finger toward the palm trees. "Stephanie, what are you doing?"

"Talking to you."

"Don't get cute."

Stephanie stuck her head out the door and looked right and left. "You mean the wash?"

Gloria's narrow eyes turned into slits while her nostrils flared from her surgically altered nose. "No, I mean the Christmas display."

Stephanie looked again and then grabbed Gloria by her boney arm. "Come in," she whispered, and shut the door. "I wouldn't want anyone else in the neighborhood to know this, but they're about to cut off my power. I'm broke. Look." She motioned toward the living room. "Max has forced me to sell off all the furniture, not that I liked it anyway. It was so *new money*."

She felt the need to add the last bit of information because Max had been so inspired by the Burnwater's living room that he'd pushed her to buy near-identical pieces. Of course, he couldn't listen to his wife's decorating ideas. No. She was merely an art history and interior design major.

"So," Stephanie continued, "unless he helps me out, I'm afraid that's the only place on the property where I can string a clothesline."

Gloria stood with her hands on her hips and continued to glare at Stephanie. Obviously, she wasn't buying a word of it.

"Sorry if it's an eyesore for the neighborhood." Stephanie turned her head down in feigned embarrassment, afraid that if she looked up she might start laughing.

Without another word, Gloria turned on her heels and stomped back across the street. Stephanie swore she could hear the woman's door shudder as it slammed shut.

She walked into the kitchen where Marta sat grinning, and bowed as though she'd starred in a play and there was applause to be had at the end.

"Any bets on how long before she calls Mr. Max?" Marta asked.

"If I had money to bet, we wouldn't be doing this."

The phone rang before another word was spoken.

"Put it on speakerphone," Marta whispered.

Stephanie nodded, braced herself, and picked up her cell phone. "Hello?"

"Stephanie, what are you doing?"

"Is that you, Maxie?"

He yelled into the phone so loudly that Stephanie's head jerked back in shock. "Of course, it's me. What game are you playing with your bras hanging on a clothesline in the front yard?"

Marta was right. The bras were the finishing touch. "I can't pay the utilities on this house and pay Patrick's school fees at the same time. So, if I have to make a choice, I'll pick Patrick every time. Besides, I thought you liked those bras. I can give them to Christie if you think they'll fit. Did you make her the same size?"

"This is blackmail."

"No, it's choices. I've made mine. Pay for Patrick's school things, and I won't have to put the wash out anymore."

"It *is* blackmail."

What a delicious feeling it was to have Max on the ropes. It had been months since she'd had a card to play. "Maxie, it's merely a statement of fact. The wash won't be coming down unless you pay for things, and I mean all of it for the rest of the year." There was silence on the other end. "I'll call the school tomorrow to see if you've complied. In the meantime, I've got five more loads sitting by the washer. Some of it's the underwear you so loved. You know, the ones you brought me from Vegas? The ones that match the bras that are flapping in the breeze as we speak."

She heard a click on the other end and smiled at Marta as the call ended. "He's going for it." Unfortunately, right now she knew Max's secretary was probably getting yelled at for some trumped-up reason, and a wave of guilt smothered her glee.

She walked over to her purse where she'd stuffed the wad of cash from the sale of her furniture. "Sorry I didn't pay you last week. As long as I have the money, let me pay you for the next three." Somehow, she'd find a way.

"Keep your money. I had fun today," Marta said. "It felt wonderful to seek my revenge on your husband and that skinny little crow with the plumped-up body parts across the street. But you're fired."

"You're firing me?"

"It's not because I don't like you. You are my favorite client and the easiest house to clean because you always clean it before I come."

"I didn't want to burden you."

Marta smiled and shook her head. "You were my weekly vacation."

Stephanie hoped she wouldn't sound weepy when she said it. "I'm going to miss you."

"I'll miss you, too. Call me if you ever get rich enough to hire me back." Marta stopped short, crinkled up her nose, then took a step back, and cocked her head.

"What?" Stephanie asked.

"I was thinking. I run a cash business."

"And?"

"And you need cash."

"That's for sure."

"Why don't you work for me? Just for a while until you get your life straightened out."

"You mean clean houses?" Part of her wanted to say, who, me clean houses? You've got to be kidding. I don't clean other people's messes, they clean mine. But those days were over and so was that attitude. Marta was talking about cash, hard, cold, untraceable cash, and it humbled her how much she needed it.

"You're good at it," Marta said. "And I've got more jobs than my sister-in-law and I can handle right now, especially with soccer season coming up. My sister-in-law always bails when her kids are playing. Anyway, I'll keep you out of this neighborhood where people know who you are, and start you in the retirement centers. I've got two condos on the same block five miles north of here that I clean on the same day."

Cash. Little, rectangular, green, untraceable pieces of paper with no receipt attached. And no one she knew would know. Her angel had come in the form of her little

Latina cleaning lady with a smart mouth and an even smarter mind. "Marta, you've got a deal."

Chapter Two

"Joey?"

Joe Schmidt braced himself for the inevitable.

His mother's voice, thick with a lifetime in New Jersey, boomed through his cell phone. When he'd been a kid, it had been the sweetest sound on the block, and when he'd been a teenager, he'd still liked it but he made sure none of his friends had known he'd felt that way. Now he needed a break from her, and somehow, he had to find a way to distance himself without hurting her feelings.

"Mom."

"Did you get my messages? Are you coming on Sunday? That's tomorrow. I made extra food and put it in those individual containers you like. One for each day. You know, so you can heat it up in single servings. Since you live alone, all by yourself."

Joe closed his eyes, leaned against the wall in his kitchen, and moved his head as though he'd been stricken with a migraine.

"Joey, are you still there? Are you coming?"

He took a deep breath and reminded himself that without his mother, he wouldn't be the person he was today. She had rescued him more than once. "Mom, what are you talking about?"

"Did you listen to your messages? I called you three times. Maybe four. I don't remember."

Yes, he had, but not really. Lately, he'd been in the habit of listening to the beginning of her messages for the tone in her voice. If it was normal, which meant she wasn't in trouble, he deleted it before listening to the whole thing.

"I got in a few minutes ago, Mom." There. That wasn't lying; it was merely avoiding the truth.

"There's a brunch at the activity center on Sunday. You know, for Valentine's Day."

"I can't come."

"A friend of mine has a daughter you should meet. Don't worry. I already checked her out. Very straight teeth, and nice hair. Wear a clean shirt with a collar."

"Mom, I can't come. Seriously."

"And don't be late. Women hate it when men are late. It makes us feel unimportant. Love you, Joey."

The phone clicked in his ear. It was as though he'd never spoken the words *I can't come.* God, she was the most frustrating woman on the planet. But she loved him, and for that he was grateful. For that, everything he put up with paled in comparison.

He was grateful for being adopted, grateful for being raised by someone who had the capacity to love endlessly, if not fiercely, and grateful for his mother's help after Lisa had died. Nevertheless, if anyone was going to make him pull out the rest of his slightly thinning hair, it was his mother. Didn't she understand that he wasn't interested in dating anyone, that he'd never be over losing his wife?

He glanced at the picture of Lisa and him on his refrigerator, the one she'd turned into a magnet. They were in Disneyland, posing with Mickey and Donald, having the time of their lives and acting like a couple of kids. Being a kid had never come easy for him.

The two of them took the trip to Disneyland during the summer of their big push to get pregnant. They thought that if they relaxed and had some fun, everything would simply fall into place. They'd be parents in no time. How naïve could you get? They had been drunk on the notion that it would all work out because they loved each other. Who knew she already had cancer?

So here he was, alone on a Saturday night. He and Jorge usually managed to do something together over the weekend, either get a few beers or try yet another new restaurant. Phoenix was full of them. They opened and closed like screen doors in summer. But this weekend Jorge was meeting the woman from dance class. What was her name? Peg something or other. All he really remembered was that she was Stephanie Ledger's friend, which made her Max Ledger's friend too, and that automatically put her in the suspect category.

Why had he agreed to take ballroom dancing with Jorge anyway? But he knew the answer. It was something he and Lisa meant to do, before she got sick. When she had been dying she'd insisted he do it without her, and she hadn't let it go until he'd promised he would. And a promise is a promise. Especially when it was one made to Lisa.

The sound of his cell phone tore him away from the refrigerator magnet. It was Jorge.

"Hey. Got a question," Jorge said.

"What's up?" Maybe the Peg person had canceled at the last minute. Well, she was Mrs. Dr. Ledger's friend. How nice could she be?

"Listen, do you know of a decent cleaning lady?"

"No, I do not." There was a reason he and Jorge always met at restaurants and never entertained at home. "Why don't you ask your new friend from dance class? She told me she grew up here, so she probably knows of someone."

"Good idea. My condo looks like shit."

He didn't want to ponder why the state of Jorge's condo suddenly mattered, but he was fairly certain that their Saturday nights of eating out would soon cease. Jorge only cleaned his place when a woman was involved.

"You know, I've been bugging my mother to get a cleaning person, too. She's getting way too old to do housework. She'll fall off something and hurt herself someday." There was a pause, then Joe spoke again. "Where are you going tonight?"

"Out for dinner, then salsa dancing. I think I've finally met the perfect woman."

The perfect woman. He shook his head, remembering Jorge in high school and their first few years of college. He'd kept a list of qualities that encompassed female perfection, and he would read them out loud to anyone who would listen. Over the years, the list had shifted away from physical attributes to personality characteristics. You could only get burned so many times before you wised up.

His eyes grazed the magnet again. Maybe he should tell Jorge that searching for the perfect woman was futile. There'd been only one, and she'd left the planet two years ago. Instead, he said to his friend, "Have a great time."

***

In the past year, since Max moved in with Christie, Stephanie's father had come up with five guys he was certain would be perfect for her. Every one of them had been as boring as skim milk. She described each of them to Peg as the best nonprescription sleep aid she'd ever had. When was her father going to give this up? A better question was, when was she going to insist he stop? But she loved her father, and wouldn't hurt his feelings for the world—if she could help it.

She parked her car in front of his small attached home and got out, letting herself in the carport door without knocking. "Hey, Dad." She spoke loudly but didn't yell. It didn't take much for noise to travel through this small, compact dwelling.

Her father met her in the kitchen, sporting his usual mile-wide grin. "Hello, princess."

She watched him try to hide his disappointment as he took in her sweatpants, matching hoodie, and athletic shoes.

"Please don't call me princess anymore," she said.

"Sorry. Old habits die hard."

"At least, try not to call me that in front of anyone, okay?"

"You bet." Her father smiled anxiously. "You know, you're really doing me a favor coming here."

She made a face and shook her head. "How old is this one, Dad?"

"Your age. About."

"About? If this is what I have to look forward to for the rest of my life, I'd rather have Max move back in."

"You're not serious." Her father's eyes looked as if they might pop out of their sockets.

"Of course not. I was trying to make a point. Please let this be the last guy you set me up with."

"Honey, you need the practice."

"I do not."

"The older you get, the harder it is to meet someone, and you haven't exactly been successful with the other dates I arranged."

"That's because I don't want a man in my life. I just want my life. Period. I want to figure out something to do and take care of myself all by myself. I'm serious. You and Patrick are enough dudes in my life."

"How is my favorite grandson?"

"He's your only grandson. He flunked his algebra test, that's how he is. He had all Thursday afternoon and evening to let me know, and he sat on the paper I had to sign for his teacher until Friday morning. Now he's over at Max and Christie's, and he knows I can't get to him over there, nor would I tell his father about him flunking a test."

Bud chuckled. "Smart boy."

"Then he should be able to pass algebra."

"Not all of us are whizzes at math like you were."

She could feel herself turning red. She had been good at math, but what did it matter? There was book smart, and then there was street smart. Maybe she was book smart, but the choices she'd made clearly indicated she was inherently street stupid. Common sense wasn't something she could go to Saks and buy in multiple colors and then charge it to her credit card.

"I may have been good at math, but I can't help Patrick. Dad, every time I try to teach him something, lately, we just end up in an argument. And things are bad enough right now with the divorce from Hades. I always end up having to be the enforcer."

"Honey, it's called adolescence."

"Was I that bad?"

"Yes."

"At his old school the class size was about half of what it is at his new one. They got so much individual attention at Country Day I never had to worry about stuff like this. I need a tutor. You know of anyone? Maybe one of your friends?" She wanted to add the words, who'll do it for free to the end of the last question, but didn't. If she did that, her father would insist on paying. He shook his head no in response.

Stephanie walked over to her father's freezer and opened it, hoping for ice cream or éclairs. Nothing. Not only was she hungry for once, she also wanted to stall the inevitable walk to the activity center.

"The ice cream's in the garage freezer. And after you scoop out a bowl for me, scoop out double the amount for you. If you get any skinnier, you're going to blow away."

"Thanks. You want a cup of coffee with it, before we go?"

By her estimate, and the amount of ice cream and coffee rumbling around in her stomach, Stephanie figured she skillfully managed to put off getting to the community center by a good forty-five minutes. Now she slowed her walk to a crawl and commented on every flower and shrub along the way. This was a challenge, given the small patches of grass people in Leisure World called a front yard.

Three years ago, she'd been appalled when her father had sold his spacious ranch-style house in the older area of Scottsdale and moved to a retirement center in Mesa. She'd thought he was making the biggest mistake of his life, not to mention that her mother would have been crushed if she'd known someone else now lived in the house she had meticulously decorated and maintained. Her mother would have also thought that Mesa was six steps down the status ladder from Scottsdale. But from the minute her father had moved out to Leisure World, he had smiled more, looked healthier, and been constantly busy. Maybe he wanted a clean break and a new start, like she did. Yet somehow, she could never bring herself to ask.

"Hey." She pointed to the last condo on the block. "What's going on there?"

They stopped in their tracks. Before them stood a series of inflatable creatures amidst a slew of lawn gnomes holding cupids and hearts. The gnomes varied in size from small to frighteningly large. As for the inflatable creatures, everything from the Easter bunny to Frosty the Snowman was on display.

Stephanie whistled. "It's truly amazing someone could manage to fit those on a lawn the size of a postage stamp."

Her father's green eyes narrowed as he sent her a look of disapproval she recognized well. Those eyes had always been the best feature on her father's handsome face, and the only thing she'd inherited from him. Now that his hair and eyebrows had turned from light brown to shock white, their color stood out even more.

"Don't you miss our yard?" she asked her father.

"Not a bit."

Well, she did. She'd grown up there, played there, and had parties in the backyard. Now it belonged to someone else.

She pointed again to the house with all the seasonal kitsch on it. "Who lives there?"

"Louise Mueller. She's from Iowa."

"Oh. That explains it."

Her father looked at her and frowned again. Stephanie knew her habit of mocking people was a trait he heartily disliked.

"Her grandchildren are visiting, and she wants to do it up. They never come for Christmas or Thanksgiving because her son-in-law's mother expects them at her house every year. So when they do come, she plays it up for all it's worth."

"Ah, so that's why Santa is mixed in with Cupid, a pilgrim, and the Easter bunny." She examined the lawn again. "I think she's missing something for Halloween."

"No, one of the gnomes has a witch hat on. See?" He pointed to the one partially hidden by the inflatable bunny.

"How could I have missed? I'm surprised the homeowner's association doesn't shut it down."

"Louise is best friends with the current president, whose grandchildren live in New York, and she never sees them either." Her father looked at his watch. "Can we hurry it up here?"

"I'll keep walking if you can promise that none of those creatures will fall and bury me alive when we pass her house."

"You know, Steph, you can make all the fun you want of Louise, but just try and understand that for some people, there's a lot of hurt feelings surrounding their kids."

She stopped smirking. "I'm sorry, Dad. I really didn't mean to sound rude. I was just joking."

"I know, but sometimes your sarcasm crosses the line. Just be glad I don't feel that way about you. And if you play your cards right, Patrick won't feel that way either."

It was true, what her father had said. Sometimes she did cross the line. "Love you, Pops."

She slid her arm through her father's still muscular one, as they crossed the street toward the community center. Red, white, and pink streamers cascaded from the ceiling, and hearts decorated the painted concrete walls. As they entered, a song by Frank Sinatra, whose voice always made Stephanie melt, boomed throughout the room. She watched as elderly couples danced the fox-trot, strutting across the floor in each other's arms.

What was it like to be in love for a lifetime? Had she ever really loved Max, or had she simply convinced herself she had, because that's how you were supposed to feel when you got married? If she couldn't answer that question, how could she ever trust herself to know what was real the next time? The simple and safe solution was that there would be no next time.

She proceeded over the next hour to meet the latest guy her father had come up with. This guy had less hair on his head than either of her father's eyebrows put together, although what few strands he did have were arranged in a comb-over. Comb-overs she could almost tolerate; bad breath she couldn't. This guy had both. They danced one dance in which she stepped on his foot and belched in his face. One act she did on purpose; the other was completely by accident. After that, she was ready to say her goodbyes to Mr. Not-Right-for-Me.

"Listen, Dad, I think I'm going to walk back to your house, blow my nose, and scamper on home. Max will be dropping Patrick off at around seven, and I want to be there when he gets home."

"I'll walk with you," her father said.

Twenty feet out the door of the activity center, he started in. "Did you have to belch in his face?"

"You saw that?"

He nodded.

"That was an accident. Seriously. Too much coffee and ice cream mixed together. A gastric nightmare."

"And trouncing on his foot?"

"I hope it didn't hurt too much."

Her father shook his head in resignation and kept walking. "Do you need any money?"

"I'm fine."

"Be honest."

"I am." She said it carefully, so that he wouldn't know how tempted she was. "In fact, I started taking dance classes, I have so much extra cash. Too late for the guy today, though. I'll be fine until Max decides to get real."

He turned to her and smiled. "Dance classes? I'm truly impressed. You weren't exactly raised to know how to budget and make ends meet, and I feel bad about that."

"Don't. What happened between Max and me wasn't your fault, Dad."

"I should have put my foot down more."

"To who? I mean, to whom? Max?"

He shrugged. "Forget I said anything. I'm proud of you, prin— I'm proud of you, Steph. Real proud."

Chapter Three

Joe tried for the third time to get from his mother's front door to his car. "Mom, I appreciate it, but no more food after this. My refrigerator is already stuffed."

He looked down at his hands. Each of them held a shopping bag stacked with plastic containers, most of which would be taken to the break room refrigerator at work tomorrow. Once there, he would tape a note onto the stack that said, "Help Joe Schmidt Stay Sane. Eat Me."

Since he'd moved from the DC headquarters to the Phoenix office of the IRS three years ago, his coworkers had sworn they had each put on five pounds. Last year, they'd developed a survey for reviewing his mother's "lunchables." The title of the survey was "Rate Mary's Munchies." So far, the meat loaf sandwich was winning. Now really, who said the IRS didn't have a sense of humor?

"I thought you weren't going to try and fatten me up anymore." He leaned over and gave her a peck on the cheek.

She ignored him and instead talked about what was always on the tip of her tongue. "I wish you would have come earlier to the get-together today. The girl was very nice."

"Well, I couldn't. I had work to do." His voice softened. "I tried to tell you that, Mom."

His mother narrowed her eyes. "Joey, you work for the government. Do you think I have *stupid* stamped across my forehead? No one works weekends." Before he could respond to that, she launched into her real mission. "You need to get over this. You have to get yourself out there again."

This? So now Lisa was a this to get over? He nodded automatically. "I know, Mom. And I will." No, he wouldn't. There was no getting over his wife.

A cloud passed over Mary's usually sunny face. "Do you think it's because of what you do that women don't want to date you? Maybe they'll think you'll audit them."

"No, Mom. That would be against the law."

"Maybe you should consider going to work for a regular law firm, instead of the IRS."

"I like my work. It's interesting. Besides, I've put in a lot of years with the government already." He took one more step. "Mom, I have to go, before the traffic gets heavy."

"It's Sunday. You don't live that far away."

"I have to get ready for work. I want to try to catch my supervisor before her morning meetings start tomorrow."

"Okay, okay."

Joe noted that his mother's balance seemed slightly off. She'd probably been overdoing it again. The woman never sat down. "Have you given any more thought to a cleaning lady?"

"Have you given any more thought to going out with someone?"

God, she was like a dog with a bone. "You know, I'm taking dance classes."

His mother perked up immediately, but it didn't wash the tiredness from her face. "That's wonderful. I'm sure there are plenty of eligible women there."

Not really. Most of the people in the group class were engaged couples accompanied by their parents who needed to learn how to dance before the wedding so they wouldn't look like idiots. "Yeah, there are. Quite a few."

"That's great, Joey."

So was it okay to lie if it made someone feel better and worry less? The answer was a resounding yes, reverberating in his head like chimes in a church. "In fact, there are more women than men, and one of them I'm thinking of asking out. That's really why I didn't want to come to the Valentine's Day party at your retirement center."

"Active living."

"Huh?"

"It's called Sunnyslope Active Living Community. It's not a retirement center. We actively live."

"Oh yeah. Sorry, Mom. You know, you look a little tired."

"I'm fine, Joey. If you're fine, I'm fine. And you're doing okay, right?"

"Yeah, Mom. Stop worrying. I'm doing great." Just great.

***

Early Monday morning at seven thirty, as promised, Marta pulled into Stephanie's driveway. She was not in her usual minivan but in a truck Stephanie could hear coming from half a block away. Without thinking, she pressed the garage door opener from the inside and then regretted it. Last night, when she'd come home from her father's, it had sputtered to a stop halfway up two times in a row and then miraculously completed its journey on the third try. If the door opener broke, she had neither the money nor the know-how to fix it. Then again, pulling the garage door up and down manually would be more exercise incorporated into her day-to-day existence. Yes, if you looked hard enough, there was an upside to everything. Unfortunately, sometimes the upside was so deeply buried you needed a shovel to dig for it.

Marta got out of the truck wearing a black T-shirt with "Marta's Maids" in white on the front. A broom and mop were emblazoned to the right and left of the words. She beamed as she pulled out two identical ones for Stephanie. "My cousin owns a T-shirt shop on Thirty-Fifth Avenue," she explained. "She did it for free. You are my very first employee, besides my brother's wife, and she doesn't count because she's family. And I'm working on a website, which officially makes me a businesswoman." Marta beamed.

Stephanie took the shirts and smiled. "Thanks. I'll go put one on."

The two of them went inside. Marta sat at the kitchen table while Stephanie ducked into the pantry to change.

When she came out with the shirt on, Marta said, "It looks good. Better on you than me, or my sister-in-law who should lose twenty pounds. Remember to change when you get home. You don't want Patrick to know, right?"

Stephanie stared, indignant. "It's not like I'm ashamed of this." The truth, she was still chewing on the fact that she was cleaning houses for money. Then again, there were only a few other things she could do for cash, and she wasn't about to go there. She'd rather move in with her father.

"I know," Marta said. "But you don't want Patrick telling Mr. Max, and if any of the gossipy matrons in this neighborhood see you with your new shirt on, Mr. Max will put two and two together and know by the end of the day, so make sure you change."

"You're right." She breathed out slowly. "Marta, I can't thank—"

She watched as Marta held up her hand. "Don't. You're helping me, too. I want to expand my business, and you are my guinea pig employee. You're the first person working for me that's not family. I figure you won't be doing this forever, and you need the money so bad you will put up with my mistakes."

"True."

"And you are nice. A little snotty, but nice. And the snotty part is from the way you were raised. It's not really you."

Stephanie raised her eyebrows and then nodded slowly. What could she say? Marta was not only right but also her boss.

"Let's get your brooms and vacuum cleaner. I only have one vacuum, and I need them for my own jobs. We can put them in the back of the truck."

"What happened to your minivan?" Stephanie asked as they loaded the cleaning tools.

"It's in for repairs. This is my stupid little brother's truck, not the other one whose wife works for me. My little brother is in Cuernavaca right now stirring up shit. Look what he did to the back of his pickup."

She motioned to where the word *Chevrolet* used to be. Half the letters were either taped over or rubbed out, leaving only the *o*, the *l*, and the *e*.

"Olé," Stephanie said. "Well, at least it's friendly."

"Ha! That's what you think." Marta peeled back the duct tape on the left revealing the word, *Che*. "See? *Che olé*. What a little smart ass my brother is. We got into a big fight about it. I said to him, 'What did Che do but help to murder a bunch of people in Cuba and preach a philosophy he never lived? People need jobs and money, not sermons.'" She threw up her hands. "He left in a huff. He thinks I should listen to him because he's my brother and he has a college degree. I said, 'I'm a businesswoman, and you're just an idiot with a college degree. This is America, sucker.'" She shook her head. "Machismo doesn't fly here. It hardly flies in Mexico anymore. Besides, I'm older than him. He should listen to me."

Stephanie nodded silently as she climbed into the passenger side, wondering what it would have been like to have a brother. Older or younger, she would have taken either. Peg had four of them and constantly complained the whole time they'd been growing up. Sometimes, things looked better on the outside than they were on the inside. Still, it was lonely having no one, unless the someone you did have was her cousin Christie. In that case, solitary confinement looked pretty darn good.

Marta fired up the truck, and they were on their way. "Today, I will go with you and introduce you to two clients. Both women are widows. I'll show you the ropes. Let you know their particulars. There are two today, then two tomorrow. All of them are in the same retirement center in North Scottsdale. And I got a phone call from a new person. I'll meet with him later today and get the specifics. Make sure he's not an ax murderer or a weirdo, or has a stupid truck with *Che olé* on the back of it. I'll tell him I'm sending one of my staff. Ha! I like that word, staff. Anyway, you'll never see him because he's gone during the day, so I figured this was okay, too. That will give you five altogether. If that's not enough, we can add more."

***

Joe made it into his office twenty minutes early, in search of his supervisor. On his way out of the break room, with his first cup of coffee, he ran into his coworker who had the Maxwell Ledger case. "Hey, Tom."

"Your mom make anything good this weekend?"

"It's in the fridge." Joe paused and then said, "I need to ask you a few questions."

Tom turned, his hand already on the refrigerator handle. "What about?"

"You still investigating that plastic surgeon? Maxwell Ledger?"

"Oh, you betcha." Tom's eyes lit up.

Joe narrowed his. "If I have knowledge of that, and I am in a social situation with Ledger's wife, what is the policy?"

"I think you should talk to Maria."

"Yeah, that was my thought too. That's why I came in early."

Tom opened the fridge and peered at the containers from Joe's mother. "She'll be in soon," he said, "because I have an appointment with her the minute the clock starts ticking. Off the cuff, in a social situation I would advise you to keep your mouth shut about what's going on. And I wouldn't volunteer I work for the IRS either. You'll never get a date that way."

"I'm not dating her. She's married."

Tom held the container up to the light. "Is this your mom's baked ziti?"

"Yeah. Enjoy. Tell Maria I need to talk to her when you meet." He picked his cup back up and had begun to walk to his cubicle when Tom called him back.

"Hey, Joe."

"Yeah?"

"Technically speaking, Ledger doesn't have a wife. They're legally separated. Have been for about a year."

"Oh."

Separated? He still had fifteen minutes and thirty seconds before he was on the government clock. The north-facing wall of windows allowed for better reception, and he pulled out his cell phone and walked in that direction.

The Federal Building, which was where the IRS offices were located, was made of glass. During the summer, when temperatures rose to one hundred and fifteen and often stayed there, they couldn't get the inside temperature below eighty-five degrees. That fact set the building up for endless rounds of sarcastic jokes, which usually started with the phrase "people in glass houses" and ended with something like "stupid federal government." Like the IRS, in particular, needed to be the brunt of any more jokes than it already was.

"Hey," Joe said, when he heard Jorge's phone pick up. "Got time for a couple of questions?"

"I'm waiting for some test results. How about lunch? I got a lot to tell you."

This was what he had to look forward to. Instead of Saturday night dinners, they would be having Monday lunches, and he would get updates about Peg, the newest perfect woman. "If you're paying, I'm going, as long as it's not that cheap burger stand you love."

"Meet me at Honey Bears," Jorge said. "The first pulled pork sandwich is on me. After that you're on your own."

Joe clocked out at noon, watching his coworkers swarm around the refrigerator until the elevator door closed.

He walked three blocks from to Honey Bears on Central Avenue and spied Jorge sitting in one of the turquoise colored booths, waiting with lunch already on the table.

Jorge pushed the white plastic bib his way to cover his shirt and tie. It was standard practice at Honey Bears.

"What's up?" Jorge asked, never one to waste time nor mince words when food was in front of him. He took a large bite of his sandwich after he spoke. Joe watched a big drip of sauce hit the bib, making a splat on the thin white plastic.

"Have you told Peg that I work for the IRS?"

"No. No offense, but you haven't exactly been the main topic of conversation."

He settled back into the booth, so relieved that he'd brushed past his friend's sarcasm. "How's that going?"

Jorge grinned his answer.

Oh, God. "Listen, could you do me a favor and not tell Peg that I work for the IRS?"

"You want me to lie?"

"No. Not lie. If she asks you what I do, tell her I'm a tax attorney like I told her friend. Just don't volunteer any extra information."

"That's pretty slippery. What if she asks me directly?" Jorge was a stickler for details.

"Then use your discretion. Why would she ask you anyway? I mean, most people don't ask, Jorge, does your friend work for the IRS?"

Joe picked up his sandwich and watched the top part of pulled pork fall onto the plate.

"Why don't you want Peg to know?" Jorge asked.

"I can't tell you."

"Are you investigating her?"

"No. Not her. Don't ask, okay?"

"Okay, but if she suspects something and mentions it, I've got to tell her."

"Well, if that happens, let me know. I'm just asking that you don't volunteer the info, okay?"

Jorge nodded silently and popped the rest of his sandwich in his mouth.

"So she's sticking around? Peg?" Joe asked, watching Jorge devour the pulled pork.

"God, I hope so." Jorge stretched out his short, muscular legs encased in a pair of cotton khakis. "I think she might be the one."

Here we go again. Joe shook his head an indiscernible quarter of an inch. "Did you know that her friend really wasn't married?"

"Stephanie? She's married. Shit, how could you miss those rocks?"

"She's separated."

"That's still married, and no, I didn't know she was separated. She hasn't been the main topic of our conversations either." He took another bite of his sandwich and spoke with his mouth full. "Where'd you hear that anyway?"

Joe dismissed his friend's question with a wave of his hand and took a bite of the pulled pork. "Around," he said from the side of his mouth.

A look of surprise appeared on Jorge's face. "Are you interested in her?"

"No. Not at all."

"I can ask Peg if she's really married or not."

"No. Please don't. I shouldn't have mentioned it." He took up his sandwich again and bit off about a third of it, chewing quickly.

"I don't like lying, Joe. 'Specially to Peg."

"God, you've known the woman for less than a week. I'm only asking you not to offer information. Technically, that's not lying." He scooped up the chunk that had fallen out of the bun with his fingers and popped it into his mouth.

"Okay, okay." Jorge frowned after he swallowed his last bite.

"Hey. Did you find a cleaning lady?"

"Yeah. I think so. Peg's referral. I'm meeting her later today. Who knew you needed to be interviewed by a cleaning lady." He shrugged. "Maybe she wants to make sure I'm not a pervert."

"Remind me to ask you in a couple of weeks if she's working out."

"Still looking for someone to clean your mother's condo?"

"Is the pope Catholic?" Joe asked.

Jorge rolled his eyes and wiped his hands on the paper napkin next to his plate. "You think anybody's going to be acceptable to your mom? We could eat off her toilet seat when we were kids, if the smell of ammonia didn't bother you."

"Want a ride to dance class, or are you and Peg going together?"

"She has to pick up Stephanie. She says, if she doesn't, Stephanie will conveniently forget." Jorge sucked up the last of his soda. "Honestly, I don't think she's into you at all, so it certainly doesn't matter if you work for the IRS, but Peg won't hear it from me, and neither will her friend."

***

By three p.m. Marta and Stephanie pulled back into Stephanie's driveway. That gave her exactly thirty minutes to clean up and change before Patrick got back from school. Even though it was all mostly ones, the wad of cash in her pocket made her feel like she'd beat the house in Vegas.

"Next time, wear gloves when you wipe down the kitchen and bathroom," Marta told her, waking Stephanie out of her thoughts. "Look at your hands."

"They're itchy, but they'll be okay." She'd spent most of the ride home scratching them. They were blotchy-red with small welts, as if an army of ants had decided they were lunch. There was probably something in one of the cleaning products she had a contact allergy to.

"And take your fancy watch off when you clean too. Cleaning ladies do not wear gold Movado watches. It's enough you have to drive your Lexus."

"It's the only watch I have."

"Use the clock on your cell phone."

Stephanie nodded. "Good idea." She'd given some serious thought to selling the watch along with the diamonds, but her father had given her the watch when she'd graduated from college. He'd been proud of her. The diamonds were one thing, but the watch was another.

"Do you have anything besides those Coach purses?"

"No." Well, she did have a vintage Louis Vuitton that had belonged to her mother, but even she had to admit, it screamed haughty. Hey, maybe she could sell them on eBay. "How about a plastic bag?" she asked Marta, intending it as a joke.

Marta nodded her approval. "That'll work. I'll pick you up tomorrow. Same time." She put the truck in reverse. It coughed dark-gray smoke out the tailpipe as the word *olé* disappeared around the corner.

Stephanie caught the outline of Gloria Burnwater from behind her plantation shutters and waved heartily with one hand, while covering up the words on her shirt with her other arm. Who knew, Gloria just might be using binoculars. She wouldn't put it past her.

Gloria's silhouette disappeared before Stephanie could mount another smile and a wave. She laughed as she watched the shutters snap shut. Ah, this was heaven. Money in her pocket, and another opportunity to piss off the snob across the street. Did it get any better than this?

She moved quickly to stash the cleaning equipment in the far corner of the garage, and ducked inside to change her shirt.

She didn't want her son to be in the position of knowing something he couldn't tell his father. Kids shouldn't have to take sides or keep secrets. In fact, Patrick didn't even know that one of the biggest disputes in the divorce involved him, and that was exactly the way she wanted it. She often wondered what damage this long, drawn-out acrimony had done to him. Would he ever want to get married or have a relationship after watching his parents go at it?

As his late teens and young adulthood loomed around the corner, would he become angry and self-destructive? So many young men she knew turned their frustration and confusion inward, attacking themselves as though they were the problem, when it was the emotional environment around them.

She heard the front door slam as she chucked her Marta's Maids shirt in the dirty-clothes basket and walked out of the bedroom and into the still-furnished family room.

"Got anything to eat?" Patrick asked the second he saw her.

"Okay. Try saying, 'Hi, Mom. How did your day go? Got anything to eat?'"

He smiled sheepishly. "Well, do you?"

"Let me ask you something first. Got your remedial math plan written out?"

Much to her surprise, he pulled a paper, with his signature at the bottom, out of his folder. "I worked on it in study hall."

"Fantastic." Her eyes skimmed his solution. Basically, he planned to study an extra thirty minutes a day and complete the sample problems that his teacher gave out at the end of each class for extra practice. It was all she needed to know.

"What's up with your hands?" he asked.

"Nothing."

"They look like you stuck them in a beehive." Patrick continued to stare. "They're all red and bumpy."

"Probably an allergy." She eyed them along with Patrick. At least the swelling had gone down a bit. "They look better than they did."

"Ready for dance class tonight?"

She'd completely forgotten. "No. I'm not." Hopefully the bumps would be nonexistent by then.

"Aunt Peg told me to remind you every Monday. She said otherwise you might forget. Personally, I think you should go."

"Of course, you do. What eighth-grade boy wants his mother around?"

"Mom, it's gotta beat laying on the living room carpeting and doing one hundred sit-ups."

"I do forty."

"Whatever."

He followed her into the kitchen where she pulled the ice cream out of the freezer that her father had packed in a cooler and insisted she take with her on Sunday.

"So you really don't want to go to dance class, do you?" Patrick asked.

"Why do you say that?"

"Because you never forget anything. It's like you've got a calendar inside your skull. You always know where I should be, when I need to be there, all that kind of stuff. You know when I flunk a test before I do."

"Funny. Honestly, I've just been so busy with other things I forgot all about it." On a lark, she grabbed his old X-Men cereal bowl from the back of the cabinet shelf.

"Hey." He smiled when he saw the bowl. "I haven't seen that thing in a while. Don't sell it, okay? I want to save it for my kid when I get married."

She smiled and willed her eyes not to water. "Deal."

Chapter Four

Peg appeared at Stephanie's a good hour before the class started, which meant she wanted to talk. A lot.

"I must have left six messages this weekend," Stephanie said, as she threw open the door. "Where have you been?"

Her friend's eyes shone with a sparkle that meant she'd either sold a house and received a huge commission, or there was a man in her life. Stephanie hoped it was a commission. She didn't know if she could watch Peg go through another breakup. Men just weren't worth it.

"I was busy practicing my dance steps," she said with a voice so melodic Stephanie knew immediately it had to be the dance guy.

As if to confirm her worst fears, she watched Peg waltz through the front door and around the entry hall, her off-white, crepe-silk skirt swirling around her knees until she stopped with a curtsey and a grin. She had such grace.

"You were with the short guy?" Stephanie asked.

"If you mean Jorge Vasquez, the answer is correcto. And he's not that short, so knock it off."

"I hope you like wearing flats."

Stephanie watched a frown pass over Peg's face like a storm cloud on a windy day. It reminded her of the standard look her father gave her when he felt she'd gone too far. Without a word to each other, they walked into the kitchen where Peg helped herself to the remaining coffee. She brought the carafe over to the table and freshened up Stephanie's own mug that read, "World's Greatest Mom." The lip sported two chips, but it was still her go-to mug for coffee.

Peg and Stephanie's frequent coffee klatches had been their routine since grade school, when their mothers finally caved and allowed them to drink the brew if it was equal parts milk and coffee. The only short breach in this ritual had been when Peg had gone through a Diet Coke phase in college, and she would knock down two cans every morning for the caffeine. That was during one of her no-fat diets when she'd eliminated coffee because she couldn't stomach it without half-and-half.

As if her memory of her friend's diet history was a segue to the moment, Peg farted long and hard, and then belched. "Sorry," she said, a look of sheepishness overtaking the joy.

"Are you on Calorie Counters again?" Stephanie asked, blunt in both word and tone.

"How'd you know?"

"Guess." Stephanie rolled her eyes at Peg.

"It takes my stomach a while to adjust to all the fruits and vegetables."

"When we drive to class, get it all out. I'll keep my window down."

"Well, I had to do something," Peg said.

"Did you ever consider that you didn't have to do anything? Maybe Jorge cares more about who you are than how much you weigh."

Peg crossed her legs. She was wearing a new jacket that was cut exquisitely for her shape, and the material brought out the honey-colored highlights in her hair. "It's only the first couple of weeks that are like this. Then your digestion gets used to the mountains of fiber."

Stephanie grabbed her sweatshirt off the back of her kitchen chair and thrust her left arm into the sleeve and then her right.

"Are you going in those sweats again?"

"Yeah."

"They smell like ammonia."

"Last week you complained I had BO. Maybe it'll cover that up."

"Hey, what's going on with your hands?"

"Rash."

"Eww. They look horrible."

"Good." The two of them started to walk to the door, and then Stephanie remembered. "My wedding rings. Hey, I'll meet you in the car."

Halfway to dance class, and several excuse-me's and unrolling-of-the-front-windows later, Peg asked, "Did you know Joe Schmidt's wife died a few years ago?"

"I didn't know he'd ever been married. He didn't talk that much after he grilled me about Max. Come to think of it, he didn't talk that much before, either. I know he's a tax attorney. That's it, and that's how I want to keep it."

"Jorge mentioned it." She softened her voice. "I'm sorry for him."

"That would be a hard one to get over, if he really loved her. You know, not everybody loves the person they're married to, which is why I don't ever want to try it again, and it's also why I suggest you don't either."

"Yeah, well, just because you voted yourself off the Love Boat doesn't mean everyone else has." Peg perked up. "I had a fantastic time this weekend. Jorge is such a good dancer, and he has the best sense of humor I've been around in years."

Peg continued talking as she lowered her window yet again. "The two of us practiced all Saturday night after we went salsa dancing, and on Sunday, we tried to work out the rumba. That's the next lesson."

"Take it slow with this guy, okay? At least wait until you're sure you won't be farting in bed." Stephanie paused to see if Peg would laugh. She didn't.

"And one more thing," Stephanie said. "Please don't tell Jorge I'm broke. I don't want him telling Joe

Schmidt. Right now, he considers me a married, money-grubbing, pampered princess, and I'd rather have the world thinking that than feeling sorry for me."

"Got it, but I don't know why. And I never thought you were money grubbing."

Peg had conveniently left the words *pampered princess* out of her defense. She wasn't about to ask for clarification. Like her mother and father, and Max, some things she was better off not knowing. Those words were becoming her motto.

They pulled into the parking lot, and once again, Stephanie lagged behind Peg as her friend barreled her way through the parking lot to the door of the dance studio. Stephanie caught up with her only because Peg stopped to smooth her hair and pass gas one more time.

"This happens every time you go on Calorie Counters. Stand here for a few minutes and get all the farts out. Considering the fact that you floored it through every yellow light to get here, you've got more than a few minutes."

If Peg's eyes had been a weapon, Stephanie knew she would be on the ground and dead.

"Some of us still believe in love." Peg pulled the heavy glass door to the dance studio open.

And some of us are big dopes. She bit her tongue to stop her from saying it out loud.

"You're on time," Jorge said, as he saw Peg come through the door. He walked right up to her and beamed so brightly Stephanie wanted to pull out her sunglasses. "I like that in a woman."

"And I like that in a man," Peg said back.

Oh, and I'd like a trashcan to barf in. Stephanie watched as Peg and Jorge walked arm-in-arm past the check-in desk. She followed behind hoping that somehow the two of them would shield her from the inevitable company of Joe Schmidt. As they approached the restrooms she ducked into the door that said ballerinas, leaving Jorge and Peg to walk the rest of the way alone. Like they'd notice she was gone.

Her plan, devised in a matter of seconds, was to stay in the restroom until class started so she could come out at the last minute and be at the end of the line. That way she would miss standing next to Peg, who of course would be standing right across from Jorge, who would be standing next to Mr. Lack–of-Social-Skills Schmidt. She sat on the toilet in an empty stall and pushed the door closed. Why did she let Peg talk her into these things? There were limits to friendship. Even theirs.

Two women came into the restroom. Stephanie watched them through the crack in the stall. They took extra care with their hair and reapplied their lipstick with the skill of master painters. She longed to open the door and tell them no one was worth it. They'd be better off taking a course in medical billing, or learning how to complete IRS forms for people at tax time, or taking a home repair course at a big box hardware store, but she didn't. She didn't want to come out of the stall where it was beginning to feel safe and cozy sitting on the toilet, listening to the hope in those women's voices. Yet when she heard Ms. Rita's voice waft through the restroom telling everyone to line up, she stood like an obedient schoolgirl, pulled up her sweatpants, and marched right out.

She got into the women's line as Ms. Rita started on her third sentence. Dressed in a leotard and a dancer's wrap skirt, Ms. Rita looked Stephanie's way and smiled tersely.

Without being obvious, she searched the men's line. Jorge and Peg were directly across from each other. She looked again for Joe. Where was that jerk?

Ms. Rita began to explain the rumba. "Men, you take your partners' hands like this." She demonstrated the move with one of the women. "And quick, quick, one, quick, quick, two, quick, quick, three, quick, quick, twirl.

Careful now," Ms. Rita warned, as the woman's hips almost ran into hers when she came out of the twirl. "These are pivot turns. You twirl on a dime."

What idiots. Stephanie laughed softly as she watched. But when she turned her gaze from Ms. Rita back to the men's line she found that Joe had slipped in and now stood directly across from her. He nodded in her direction. So much for strategies.

"Now," Ms. Rita said. "If you'll walk up to the person standing in front of you, we'll all practice what I demonstrated. And, girls," she said winking, "watch those twirls."

Stephanie veered toward the man next to Joe. He looked her up and down through a pair of thick, black plastic glasses. "Honey," he said, "if I don't dance with my wife, I'm going to be in hot water for the next decade, and I don't know how to cook."

"Sure. Sorry." She moved back over.

"Looks like we're stuck with each other," Joe said, as he took three more steps in her direction.

"Lucky you." She made sure her face was absent of any trace of a smile and that he didn't see the top of her hands, still somewhat red and splotchy from cleaning.

"Lucky you too." He counted out the steps without paying her any heed whatsoever. She could have been a robot.

Ms. Rita hopped over to them and started squawking in little bird-like pecks. "This isn't war; it's the rumba. Don't twirl her like that, she's not a top. You're trying to spin her to the other side of the room, when your hand should guide her for a sweet, close turn right back to you."

Stephanie smirked.

"And you," Ms. Rita glared at Stephanie. "Don't resist so much. The look on your face shouldn't say *torture*. It should whisper *attraction*." Before she moved on, Ms.

Rita delivered two more pieces of advice to them both. "Your steps are too big. And don't look down. It makes you look like clunky baboons. The rumba is a Latin dance. There's eye contact. Eye contact that says you're enjoying yourself in each other's arms."

Joe looked at Stephanie and smiled, but only slightly. "Well, I feel good. How about you?"

Stephanie nodded. "Wonderful."

At the sound of giggling, they stopped in the middle of a poorly executed pivot turn to see Jorge pulling Peg up from a dip. He twirled her into his arms as though she was a yo-yo on a string. Without a doubt, they were the best dancers in the class.

"They went over the steps all weekend," Joe said.

"I know. I heard all about it."

"Me too. Obviously, practice makes perfect." Joe watched Jorge's steps.

"Look at them," Stephanie said, as Peg beamed at Jorge. "I hope you don't expect me to look like that." She added quickly, "I can learn to dance, but I can't act like I'm in to you at all."

"And the same for me."

"Besides, I'm married."

"Of course you are."

They kept their eyes on Peg and Jorge as he twirled Peg, pulled her into his arms again and, this time, did a side rock at the end.

"God, love sucks," Stephanie snorted.

Joe nodded in agreement, and they resumed dancing for a few minutes until Joe planted his right foot firmly on top of Stephanie's.

Stephanie winced. "Ow. Did you do that on purpose?"

"No. Who steps on someone's foot on purpose? If you'd pay attention, you'd know your foot shouldn't have been there." He pulled her closer.

"The rumba is a dance of seduction," Ms. Rita called out to the class. "Move your hips, ladies. Gentlemen, look like you mean it."

"Mean what?" Joe asked Stephanie. "What am I supposed to mean?"

"You don't have to look me in the eyes, okay?" Stephanie murmured.

"It's part of the dance."

"No, it's not."

"Yes, it is. In the rumba, you look at your partner. In the waltz, you look over their shoulder, through the window." He pulled her in and looked her in the eyes until they both started laughing, and then he turned slightly away and looked over her shoulder.

The next thing she knew Joe was grabbing at her pants, right above her butt.

She pulled away quickly. "Hey, that's not part of the rumba. That'll get you a swift kick to your nuts, buster."

He pulled his hand away from her backside and showed her what he'd been after. It was a stream of toilet paper that had been stuck in her sweatpants, and it fluttered slightly under the ceiling fan they were standing beneath as he held it out to show her.

Stephanie grabbed it from him and wadded it up in her hand.

"You could say thank you."

"I could," she nodded, "but you're not that lucky."

"Okay, the next time you have toilet paper streaming down your backside, I won't say a word. I'll let you humiliate yourself in complete ignorance, that's how lucky you'll be."

"Sounds like a plan, Stan." God, she sounded like she was in high school.

"Fine." He nodded emphatically.

The music ended and the two of them immediately withdrew their hands. Stephanie expected him to walk away, but instead, he stayed next to her and kept silent.

She examined the tops of her athletic shoes, the ceiling, the ceiling fans, and the framed pictures of famous dancers that hung on the wall, Fred Astaire, Ginger Rogers, Gene Kelly, and John Travolta. Anything but Joe Schmidt.

Everyone else seemed to know someone, and as far as Peg and Jorge were concerned, no one else was in the room to begin with. She eyed the other dancers while she picked at the fuzz on her cheap, cream-colored hoodie. Finally, she turned toward the clock on the wall. Thirty more minutes and she would be on her way home. When the music resumed, she turned toward Joe.

"Peace?" She let the white toilet paper she still had wadded in her hand fall into a white flag of surrender.

He grinned, and she wished she hadn't liked it.

"I think everyone else is partnered with someone, anyway." She held her hand out for Joe to take. "We're the only ones here who need someone."

His eyes widened when he noticed the redness on the top of her hands, and then a sarcastic grin spread over his face. "Allergic to your diamonds?"

She ignored his rude comment and thrust her left hand into her pocket. She'd shoved the rings in there on the way out of the house and then forgotten to put them on. Careless. Maybe she detested them, but they were worth at least a couple thousand on resale. Probably more. She pulled them out, pushed them onto her swollen fingers, and then lifted her hands for him to take.

"Seriously, what's wrong with your hands?"

"I tried a sample of hand cream at one of the boutiques I went to today, and I guess I had an allergic reaction to it."

"Oh." He nodded in understanding. "Yes, it happens to me every time I go into a boutique, too."

She smiled, and looked around the room. "So I guess you're stuck with me again."

Joe stood in silence.

"Things could be worse, you know," she said. "You could get Ms. Rita."

His laughter caused Ms. Rita to look over at the two of them and glare. "Agreed," he whispered.

They danced in silence for the rest of the session, neither of them stepping on the other, until Ms. Rita shouted to the group. "Good job everyone. Next week we review the waltz and rumba, then we start on the cha-cha."

"Hey, can you catch a ride home with Joe?" Peg asked Stephanie quietly.

Stephanie stared wide-eyed at Peg. "No."

Peg's face took on a pleading look. "Jorge and I are going out for coffee." She leaned closer and whispered in her ear. "Please."

Joe appeared at Peg's side. "Jorge told me you were going out for coffee, so I'll give her a ride home, Patricia."

"Actually, my name is Mary Margaret. O'Malley. I'm called Peg for short."

Joe's eyes danced. "There was a girl in my grade school with that name."

"Where'd you go to school?"

"St. Gregory's in Camden, New Jersey."

"Oh, that explains it," Peg said. "Didn't you know there's a requirement that every Catholic school has to have at least six Mary Margaret's to stay open?"

Joe laughed outright. "Mary Margaret, I'm happy to take Mrs. Ledger home. For you."

"Thanks." Without another word, Peg sprinted away from them toward Jorge.

"Nothing like being ditched." Stephanie headed for the door. She turned around to Joe after she pushed it open. "Lucky you, again. That's three times in one night you've had the privilege of being stuck with me."

The two of them walked toward the parked cars, with Stephanie falling into an I'll-follow-behind-you pattern. Anything but walk right next to him. He hit the unlock function on his key when they were ten feet from a white, four-door Camry.

She climbed in and twenty minutes later found herself staring at her front door.

"This is one big house," he said as he pulled into her driveway. "You and Max use a megaphone when you want to find each other?"

He grinned and craned his neck out of the car window, whistling like a country yokel. "Whew-eeee, where does your house end?"

"On the other side." Stephanie tried to look put out, but she really thought it was quite funny, especially the megaphone comment.

He pointed to the house across the street, flooded in an unnecessary abundance of electric lighting from all angles. "Is that house pink?"

Utter the word *pink* in front of Gloria Burnwater and you were banished from her social calendar for life. Not that someone like Joe knew or would care. Stephanie looked at him and smiled. "The owners call it *desert rose*."

"Isn't that another word for pink?" He whistled again as he looked at the house. "That house is even bigger than yours. You could probably go for a week in that thing and not see someone if you didn't want to, megaphone or no megaphone."

"I won't be telling Max you said that." She tried very hard not to smile. She did not want to like this guy.

"Is he in there?" Joe asked. "Because the front of your house is all dark, almost like no one lives there."

Stephanie frowned. "Not that it's any of your business, but of course he is. And it's dark because we strongly believe in energy conservation. Thanks for the ride."

"Anytime. You know, if you were my wife I wouldn't want you going to dance class alone. You should take him sometime."

She shot him a quizzical look and then got out of his car without looking back, and walked to her darkened front door. Habit led the key to the lock, as she heard Joe's car pull away.

And then it hit her. Why hadn't he needed directions when he drove her home?

***

The next morning Stephanie woke and reached for her Marta's Maids T-shirt, then put it back in the drawer, remembering that she had to see Patrick off first. Today was one of those wretchedly annoying late-start days due to preparation for parent-teacher conferences. Given her son's one-toe-over-the-line sense of humor, parent-teacher conferences were something she never looked forward to.

She stuck her head out of her bedroom and looked down the hallway. The door to Patrick's bedroom was open, which was a good sign. Usually the door was shut, and she had to knock to get his attention. She made her way to the kitchen and then walked back down the hallway to her son's room, a cup of coffee in her hand.

"Hey, Mom."

"Morning, sweetie. What's up today? Anything besides school?" She leaned against the door frame to his room and wondered when the last time was that his sheets had been changed. His bedroom stunk like a locker room in the dead heat of a Phoenix summer when the rains came.

He looked up from his task of piling books and papers into his backpack. "No."

"Don't forget your lunch."

"You say that every day."

There was a testiness to his voice that made Stephanie refrain from the reply that was ready to launch from her lips. The reason she said that every day was that he forgot to take his lunch at least three times a week.

"You know, your room really stinks. Can't you smell that?"

"No."

"I'm about ready to go out and buy one of those plug-in scented things and stick it in your outlet. When's the last time you cleaned up in here?" His dirty clothes were strewn on the floor like wall-to-wall carpeting, and when she looked around his bed, she realized everything he'd worn for the last two weeks surrounded it like a moat.

"When Marta quit, you told me my room was my business."

Amazing the way Patrick processed information. "What I meant was that it was your business to keep it clean. And now it stinks."

"I'll keep the door closed." He smiled mischievously and shut the door in her face.

"Funny, Pat, real funny." Stephanie knew it was both a challenge and a joke. The two of them had always clowned around, but sometimes he crossed the line where adults were concerned, and it worried her.

"Patrick, open the door."

He mimicked her perfectly. "Hello, Patrick, did you sleep well? Can you open the door, pleeease?"

"Knock it off, buster."

The door opened.

"This weekend, you clean up your room and do your wash."

"I don't know how to do wash."

"I'll teach you. Then when you go to college, you'll know how to do it, and you won't have to ask anyone else for help. It's good to be independent." She remembered Peg teaching her their freshman year. It was embarrassing how ill equipped she'd been to live away from home. With a cleaning lady coming three times a week, she'd never been expected to lift a finger.

"Can I close my door now?"

Why feed the bear by answering him? Instead, she went back to the kitchen to have another cup of coffee and wait for Marta, who showed up in her minivan at eight thirty.

Patrick rushed to open the door when he saw Marta through the living room window, where he waited for his ride, getting out of the van. "Are you back?"

Stephanie, who stood behind Patrick, made a face to Marta over his head that conveyed the message *roll with it, please.*

She watched as an impish grin appeared on Marta's face. "No. I am here because I like your mother, so you should be nice to her. And I need to borrow her vacuum cleaner. Mine broke." She sniffed the air. "What smells in here?" Marta asked, sniffing again. "It's coming from down the hallway. It smells like a toilet." She walked toward the hallway and stopped. "Ha! It is your room."

Oh, this was too perfect. "Told you." Stephanie chimed in.

Patrick made a face and turned to look at Marta with sudden suspicion. "Did she pay you to say that?"

"People do not pay me to tell the truth. They pay me to clean their houses."

Patrick shook his head and grabbed his backpack as his ride pulled up and honked. "I have to stay after school today," he said halfway out the door.

"Why?" Stephanie asked Patrick's silent, fleeting figure. She got no answer and shut the door behind him.

"He is at that age," Marta said softly.

"I'm afraid he's hiding something."

Marta nodded her head in understanding. "Maybe, but it might not be a bad thing he is hiding."

"Good point." She stood for a minute, not knowing what to say. "Let me change into my shirt, grab my equipment, and we'll get going."

They pulled Marta's minivan into the garage, piled the equipment into it, and pulled out with Gloria Burnwater watching them from her living room window again, this time with the shutters wide open.

"Do you think she's spying on me?"

"I think the woman has nothing to do but pick at herself and other people."

"Maybe I should come up with a story in case people ask."

"Yes," Marta agreed. "Also, this is the last day I will be with you, so that will lessen any suspicion. First, we will go to this new job in North Central Phoenix. Uh! Now they call it Uptown. How silly. Anyway, no one knows you there, and then we will double back, and I will introduce you to the people on the other two jobs, and stay to show you the ropes. Then, after today you are on your own."

No one in North Central Phoenix knew her, except her cousin Christie. Marta didn't know, but that was where she lived. Really, what were the chances of running into her? It wasn't as though she was going to stop and do her shopping there.

Marta continued talking. "The guy whose condo we will clean, I met him. He's nice. Not a pervert. But I need to let you in and show you his particulars. Then I'll give you the key." She shrugged and shook her head. "Everyone has a particular, but not this guy. He just wanted it cleaned, and he seemed grateful." She blinked and then said, "Something else."

"What?"

"Your car."

"What about it?"

"That Lexus is too fancy for a cleaning lady."

"I can't buy another one."

"I know. And I need a place to store my brother's truck while the idiot is in Cuernavaca. If I can keep it in your garage, you can use it to go on jobs for the next few months. It will keep the battery charged, and maybe by the time he gets back, your problem will be finished. I tell you, if those ladies in the retirement center see you drive up in that Lexus, they'll start tut-tutting about how much they pay you, and you won't ever get any tips. Not that they're generous in those ways in the first place, but they'll ask questions about why you are cleaning houses. People with too much time and money can cause big headaches."

"You wouldn't mind if I use it?"

"You wouldn't mind if I stored that piece of junk in your garage?"

"No."

"Good. We will drive by my house when we are finished. You can pick it up there. I should probably get the muffler fixed."

"No, don't. I sort of like it." *Mostly, because Gloria Burnwater doesn't.* "It makes me think of firecrackers going off, like the Fourth of July."

"Well, make sure you keep the Che part covered up, otherwise your neighbor across the street will probably call the FBI."

They drove in silence down Camelback Road to Central Avenue. Stephanie had always liked the North Central Phoenix part of town, but her mother preferred Scottsdale. Aunt Gigi's house was in North Central Phoenix, and it was bigger and statelier than theirs, something that had always rankled her mother. But her mother had a somewhat snottier Scottsdale address to laud over Aunt Gigi, and even up the score. The two of them were always in competition.

Marta turned off Central, onto Maryland Avenue, and into a group of well-kept townhomes.

"It's number six," Marta said as she grabbed the bucket and mop.

Stephanie pulled out the vacuum and rolled it behind her while Marta turned the key in the door and then stuck her head in. "So far so good," she said, turning back to smile at Stephanie.

She followed Marta into the house and gave the living room a quick scan. The condo was definitely a man's domain, with an oversized suede couch and matching recliners on each side. All three pieces of furniture were centered around a big-screen TV. If there were video games, Patrick would love it.

"Dios mio," Marta muttered from the room beyond the man cave. Stephanie found Marta in the kitchen, holding an envelope full of cash, and counting it silently. "Look at this mess," Marta said, putting the envelope down. "It's worse than my bratty little brother's studio apartment."

To call the kitchen a mess was polite. It reminded her of the time Patrick had decided to bake a cake for her birthday. Not a utensil, bowl, or pan was left clean. The cake-disaster birthday marked the first time Max had forgotten to get her a present, and he'd never bothered to get her a card. After that, forgetting her birthday had become habitual. No matter, she went revenge shopping the very next day.

"Wow." That was all she could muster when she looked at the mess.

"Yes," Marta agreed. "But at least he left an apology note and paid us three times the amount I quoted him. He also writes that he will never leave it this messy again."

She watched Marta stare at the sink, piled high with plates, pans, and a dirty casserole dish balanced precariously on the top. "Oy vey," Marta muttered, her head shaking back and forth.

Stephanie laughed. "That's not Spanish."

"I cleaned house for a woman who was Jewish. They have great words. Other words she taught me were schmutz, schlep, schmuck, and schlemiel. Those are good, too, so I use them." She pointed her index finger and wagged it back and forth. "This is America. You use what you want, and what you don't want, you don't use."

They worked relentlessly on the condo for the next three hours, and when they were done, they loaded the equipment back into the minivan.

"We did good," Marta said. She handed her the key to the condo. "Now we are on to the ladies of Scottsdale. They live right next to each other in a retirement, I mean active-living, center, so I will introduce you and then leave."

"We have to make a stop and get some more vacuum bags," Stephanie told her. "Sorry, I didn't check how full this one was when we left my house, but I didn't anticipate how dirty the condo would be either. It's about ready to explode." Really, who lived like that?

"Not a problem. There is a vacuum-and-sewing-repair store in the same shopping center as that fancy grocery on Central Avenue and Camelback."

She remembered the grocery store well. M&N's Gourmet Foods. It was within walking distance of her aunt's house, the house where Christie now lived with Max. The house that was both stunning and completely out of place in Phoenix. Much of North Central was an area of sprawling brick ranch houses, many built in the fifties and then added onto over the years.

Christie's two-story house, a Phoenix rarity, had white pillars in front, and a domed entry room. Set back far from Central Avenue, and complete with a paved, brick horseshoe driveway, the house hinted at a life where carriages were drawn up to the front so that the help could assist the ladies into the house. Stephanie used to jokingly call it Monticello, but quit because Christie missed the sarcasm and took it as a compliment.

This was where Patrick went to stay every other weekend since Max had decided it was better for him to fulfill his parental visits than pay her more money. As they passed the house on the way to the store, Stephanie made a point of not looking.

"How is your friend, Peg?" Marta asked, pulling Stephanie out of her thoughts.

"Peg? Oh, she's fine. Why do you ask?"

"No reason. She has given me many jobs over the past few years with her real estate business. You know, people who need to clean their house before they put it on the market. And she has thrown many handyman jobs my brother's way, too. She's nice."

"Yeah, she is." Not at all like her cousin Christie.

They turned into the shopping center and parked as close to the vacuum store as they could. Stephanie got out and took off walking toward M&N's. The gourmet grocery store had been there for decades.

Years ago, when her mother was visiting her sister, she and Christie would walk there for candy. They always went for the chocolates, which melted before they managed to get halfway home.

Even back then, Stephanie couldn't stand her cousin, and she recalled how horrible she'd felt because her mother and aunt wanted them to be like sisters. Come to think of it, she really didn't like her aunt all that much, either.

She looked up from her thoughts and stopped so abruptly she heard her running shoes squeak as they lurched against the concrete. There she stood, Cousin Christie, holding a bottle of wine sticking out of a paper bag, and carrying a chunk of something wrapped in white butcher's paper with M&N stamped on the sealing tape. It was either a big chunk of overpriced fish or two disgustingly thick steaks. Nothing at M&N's was ever a bargain.

They were upon each other before Stephanie could duck behind a car or make a run for the vacuum store. She hadn't seen Christie since catching her in bed with Max. It was an image far too vivid and humiliating, and one she'd tried to rip from her memory but couldn't.

Stephanie steadied herself and took a big, deep breath. Time to be bold, brave, and a bitch. She held her purse against her chest so that the part of her shirt with the words *Marta's Maids* was hidden.

"Christie." Her voice sang with mockery. "It's been too long. Why, I think the last time I saw you, you were in my bed with my husband. Wasn't that about a year ago? Or was it a year and a half? I don't remember."

"Wha ah ew ewing ere?"

Stephanie scrutinized her cousin's face, which was showing minimal signs of surprise upon seeing her. A small bit of drool at the corner of Christie's mouth appeared, and with that, the clues converged.

"Oh, my god." Stephanie burst out laughing. "You've had a collagen injection, and you can't talk. Or is it Botox?" Out of the corner of her eye, she caught Marta staring at her from the minivan, a question mark on her face.

She turned back to face Christie, whose hateful eyes made up for her vacuous face. The drool was beginning to work its way down her hairless chin, but Christie probably couldn't feel the meandering spittle. Stephanie wasn't about to tell her. Instead, she watched gravity take its sweet time.

"Tell Max he needs to be a little more careful where he sticks that needle next time."

She watched Christie blink and turn away. "Oh my god," she said, realizing the full implications of what Christie had done. "You didn't have Max do your injection, did you? You had somebody else, because you didn't want him to know. That's true desperation, Christie. I'd feel bad for you, but you and Max didn't even offer to wash my sheets when you two were done. I mean, how disgusting can you get?"

Christie turned to walk away, but Stephanie blocked her.

"You don't get to run away this time, Cuz. Now's my chance to tell you what a lying, duplicitous bitch you are, and you can't form a single, coherent word back at me. This is really too choice."

She faked a yawn and continued.

"It's almost worth Max leaving me and sleeping with you. In fact, it's better."

She knew Christie would be glaring if she could make a face.

"But you know," Stephanie started in again, "I'm not going to tell you what a lying, duplicitous bitch you are, because you're not worth it, given the fact that you are a lying, duplicitous bitch. Don't get me wrong. I don't want him back, but you are my cousin, so how could you?"

She paused again and took a long and deep breath. Enough vitriol for one day.

"You better get that fish or steak or whatever you've got for your overpriced dinner wrapped up in that paper, home quick. We wouldn't want Max to get food poisoning. Then we'd both be out of luck. Or maybe you'd be the one out of luck, because, legally, I'm still his wife. I'd inherit everything. Oh, on second thought, don't bother getting that—what is it, steak or fish—home. You just take your sweet, little, self-absorbed time."

"Uck ew."

She stuck her finger out like a prim-and-proper school marm. "Ohhhh, did you just say what I think you did? I'm telling Aunt Gigi on you. Your mother seriously thinks you never cuss, much less drop an f-bomb."

Stephanie thought about slapping Christie hard on the back, as though they were two buddies playing baseball, but then she remembered what her folded arms were hiding on her shirt. "See ya around."

She started to walk away and then thought about Patrick and stopped.

"One more thing. If I ever hear from my son that you are mean to him in any way, I'll drag that Saran Wrapped face of yours through the dirt, like I did when we were kids. Only this time, the ER won't be able to extract the mud out of your surgically altered nose with those extra-long tweezers they used last time."

"Uck ew, ich! Eye ose is ot ixed."

"It is too fixed. Your mother told my mother years ago. It happened the summer before high school when you supposedly went to international world peace camp." Stephanie left Christie drooling on the sidewalk and never looked back.

God, that felt good. Sort of. Her legs were trembling when she climbed into the minivan and shut the door. Marta turned to look at her. "Was that—?"

"Yep."

"Dios mio," Marta uttered.

"Oi vey," Stephanie said, grinning.

Marta smiled like the rascal she was. "Holy shit."

Chapter Five

After her run-in with Christie, Marta and Stephanie drove to the retirement center where the two women she would be cleaning for lived. She and Marta worked hard and quick in both condos, and by midafternoon Stephanie was driving the Olé truck she'd picked up at Marta's house into her garage. She checked in the rearview mirror to see how many of her neighbors were looking. There was only the usual suspect.

After changing, she washed her face and hands, and was looking forward to relaxing on the sole existing couch in the family room when her phone rang.

"Steph." Her father's voice came over loud and clear, with a pinch of the old disciplinary dad in it.

"Hey, Dad."

"What did you say to your cousin?"

"How do you know about that?" Stephanie asked.

"Your Aunt Gigi called."

The negative effects of Christie's injections must have worn off quickly. "I thought Aunt Gigi was in assisted living."

"That doesn't mean she can't make a phone call."

Stephanie let the air escape from her lungs. "So my sweet cousin, who put her mother in a home so she and Max could occupy Monticello all by themselves, called to whine about me? Some things never change."

"No, they don't, but what I wish would change is your mouth."

She sprang off the couch and started pacing between the kitchen and the family room. "Hey, she was the one that unloaded the f-bomb today, not me. I only told her the truth, that she's a lying duplicitous bitch." Three times.

"And then you said something about poisoning Max?"

Now she was mad. "No, I said she should get her food home so Max *wouldn't* get food poisoning."

"Well, you might want to call and apologize."

"What? Let me get this straight, she messes around with my husband and gets him to move in with her, while she moves her mother out. Then the little Girl Scout helps Max initiate the divorce from hell, humiliates the shit out of me, and you're on their side? I am so *not* calling her."

"Hey, Steph. I'm on your side."

"Then why are you calling to yell at me?"

"Because you're better than your cousin and your aunt. And I'm not the one yelling, by the way."

That stopped her cold. "Dad, Christie's had that coming for decades."

"Everyone with an IQ over fifty knows that. But you didn't need to say it. Like I said, you're better than that."

"No, I'm not. I had money, so everyone in Scottsdale thought I was just jim-dandy, and the money wasn't even really mine. It's Max's. And now everyone considers me shit on a stick, because the only things that matter in this stupid-ass town are money and Botox."

She heard her father sigh his exasperated sigh. "Sometimes silence says more than words. You should have walked away when you saw her."

This was getting her nowhere. "I have to go."

She threw her cell phone down on the kitchen's granite countertop and watched with relief as it skidded to the edge and stopped before hitting the tile floor. It wasn't like she could afford to buy a new one. Making a beeline for the empty living room, she laid on the floor with the intent of working off her anger by doing sit-ups. Instead, she curled into a fetal position on the carpeting, next to the newly purchased beanbag chair.

Since she'd been a little girl, it had always this way. Christie did something, and everyone made excuses. Stephanie did something, and everyone got on Stephanie about it. How could you? You're better than that. And, the one she always got from her mother, what did you say to your cousin to make her that mad? Most of the time, the only one who ever understood her feelings about it all was Peg, and now Peg was busy playing doctor with Jorge Vasquez, MD.

She sat up and leaned against the wall, realizing that her thoughts were that of a twelve-year-old's. Enough whining. Enough feeling sorry for herself. She shouldn't have said that to Christie. She knew that. But she hadn't seen Christie for an entire year, a year in which her world, for better or worse, had completely come undone in large part because of her cousin's actions.

But in some rebellious corner of her being she liked herself better than she ever had. *Forgive yourself, Stephie girl,* a voice from the back of her skull echoed to the front. *Let it go. Walt Disney was wrong. There is no happily ever after. There's just life, and even blond, little princesses aren't perfect. Learn from what it is that you shouldn't have done and forgive yourself for it.*

The doorbell rang. She scrambled up off the floor and walked to answer it, barefoot, in dirty jeans, but with a clean shirt on. Her toenails looked horrible, and the cuticle surrounding them looked even worse. A pedicure was the thing she missed the most about not having money to throw around. Screw the clothes, the haircuts, and the exclusive makeup lines.

She pulled open the door without looking through the peephole. "Peg. Boy, do I need to talk to you."

Peg swept in with a smile that went from one side of her lightly freckled face to the other.

Now, to find a way to tell her what happened today without telling her that she'd become a maid.

***

"Happy Friday." Maria Hernandez, Joe's supervisor at the IRS, greeted him as he opened the door to the conference room. "Sorry I couldn't meet with you earlier this week."

"Not a problem. At least not yet. Really, all I need is to let you know what's already transpired and get some legal clarification."

Gloria laughed. "Oh, that's rich. A lawyer needing legal clarification."

"Perhaps I should have said policy interpretation. And you are my supervisor."

"Whatever. I already talked to Tom. He said it had to do with a case he's investigating. The plastic surgeon. What's his name?"

"Ledger. Maxwell Ledger."

She nodded in affirmation. "And what's your concern?"

"I know he's being investigated—"

"Him and a boatload of other people."

"And I met his wife." Joe finished his sentence.

"Yeah, okay." Gloria cocked her head. "Did you say anything?"

"No. But we're in the same dance class."

"You take dance classes?" Her eyes lit up.

"Yes."

"I always wanted to take dance classes."

"Also, her friend is now dating my friend."

"Does your friend take dance classes too?"

"Yes. That's how we all met."

"Sounds cozy. You know, I want to take dance classes, but my husband keeps stalling. Does Ledger's wife know?"

"Know what?"

"That you work for the IRS."

"I told her I was a tax attorney."

Gloria raised her eyebrows and shrugged. "Well, you are, but it's sort of stretching the truth. I guess you don't have to tell her everything, but that's a bad way to start a relationship. What are you doing dating someone who's married, anyway?"

"Tom told me she was legally separated, and I'm not dating her. Not now, not ever. We're in the same dance class, that's all."

"So why are you worrying?"

"Because my friend and her friend are dating. My friend could spill the beans to her friend, and I think it would take less than a second for Stephanie Ledger to figure out why I lied in the first place. She's pretty sharp."

"Don't say anything, and you won't have to worry about it. If she finds out some other way, you aren't the one who's culpable."

"Okay. But if it comes up?"

"Don't tell her."

"What if she tells me something that could influence the case?"

"If you haven't asked, and she volunteers, tell Tom. I see the fuzzy line you're concerned about. But you haven't gone looking for anything. If you tell Tom, then it's his job to gather the evidence. But if you're not assigned to the case, and you're not deliberately trying to dig up dirt, then I think it's okay."

"Rumor has it that they're separated," Joe said.

"Yeah, you just said that. She could still be knowledgeable and therefore liable if he's been squirreling money offshore and she knew."

"Is that what Tom's investigating?" Joe asked.

"That and Medicare fraud," Gloria answered.

Joe stood to leave. "Okay. Consider yourself informed."

"You're keeping a log of our conversations, correct?"

"Yes."

"Good. I'll keep one, too. Make double sure you keep a log of your conversations with Tom, and have fun at dance class."

He turned to go and then stopped. "You know, you can take them by yourself. Lots of people do. Or you can come to class with me." That would end his problem right there. Dancing with his boss, instead of Stephanie. But that might start a different problem. If he remembered correctly, Gloria's husband worked for the Maricopa County sheriff's department.

"Thanks, but I think I'll keep nudging my tubby hubby."

"It's good exercise," Joe said.

"He's afraid people will laugh at him."

"Gloria, everyone looks stupid at the beginning. That's half the fun of it, being our age and forcing yourself to learn something new besides how to get the DVR to record a show."

She smiled ruefully. "I can't do that either."

"No one can."

***

Surprisingly, Stephanie started crying. She didn't cry when Max left, nor had she cried when she found out he'd moved in with Christie. And most certainly, she hadn't cried when the first round of furniture got rolled out on dollies. Come to think of it, she hadn't cried when her mother died either, which was something her Aunt Gigi repeatedly told her was both strange and rude.

Yet here she was bawling like a baby as she told Peg about her encounter with Christie and about her phone conversation with her father. Peg, for her part, listened like the friend she was. When Stephanie finally came to a stop, she took a long breath, letting it out like a deflated balloon.

"Life sucks," Peg said, from the beanbag chair she'd lowered herself into.

Stephanie, who sat cross-legged against the wall, smiled. "Life is a shit sandwich, and the bites keep getting bigger all the time." Ah, now they were in their groove.

Peg nodded and added on. "Life is a shit sandwich, and when you're done eating it, you regret you swallowed it in two bites instead of one. You know, less knowledge regarding the fact that it's shit."

"No foolin'. Okay, give me a second. Life is a shit sandwich, and you regret you swallowed it in two bites, but two big bites are better than— I can't top it, Peg. My mind's gone to shit."

Peg laughed. "Yeah, too much shit's happened. Okay, how about, a life spent making mistakes is far greater than a life spent doing nothing."

"Wow. Did you make that up?"

"No. George Bernard Shaw did."

"Nice," Stephanie said. "I should have that one tattooed on my forehead, but then I'd have to constantly look at myself in the mirror to read it, and it would be backward. Got any more?"

"It sucks to be the only grown-up in the room?"

"But I wasn't the grown-up. That's the problem."

"Nobody's perfect, Steph. What did your dad expect? Look at all you've been through this year. Not to mention that Christie really is a—"

"Yeah, that phrase."

Peg nodded. "You nailed it. That's probably what really made Christie and Aunt Gigi mad. Somewhere inside those tiny and mercenary little minds of theirs, they know it's true. By the way, I never liked your aunt."

"Me neither. I'm not sure why my mother was so close to her, besides the fact that they were sisters. She never saw through my aunt's baloney."

Stephanie watched Peg's face contort. She was about to ask what was going on in that head of hers when Patrick crashed through the door, dropping his backpack on the hard, marble tile and shutting the door so hard it shook. One look at him told Stephanie that there was nothing wrong with her son, other than the fact that he was fourteen and male. Oh, to have that energy for one day. Whatever was keeping him late at school was not a major life issue.

"Aunt Peg," he said.

"Paddy Pie," Peg returned his greeting.

Stephanie watched them interact. Patrick made a face but didn't correct Peg when she used the name Paddy Pie, as he would have if she'd said it. Peg was Peg, not his mother.

"What are you here for?" he asked.

"I need a reason?"

Patrick smiled but said nothing.

"Hey, Einstein," Peg said, "I'll tell you one thing I'm not here for, and that's to clean your stinky room. I peeked into that chaos you call a bedroom. After that, the smell was too much. You even beat my little brother, Sean, when it comes to stink."

"Thank you. Thank you very much," Patrick said, in his Elvis imitation voice.

Stephanie watched the two of them go back and forth, upping the ante with jokes. It felt like old times. Maybe she'd get along with Paddy Pie too, if she wasn't his mother.

"Hey," she said, breaking into the conversation. "I've got some cash in my hot little pants pocket here. How about I take you all to Whataburger?"

The two of them stopped short.

"Did you sell your wedding rings?" Peg asked.

"No."

"Did you sell more furniture?" Patrick asked, giving the living room an unnecessary scan.

"No." She realized it two seconds too late that she should have lied. No one could know how she was getting money.

"You're not going to believe it," she said. "But I found eighty bucks in a pair of pants I haven't worn in over a year. Isn't that wonderful? I think that kind of luck should be celebrated."

"Me too." Patrick glowed.

Poor kid. He hadn't been out to a real restaurant in quite a while. When he spent the weekends with Max, he always came back and told her they had takeout of some kind or a microwaved dinner. Max didn't know the difference between a pan and a plate, and Christie wasn't about to lift a finger feeding Patrick, nor spend money at a decent restaurant when he was around.

Peg's face clouded over. "I'm having dinner with Jorge. And we were going out for pizza. The good kind."

"Who's Jorge?" Patrick asked.

"Peg's new boyfriend," Stephanie told him. She would have to get used to the fact that if she wanted to hang out with Peg, Jorge was going to be there, too. At least for a while. She liked him, but getting used to someone new was hard, especially someone she didn't know she could trust. Someone who might hurt her friend worse than Max had hurt her.

"We can go for pizza. Right, Mom?"

Stephanie nodded.

"Mom's got eighty dollars. How much does your boyfriend eat, Aunt Peg?"

"I'll give him a call." Peg whipped her phone out of the front pocket of her purse. Stephanie and Patrick watched as the smile on Peg's face got even bigger when she was talking, then shrunk in size at the very end. She put her phone down and turned to them. "He's says that'd be great, and thanks for asking him. Also, he's bringing Joe."

Shit, shit, double shit. "Oh. That's nice," Stephanie said.

"Who's Joe?" Patrick asked Peg.

"Your mother's dance partner."

Patrick burst out laughing and turned to his mother. "You have an official dance partner?"

Stephanie frowned. "Not official. He's a friend of Peg's new boyfriend, and he usually ends up across from me in the guy's line."

He turned to Peg. "Your boyfriend dances, too?"

"He's good," Peg said, nodding.

"What's his name, John Travolta?"

"Funny. No, Fred Astaire."

"Who's that?"

"Google him, Einstein. And my boyfriend's name is Jorge. Jorge Vasquez."

"I'll google him too." Patrick gave Peg a hand as she struggled to get up from the beanbag chair, leaving Stephanie to fend for herself.

When she got to her feet, Stephanie said softly, "I have a favor to ask you two. Could you, would you, mind trying not to mention to either of the guys that I'm currently broke?"

"There's nothing to be ashamed of, given the circumstances," Peg answered.

"Yeah," Patrick chimed in again.

"Well, would you try not to?"

Peg and Patrick nodded silently. The two of them looked slightly uncomfortable, until Peg broke the ice.

"Hey," she said, "you know I've got a couple of really nice folding chairs stashed in my garage. They're collecting dust out there." Peg pulled her blouse down in the back. "Want 'em?"

"Not to keep," Stephanie said, firmly.

"Steph, they're folding chairs."

Stephanie smiled. "They might not blend in with the rest of my décor. How do you think they'd look with beanbag?"

"Yeah," Patrick joined in the joke. "Might make the room look too crowded. I think we should take a pass, Mom."

Peg shook her head. "You two."

The levity created by Peg's visit bolstered Stephanie's mood to the point that she thought she could make it through dinner with Joe and Jorge. But she was nervous about Patrick being there. He might let it slip that she and Max were separated, when she'd insisted to Joe that she was married. These days, she found herself keeping too many secrets from one person or another, all in a vain attempt to get through this divorce without surrendering or being pitied.

The three of them piled out of Peg's Mini Cooper and trooped into the Italian restaurant that boasted wood-oven-baked pizza. Stephanie saw that Jorge and Joe were already seated, and Jorge rose from the table the second he set eyes on Peg. He smiled at her as though she was dinner. Joe followed Jorge's lead and stood, although it was with an observable degree of reluctance and absolutely no smile whatsoever.

They settled in around the table, Peg next to Jorge and Patrick next to Peg. Unfortunately, she ended up directly across from Joe, just like she did in dance class. Why did this always happen?

Patrick perked up as Jorge and Joe took the time to talk with him about school. He confessed that he was struggling with algebra, and then pulled out his tablet to show them the problems he was working on.

"You're in luck," Jorge said to Patrick. "Both of us were pretty good at math."

Jorge and Joe studied the algebra problem and then took turns explaining the strategy for figuring out the answer. The relief on Patrick's face was palpable. Stephanie wanted to reach out and hug them both. Thankfully, the pizzas came.

"Do you have anyone helping you when you get stuck like that?" Joe asked Patrick, after he swallowed his first piece of pizza.

"Today my teacher let me and some of the other kids stay late and work on some stuff with her." Patrick looked quickly at Stephanie, then turned away. "I already flunked one test, and I got a D on the last one. But she told the class that she'll drop the two worst test grades if we show improvement over time."

Her eyes widened, but she kept her mouth shut, stealing a glance at Peg who, she could tell by the look on her face, had a plan.

"Hey," Peg said to both Jorge and Joe. "Since you two are such numerical geniuses, why don't you give old Paddy Pie here a little help? You know, tutor him."

"Your husband doesn't care?" Jorge asked Stephanie.

"Not if it's free." Patrick chimed in.

"No, Peg." Stephanie interrupted. "You can't expect them to do that. They're busy people. Guys, thanks, but no." She reached for another piece of pizza and took an unusually large bite, chewing furiously and adjusting a chunk of Italian sausage that was about to fall off the edge.

Joe looked at Stephanie in a way that made her feel as though he had found a hole in her skull and was looking through it. She turned away quickly.

"Anytime you need help, call me. I could come by before dance class," Joe said.

All eyes turned to Jorge while Peg's eyebrows raised in expectation. "If Joe can't make it, I'll be your backup guy," Jorge volunteered.

Patrick and Peg beamed. Stephanie pasted a smile across her face while wincing on the inside. Her wish had been granted. She'd found a tutor. But why did the good fairy have to come in the form of one Joseph Schmidt, with Jorge Vasquez as the backup angel? No. This was not happening.

"I can't let you do that," Stephanie said, softly.

Peg flashed her an "are-you-nuts" look while she gave Peg her standard "shut-up-if-you-know-what's-good-for-you" glare.

Jorge broke the face fight. "Joe and I were in AP algebra. And Joe almost became a math major. But he decided to have a personality instead."

Now was not the time to heap on sarcastic comments, although she was tempted. For once, she stayed silent and watched as Joe flashed Jorge a look like the one she'd given Peg seconds before.

"Look, let's make a trade. How about food? I'm a decent cook." This time she shot the shut-up glare to Patrick, who was snorting over her declaration.

"Joe's mother has the food thing taken care of. Trust me." Jorge answered.

"No, really it's fine," Joe said. He turned to Patrick, winked, and then said, "He needs a little practice, that's all. A couple of sessions ought to put him on the road to straight As. You won't owe me anything."

Ah, shit. How could she explain her near vacant house to Joe? She'd have to come up with something that sounded like the truth but wasn't. "Look, if you do this, and I'm not expecting you to—"

Her cell phone went off as all five of them were eyeing the last four pieces of pizza. As she grabbed for her purse, the contents, including her phone, slid toward the other side of the floor. They came to a stop between Jorge and Joe, who bent down to retrieve her things.

Joe picked up the ringing phone. He glanced at the face of it. "I think it's your husband."

"What's Dad calling you for?" Patrick asked.

Stephanie avoided everyone's eyes as she answered the call. "Hello, dear, what's up?"

"Dear? Oh, that's a laugh," Max said over the phone. "What do you think is up? I heard what you said to Christie."

She stood and made a beeline for the front door of the restaurant. There was a slight humming on the other end that she thought was cell phone fuzz. Then she got to thinking, what if it wasn't? What if he was recording her? But he'd called her on his cell phone. Was that possible?

"What did she tell you I said?" God, she had to be so careful.

"That you wanted to poison me."

"I didn't even imply that. I told her to get that fish home fast, so you *wouldn't* get food poisoning. Or was it a steak? And how was dinner by the way?"

She heard him breathe out. "And what did you call Christie?"

Not falling for it, Maxie. "What did she think I said?"

"Just tell me what you said."

"If she was wrong about the food poisoning comment, she probably misunderstood what I said to her, too. I love Christie. We're cousins. She's like the sister I never had." She heard him snort on the phone, and in the background, she heard a muffled yelp. God, what a couple of amateurs.

Stephanie continued. "You know, she had all that stuff pumped into her sweet little face today. Did she tell you? Maybe it affected her hearing."

"What stuff?"

"Oh, I shouldn't have said that. You'll have to ask her, Maxie. Girls never tattle, especially when they're cousins. They may sleep with the other person's husband, but they don't spill the beans on beauty secrets."

"Are you going to tell me what you called her?" The rage in his voice was barely kept in check.

"I called her a sly, darling, good witch. It's from a book we read when we were little, but she probably doesn't remember it. Maybe her hearing was bad, even back then.

"You know, I'm out with Peg. She's paying for pizza for Patrick and me, because I'm a little short on cash this month— again. In fact, on the small bit of money I get from you, I'm short every month. But I try to be the best person I can be and make do with what I have. We can talk about money some other time, dear. Maybe do lunch." She hung up and laughed, even though her hands were shaking.

By the time she made her way back to the table, the waitress was walking away with a mound of bills on top of the check tray, and Joe and Jorge were waving goodbye to Peg and Patrick as they exited the side door.

"Jorge and Joe insisted on paying," Peg told Stephanie.

She had to admit she was secretly relieved.

"Why did Dad call?" Patrick asked.

"Patrick, can we ... can we talk about something else?"

He put his arm up on her shoulder. "Sure. It's okay. You never used to call Dad 'dear,' but I guess you have a right to go a little crazy, Mom."

Chapter Six

Joe wondered more than once why in the hell he'd volunteered to help Stephanie's son with his math. Talk about idiot moves. But the kid seemed sincerely nice, and quite concerned about getting his grade in algebra up. Given what he knew about the kid's father, and how Stephanie sounded from time to time, he was shocked that Patrick had manners. And he was funny, but that part didn't really surprise him. Stephanie was too, in a condescending, sarcastic, aren't-you-an-idiot, it's-good-to-be-the-queen sort of way.

He shook his head. In the neighborhood he and Jorge had grown up in, she would have lasted about five minutes before someone tongue-lashed her to death. Being uppity was against the law in Camden, New Jersey.

He parked his car in front of her house, got out, and glanced at the pink stucco monstrosity across the street. The front window shutters snapped shut, as though he'd caught someone scrutinizing him. He pretended not to notice, and proceeded up the front walkway. Before his finger hit the bell, the door opened.

Patrick smiled broadly. "I've got the problems all laid out on the table. There are two I can't figure out."

Joe stepped in and looked to the left and right. Both rooms were empty.

"On the table in the kitchen," Patrick told him.

"We're redecorating." Stephanie got up from the beanbag chair and walked toward him, her arms crossed tightly in front of her. "Thanks for doing this."

"Not a problem." He noted that she looked at him suspiciously. He didn't blame her. If she only knew, she'd boot him right out of here with her foot, and he wouldn't be sitting down for a week. "And I'll be happy to give you a ride to dance class tonight." Maybe then he could ask her some questions.

She shook her head vehemently. "Thanks, but no."

"Hey, Mom, take the ride. Save on gas," Patrick said.

"We care about the environment," Stephanie told him.

"And money," Patrick added.

Joe watched Stephanie's eyes widen. She looked from Patrick to him and then out the window, breathing out a defeated sigh that sounded like she'd lost at something she'd desperately wanted to win at.

"Fine," Stephanie said. "I'll catch a ride with you. I'll be in the living room reading a literary novel whenever you're ready."

An hour later he was busy stealing glances at Stephanie as she sat in the passenger seat of his car, her face turned to the side window. In fact, she was so resolute about not turning his way that her nose, about a half an inch from the glass, kept fogging up the window.

"He's not bad, you know," Joe said, softly. An awkward attempt at conversation, he had to admit, but it was the best he could come up with.

"Who's not bad?" she asked, her face still glued to the side window.

"Patrick. Your son."

She turned to stare at him indignantly. "Of course, he's not."

"I meant at math."

"Oh. That's good to know. Thank you. I worry about him."

He watched as she turned back to stare out the side window.

When she started talking he could see a slight smile on her face, reflected in the glass. "Yesterday, I made him clean his room and taught him how to do the wash. He didn't complain too much, for someone who's fourteen. I made a checklist with directions for him to follow. Kids need to know how to organize."

"So you make your kid clean his own room and do his own wash?"

"Is there something wrong with that?"

"Absolutely not. In fact, there's everything right with that. My mother did it all for me. She'd still do everything for me if I'd let her."

"Ouch."

Joe glanced over at her and noticed that she had turned from the window and was now looking his way. Progress in small steps. Progress in small steps? What in the hell was he thinking?

"Yeah," he agreed. "She's someone who should've had six kids. Instead all she got was me."

They laughed, then Stephanie resumed looking out the window. "It's quicker if you take Indian School to Forty-Fifth."

"You hit the irrigation canals that way."

"I'll show you a little dipsy-doodle."

She directed him though an older neighborhood where they weaved in and out of the connecting streets and arrived at Let's Dance ten minutes ahead of schedule.

Joe grinned. "I'll have to remember that."

"Yes, well, it's a secret. Sort of like the short route to China. So don't tell anyone. I don't want those residential streets all clogged up with foreigners, okay?"

"Foreigners?" He asked.

She turned to him and smiled. "You know, like people from New Jersey."

"That's over half the city, plus Jorge and my mother."

"How did you and Jorge end up here?"

"He did his residency in Phoenix and never came back. I went to visit him and never went back either. The same with my mother after my stepfather died."

He watched as she nodded her head, still smiling. "Yeah, everybody loves Phoenix, until June, July, and August roll around."

"True, but I'd also add May and September. Also October. So, you got any other secrets you want to tell me?" He knew instantly he shouldn't have said that. He didn't even really mean that. What he meant was, do you have other secret routes, but judging by the look on her face, she was taking his words exactly the way he hadn't meant them.

"No," she said, crisply.

"Sometimes, I get the feeling that something's going on with you." Why was he pushing?

"I don't have a single thing to tell you, besides the fact that my life is none of your business. I live it as honestly as I can. That's all you have to know. And, hey, talk about telling the truth, do you want to tell me how you knew the way to my house without asking for directions last week?"

"Your friend Peg told me your address."

"Really? When?"

Buy some time, buy some time, stall, stall, stall. "When you weren't around, I guess. Or maybe she told Jorge, and he told me. Jesus, Stephanie, you act like there's some spy ring out for you. I don't work for the FBI, the NSA, the CIA, or the MIA—"

"That's missing in action."

"Or any of those organizations that end in a vowel. And I'm not stalking you. Trust me on that one. You know, you really need to get over yourself." He watched her face turn red, and realized that, without meaning to, he'd found her Achilles' heel.

"Thank you again for helping Patrick. And I'll find some way to pay you back. Count on it."

She said the words so stiffly he could snap them in two. He watched her open the car door, get out, and without saying another word, march toward the studio.

Shit. He'd lied about the address incident, but the IRS really didn't end in a vowel, so at least that was the truth. And she was right, none of this was any of his business. Her husband wasn't his case, and he sincerely doubted she had anything to do with what the agency was investigating anyway. But redecorating? My ass. He hit the lock function on his keys and proceeded into the building.

In the far corner of the studio, Jorge and Peg were standing so close they might as well be sewn together. There was something about the way his friend looked at Stephanie's friend that told Joe that this was serious. Peg was here to stay.

Stephanie stood by them, looking as if she wanted to be anywhere but next to Jorge and Peg. He could sympathize with the feeling. He didn't want to be the odd man out either, but that's what would begin to happen if he didn't make friends with Stephanie Ledger. When Peg and Jorge went out and wanted company, they would have to choose between Stephanie and him.

Jorge was like a brother, and his five sisters were like cousins to him. He'd lost his first mother, his adoptive father, the guy his mother had married after that, and of course, Lisa. He didn't need to lose anyone else, especially when they were still alive.

"Hey!" Jorge motioned.

He walked over to where the three of them stood. No one said anything until the class started.

Ms. Rita began with an announcement about the beginners' dance competition. It would take place in two months and required more lessons and practice at the studio, not to mention recommended practice time away from the studio as well. Several of the couples, including Peg and Jorge, looked interested. He watched as they murmured amongst themselves.

Stephanie looked at the ceiling, the floor, the pictures on the wall, and her overpriced wristwatch. Anyplace but at him. He didn't blame her. When they broke into partners for the cha-cha, he gave it his best shot for detente.

"I'm sorry if I seemed rude," he said. "And you're right, your life is none of my business."

To his surprise, she gave him a weak smile. "And I'm overly sensitive. Especially when people think I'm haughty, because I'm really just snotty. You should never confuse haughty with snotty."

"They're the same thing."

"That's the point of the joke, Einstein."

He smiled and shook his head slowly back and forth. It was so like her to turn this into a joke. "You're definitely spunky. That's for sure." He took a breath and then asked, "Dance?"

"Deal." She held out her hand, and he took it.

***

No matter how tightly Stephanie closed the shutters, the Phoenix sun had a way of sneaking through the smallest of cracks, waking her up before her alarm went off. As she rolled out of bed and pulled on a pair of pajama pants, she wondered why she even bothered to set an alarm. For a split second, she pondered the energy savings from unplugging the clock. "Jesus, Stephanie," a voice in her head that sounded strikingly like her father's spoke. "Give it a rest." She plodded down the hallway into the kitchen for her morning cup of coffee and came face to face with Patrick.

"What are you doing up so early?"

"Homework. How was dance class?"

"We learned the cha-cha."

"We're out of milk."

"No, it's in the pitcher, remember?"

Yesterday, she'd made powdered milk in her favorite blue glass pitcher, telling Patrick that she couldn't stand to look at the sight of a plastic carton when she opened the refrigerator. Amazing how much money she could save if she put her mind to it.

If she used ice water when she mixed the milk powder in, the stuff didn't taste all that bad, especially if she gulped it down without breathing. The only thing that bothered her about it was that Patrick bought her excuse, which was that looking at a plastic carton of milk bothered her sense of aesthetics. Did she really come off like that?

He made a face when she brought the pitcher out of the refrigerator and placed it on the counter. "Could you handle looking at a plastic carton in the fridge again?" he asked.

"You don't like milk like that? All nice and Martha Stewartish?"

"No." He looked momentarily uncomfortable and then said, "Um, can you do the pretty pitcher thing when I'm at Dad's? I think that pitcher does something weird to the milk."

She straightened. Caught, but not red-handed. What had she been thinking? The stuff tasted terrible. "Really?"

"Really."

"Sure. No problem. Want some toast with peanut butter? That's almost a complete meal." She popped the bread into the toaster, grateful not to have to look at him.

He handed her the peanut butter. "Thanks. Hey, there's something else I want to ask you."

She turned around to face him. "Shoot."

"When all of this is settled, you know all the divorce issues, and when you and Dad aren't married anymore, I'd really like to not go over there so much. Can you put that in the divorce paperwork, or whatever it's called?"

"I'll try. What made you bring this up now?"

"That phone call from Dad in the restaurant a couple of days ago. You looked upset when you came back to the table, and I got to thinking." He started to walk toward the archway, then stopped. "I don't really like Aunt Christie."

She nodded.

After all the nasty exchanges lately, she was in no mood to heap on any more criticism, even if it was about her cousin. "She's not really your aunt."

"She cusses."

"So do I."

"More than you."

Now she was alarmed. "Is she mean to you?"

"No. She either ignores me when I'm there, or she makes sure I hear stuff that she says when she's in another room. You know, like I'm overhearing her conversations with Dad or her mom by chance, but I know she talks loud on purpose. Sometimes it's stuff about you, and sometimes she's yelling at Dad."

"I'm sorry you have to hear that."

"And they live far away from my friends, and Dad and Aunt Christie never want to drive me anywhere, so I spend the whole weekend alone. It's weird."

"I bet."

She watched his figure start to walk through the family room while she leaned against the door frame. "Patrick."

He stopped and turned around.

"I haven't been honest with you."

"About what?"

"You know that milk in the pitcher?"

"Yeah."

"I made powdered milk, and didn't tell you. That's why it's in the pitcher, and that's why it tastes weird. I was … I've been trying to find ways to save more money. That one, I have to admit, was an epic fail. I'll pick the real stuff up later today. We're not that broke."

He turned to go.

"Patrick." She stopped him again. "I know your dad loves you. Some people … some people, they have a lot of stuff in the way."

He smiled and then disappeared around the corner. She heard his bedroom door close. This time, softly.

***

Joe slipped his head around the corner of his cubicle and spoke to Tom, the agent investigating Max Ledger. "Hey, I don't think Ledger's wife is involved in any of his tax-avoidance activity."

Tom looked up from his paperwork, his face clouding over. "What did you say about Stephanie?"

It bugged Joe that he knew her name and used it so casually. "I said I don't think she's involved in anything, and I don't think she has any prior knowledge."

"I don't think so either, but we still need to look at it all very thoroughly. We think what he's doing has been going on for a while, so she might know something."

Joe leaned against the four-inch-thick edge of the cubicle wall, wondering if that was a good idea, but there was nowhere to sit. "But she is separated."

Tom nodded. "Yeah, I told you that. Legally separated, meaning they don't live together. He lives with his office assistant, who we're also investigating in conjunction with him."

"So you don't think that Stephanie Ledger is involved in any of this." He realized he was repeating himself, but he wanted some reassurance, and he was hoping Tom might tell him more if they kept talking.

"I can't tell you much more. I already told you too much, especially if you want to stay out of it."

"Right." He knew he'd overstepped. Hell, he was a lawyer. "You know they have a kid who's at the age where rumors about their parents really affect them."

Tom let out a sigh. "What would you have me do? Wait until he goes to college or he's an old man? His father is cheating the government."

He didn't want the kid to get hurt when it all came down. Stephanie might be a comedic terror, but she had raised a nice son, something he didn't think the husband had much to do with. "Forget I said anything. I would do the same thing you're doing."

Tom put his pencil down and looked Joe straight in the eyes. "People get hurt. People who had nothing to do with any of the things we investigate get their lives ripped up. Some jerk's always got a parent or a wife or a husband or a brother who's mortified when it all comes out." He shrugged. "Greed's a nasty vocation."

Joe nodded.

"Hey," Tom said. "Speaking of family, where's the food you usually bring in from your mom? I might have to go out and buy lunch today."

"Haven't seen her for a week." Come to think of it, that was a record.

"You're starving us."

On his break, Joe walked down the hallway that led to the stairs, and called his mother. He wanted to do it privately, in a place that no one went, and no one took the stairs.

He shook his head, waiting for her to pick up the phone. What was taking so long? She usually answered in two rings.

"Hello?" Her voice sounded tired and weak.

"Mom?"

"Joey?"

Of course, it was him. Who else would call her 'Mom'? "You okay?"

"I'm fine," she said. "I'm always fine. Why wouldn't I be fine?"

"I haven't heard from you in a week. Got a new boyfriend?"

"No. I've been busy with the girls. Lots of things to do. Plenty."

"Look, I thought I might drop ov—"

"No, no, don't do that. I'll be out."

"How can you be out? You don't even know what time I'm coming over."

"Are you on your cell phone?"

"Yes."

"Well, I can't hear you. And the call is dropping."

"If the call dropped, you couldn't hear me at all. What's goin' on, Mom?"

"Nothing. Nothing at all."

"I'd like to come and see you."

"You can't come. I'm very busy. And I … I haven't made anything for you to eat."

Since when did his mother not want to see him? And since when had she not cooked something for him to drag home?

"Oh, and I'm going on a cruise with some of the girls. For a month. Maybe five weeks."

What in the hell was she hiding? "Okay. Have fun, Mom. I'll see you soon."

"I'll … I'll call you after the trip. Don't come over before that."

Don't come over before that. He knew where he would be spending his lunch break today.

***

"Now, Joey, don't be mad at me."

Shit, god damn it. Of course, he was mad. In fact, he was furious. "When were you going to tell me you broke your arm? When the cast came off or when you got back from your fake cruise?"

Joe watched as his mother avoided his stare. She sat on the couch, looking like a dog who'd gotten caught eating the middle out of a birthday cake.

Mary Sterling turned her gaze to the framed photographs on the wall of the dead. At least that's what he and Jorge called it, until Lisa's picture had been moved to that side of the living room two years ago. After that, they'd quit mentioning the wall altogether. There was a picture of his birth mother, who was his mother's cousin, a picture of the Leone grandparents, one picture of his adoptive father in his navy uniform, a photo of his Schmidt grandparents sitting stiffly beside one another, and one of his mother's second husband in a golf cart at the nineteenth hole, as he had jovially liked to call the outside bar at the country club.

On the opposite wall were the living: Jorge's adoptive parents, his mother's two sisters, and a picture of himself at his first communion. The whole New Jersey clan of his childhood years, plus the picture of Lisa, was on one wall or the other. Unfortunately, the wall of the dead was getting larger than the wall of the living. Either way, there was no escaping them when he came to visit his mother.

Today all the photos, alive and dead, seemed to glare at Joe. He could almost hear them muttering, "What are you talking to your mother like that for? What's wrong with you, kid? You oughta get a smack on the head for the tone you're taking with her." And they were right. He had no business being that terse. But losing her scared him. First, it'll be her arm, next it'll be her hip, and then, he couldn't even think it much less say it. God, he was so tired of people dying.

"I'm sorry I yelled, Mom. What were you doing when you broke it?" He watched as she looked away again, this time into the kitchen. "Were you on that damn step stool again?"

"Joey, you cuss too much."

"Mom. I've told you repeatedly you need a cleaning lady. Jorge has one. I can call her and set it up."

"Really? Jorge has one? Hmm. That's good. He was always on the messy side."

"Yeah, and I can give her a call."

"I have a cleaning lady now."

"Really, Mom?" He sincerely doubted it.

"She comes over twice a week. I don't touch anything until she gets here."

Maybe she did have one, and whoever she was, she must be a saint. His mother could have run the janitorial staff at his school into an insane asylum.

"Do you want to come and stay with me?" The phone in his pocket began to vibrate.

"Answer your phone. Maybe someone is having an IRS emergency."

Nice try. "Mom, no one has an IRS emergency. Whoever it is, they can wait. Do you want to come and stay with me?" he asked her again.

"Mothers don't stay with their sons. Sons stay with their mothers."

What was the difference? Either way they were living together. "Do you promise you won't do anything risky?"

This time she looked up at the ceiling. When she did that, he knew she was asking for forgiveness for the lie she was about to tell. "I promise."

"You'll wait for the cleaning lady?"

"I always do."

He didn't believe her. Somewhere there was a loophole. "Okay, I'm checking on you. You can count on it. You won't know what time or what day."

"Pop over all you want, Joey." Her eyes scanned the wall of the living and the wall of the dead before she looked at him with a face full of defiance. Well, he thought, she must not feel all that bad.

He returned her look with one of his own. "Maybe I'll come every day. Unannounced." Every goddamn day.

Chapter Seven

It had been a long day but a good one. Stephanie loved days when she was so busy she forgot to eat. She remembered around two o'clock that she'd been running on nothing but this morning's coffee. Now, she was headed home with another pocketful of cash. Granted, the bills were mostly ones and fives, but she could buy real milk and a few extra treats.

As she headed up Camelback Road, driving the sputtering, backfiring Olé truck, her thoughts meandered from her father, who she hadn't heard from since he'd chewed her out, to Joe Schmidt and dance class.

If it wasn't for the fact that Joe was helping Patrick with his algebra, she'd probably never go to another dance class again. Even though the cha-cha was a blast, and even though Joe was a decent dancer (something she'd never tell him), she'd still never go. Ever.

First, she didn't want Joe and Jorge to figure out she was separated, after she'd insisted that she was married. That would be hugely embarrassing, although she seriously considered, for at least a few minutes every day, fessing up just to get it over with.

She could only imagine what Joe would say when she told him the truth. Something to the tune of, what makes you think a guy would be that instantly attracted to you that you would have to put those big rings on to fend him off? You think too much of yourself, Stephanie. Okay, she could take a few minutes of utter humiliation, and after confession time was over, she could sell those diamonds like she'd meant to the week Peg dragged her to class. That would be some serious cash. Then again, maybe she should just save them for a rainy day, since now with the cleaning jobs, she was making ends meet a little bit better.

She had Patrick to consider too, and she wasn't about to ask him to lie to anyone on her behalf, including Joe and Jorge. Luckily, no one seemed to notice she wasn't wearing her rings when they went out for pizza the other night. On the way to the restaurant, when she realized she didn't have them with her, she'd concocted a story, in case Joe asked her where they were. I didn't want to get sauce and cheese in the setting, she was going to tell him, if he asked. It was something prissy enough that Joe would believe her, like Patrick completely bought the plastic-milk-carton-offends-me baloney. What must people really think of her?

She downshifted to second gear, then put the Olé in neutral, and applied the brake when she saw a red light up ahead. The truck farted to a stop and protested with an emission of dark-gray smoke. The driver in the Prius behind her looked none too happy. She didn't blame him. "Talk to Max," she said, staring at the driver in her rearview mirror. "Tell him to pay for his son's education. Then I can return the Olé, and we can save the world together."

The light turned green, and she continued her way home, getting back to her thoughts, which again jumped to Joe, Jorge, Peg, and Patrick. She cleaned houses for the cash. If either Joe or Jorge knew, they might tell Patrick when they tutored him, or Patrick might figure it out and tell them, and then the whole thing would unravel like the hem on a cheap pair of pants.

If Patrick ever put two and two together, he might slip in front of Max and Christie, and they'd all be back in court. Too much lying while trying to do the right thing. Or was this the right thing? Maybe she should cave, get the divorce over with, and take out student loans for herself and Patrick.

At least cleaning houses was honest work and better exercise than doing those stupid sit-ups on the empty living room floor. And cleaning houses was far better than being paraded around on Max's arm at the right functions, smiling when she didn't want to smile, and being nice to people she didn't like much less respect. That was whoring. This was cleaning.

Max had used her as an example of the work he did, when the truth was she'd never had plastic surgery and never intended to. Now, she would wrinkle and grow old with grace. And when she could afford endless supplies of chocolate, maybe she'd even put on a pound or two, or ten, or thirty. Her mother wasn't around to comment about her weight anymore.

No matter what anyone thought, she was not a princess. Come to think of it, she wasn't even a lady in waiting. Hell, she burst out laughing, she was the maid.

***

Joe was halfway home before he remembered the text. He wiggled his cell phone out of his back pocket when the light at Forty-Fifth and Indian School turned red. A glance at the screen told him that Patrick Ledger needed help with an algebra problem he couldn't figure out. Could you come by for a few minutes, he wanted to know.

The car behind him honked. He tossed his phone onto the passenger seat and proceeded through the intersection seconds after a Mustang from the other direction turned left fifty feet in front of him. The car behind him honked again, as he slammed on his brakes. "Sorry, sorry."

So why not drop by and help the kid? Patrick had asked him. Yes, his father was being investigated by his office, and yes, he wasn't exactly being forthright with the kid's mother. But the kid needed help. Period. When he was young and he'd needed help, people had reached out to help him. It was time to pay it forward.

Patrick had shared his desperate desire to get a scholarship, something Patrick had begged Joe not to tell his mother. Patrick didn't want Stephanie worrying about him any more than she already did. Joe had watched the two of them interact. The fact that Patrick worried about his mother would never occur to Stephanie, and he figured that was how every teenage boy wanted to keep it. He could certainly sympathize with that one.

While he understood Patrick's concerns, fourteen was a little young to be thinking about those sorts of things. Fourteen should be filled with friends, sports, and finding ways to do things without your parents always finding out about it. At least that's how his adolescence had been, and Jorge's too. But with his sisters hovering around him, Jorge had spent a lot of time sneaking around trying to lead a normal teenage boy life.

He shook his head, thinking about Patrick's dilemma, as he pulled up to the curb in front of Stephanie's house, hitting the lock function on his key without thinking as he got out of the car.

Yes, there was more going on in the Ledger family than anyone was spilling the beans on. Why the empty rooms? Why no lights? It looked deserted, but Patrick said they were home.

Seconds after he rang the bell, he heard scuffling behind the door, along with the whispers he took to be conversation. Finally, he heard Stephanie say, "You never open the door without looking first."

"It's Joe," he heard Patrick say. His tone, soaked in teenage self-righteousness, carried through the thick wood along with his words.

After a few more muffled sentences, the door opened. There stood Stephanie in her full-throttle indignant mode, wearing a pair of sweatpants that even he noticed were a mess, and he never noticed stuff like that. On the front of her T-shirt, three sizes too big, were the words that commemorated a plastic surgery convention in Vegas, four years ago.

"Patrick didn't tell me you were coming. And now, here you are." Her body blocked the entrance, and he was stuck outside. So much for good deeds.

"Mom, he's here to help me with this algebra problem I can't get. You said I need to bring my grades up. So let the guy in, okay?"

He watched Stephanie weighing the matter in her head, then her body deflated an almost indiscernible amount, and she moved out of the way.

"I should have called, but I was cutting past your neighborhood on my way home anyway."

"Where is your law office?"

Shit. "Um, around Scottsdale and Sixty-Forth. But we're moving soon."

"Where to?"

"Somewhere around Coral Reef, I think. Stupid name for a street in the desert, don't you think?"

Both she and Patrick looked at each other and laughed.

"It's better than Mountain Vista, or Mesa Vista, or Mountain Mesa Vista, or Vista Mountain Mesa Canyon." Patrick beamed.

"Or Verde Vista Mesa Canyon," Stephanie added.

Joe caught the joke. "Yeah, there are a lot of places in Phoenix named after those words."

"It's Scottsdale, really. In Phoenix, you have words like Maryland, Jefferson, Adams, Myrtle, Fillmore, and Orange Grove. You know, real names." Stephanie looked down, then up at him. "Do you think we could talk for a few minutes after you help Pat?"

"Sure."

"I'll be sitting on the living room," she said. "I mean in the living room. On the floor. Waiting. Probably reading another literary novel."

***

Stephanie sat cross-legged on the carpeting, her back against the wall, and tried hard to ignore the conversation going on in the kitchen. Instead, she focused on her notepad and pen. She wrote the title at the top of the page, "Possible Career Paths for Stephanie Ledger—Big Girl," and then laughed. Well, it was funny. Much better to laugh than to cry. And her situation was temporary. She would make sure of that.

She wrote down number one, and next to it the words *cleaning professional*. Pros, cash. Cons, not much cash. Probing minds would want to know, and judgmental minds would snicker behind her back as well as in front of her face. She'd be the laughingstock of Scottsdale, but who cared? The answer to that question unfortunately was herself. She cared. And honestly, it wasn't enough money.

Number two, professional organizer. Now she was talking. Pros, her obsessive need to straighten could go full speed ahead without driving what was left of her family nuts. She could even give organization classes to teens, whose mothers would thank her profusely. Yeah, right. Con, she would be self-employed, and that meant she'd need a stash of cash up front until she built up a business, and her own health insurance. And how much potential business really was there in Scottsdale and neighboring Paradise Valley? They had to be the two most anal-retentive places in the entire United States. Nobody needed much help being organized around here. Maybe she could spread out to other parts of Phoenix and the retirement area of Sun City. But it all came down to money. Never had she both hated and wanted something more than money in her lifetime.

She stared at the rest of the blank page and sighed in relief and frustration when she heard the kitchen chairs scrape against the floor. At least she could put aside pondering her future for a while longer.

"Are you two done?" she called to Pat and Joe.

"Yeah." Joe appeared at the entrance to the living room, and stood uncomfortably. "He gets it more than he thinks he does. He needs a little more practice, so I made up some problems for him."

"Good." She got up off the floor and wrapped her arms tightly around her chest, the same way she had when she ran into Christie at M&N's. "Look, there's something I need to tell you."

He stared at her in earnest but said nothing.

"I'm not really married. Well, technically, I am, but I'm separated, and my husband and I are fighting over the division of ... the stuff."

"Oh."

"And I'm not in the middle of redecorating. Max has me on a tight financial leash, so I have been selling stuff off. He likes to jerk the leash from time to time in the hopes that I'll cave." She looked at him directly. "I won't. I won't sign those papers until I get what I want."

"And what's that?"

"Not what you probably think." She sighed and said, "What I want is the legal commitment that Max will pay for whatever college Patrick gets in to. I want it written into the divorce decree. There are a few other things, but that's the big one."

"Well, thanks for telling me. Now I don't feel so uncomfortable." He indicated with a jerk of his chin toward the kitchen and Patrick. "Around here."

"Trust me. If Max thought some guy was hanging around, he'd probably try bribing him to take me off his hands." Why had she said that? "And you can tell Jorge, too, if he doesn't know already. Peg has a tendency to spill the beans, so he might know by now. It's not really on purpose," she added quickly, "she just talks a lot."

Stephanie changed the subject. "Look, I just wanted to thank you again."

"You've thanked me enough."

"Yeah, but now you know why I'm so grateful." She glanced toward the kitchen and then lowered her voice. "There's no way I could afford a tutor for Patrick, and Max certainly wouldn't help."

Joe nodded.

"So if there's any way I can pay you back ..."

"There are two things I can come up with."

"Two?"

"Yeah. One is fun. The other is, well, I'm asking you to lie."

It wouldn't be the first time. "Okay, start with the fun thing."

"You know that beginners' dance competition?"

"Yeah. I can't afford it."

"I'll pay for the entry fee and the extra lessons, if you'll agree to work up a cha-cha routine with me. It'll involve one-on-one lessons with Ms. Rita, and lots of extra practice."

"Okay."

"There's more."

She looked down at her feet, then met his eyes. "This is the lie part, right?"

"Yes. Look, I have this mother."

"Nice to know you weren't cloned."

"Funny."

"Or came out of a cabbage patch."

"Stephanie."

"Sorry."

"Look, my mother ... my mother worries about me. A lot." He stopped and cleared his throat. "My wife died a few years ago."

Peg had already told her, but she hadn't told him that. "I'm sorry."

He nodded and looked away. "Anyway, my mother thinks I should date, you know, get back out there, and I really don't want to. And she worries ... she worries about my dating. Someone. Anyone. She's driving me nuts. The woman is relentless. And she's not getting any younger, so I worry that she worries about me."

Stephanie's eyes widened, and a smile broke out on her face. "We live in a parallel universe." She crinkled her forehead. "So, what do you want me to lie about?"

"I'm going to invite my mother to the competition and tell her I've been dating you. And you have to act like you've been dating me. Okay?"

"Can I invite my dad and tell him the same thing?"

"Sure. It would make my story even more valid, and if we're lucky, it should buy both of us a few months of peace at the very least."

"Well, mine isn't exactly talking to me right now anyway, so I'll probably get more months out of this than you will."

"So we'll dance together?"

"You've got a deal."

He extended his hand, and she took it.

***

Joe turned the key in his front door and made a beeline for the fridge. Upon opening it, he found nothing good inside. Sort of how he felt right now about himself. Nothing good inside.

Why had he done it? Asking Stephanie to enter the dance competition just so he could get his mother off his back? It was sleazy and dishonest, but he knew this scheme wasn't just about his mother. Be honest, Joe. You like her. She's fun. You like her son. They both make you laugh, and you feel weirdly comfortable with them because they find ways to enjoy life, even when it's coming down around their heads.

Stephanie had told him the truth today. Why couldn't he return the favor and tell her what he'd been keeping silent about? Why couldn't he say, you know, I didn't exactly lie when I told you I was a tax attorney? I am a tax attorney, except I'm an attorney for the IRS. Yeah, that might work.

But that wasn't the entire truth either, so he should just keep his mouth shut. They were investigating her soon-to-be ex, which technically meant she was still married to him. And she wasn't stupid. If he told her a little, just enough to alleviate his conscience, she'd put two and two together and figure it all out. And then what?

He shut the refrigerator door and looked at the magnet picture of Lisa. Tonight, she looked as though she was staring right at him and saying, a lie is a lie. You can never parse the truth. Sweetheart, you've backed yourself into a corner. Why did you really ask Stephanie Ledger to enter the dance competition with you? Because you like her. And that's okay.

No, it's not.

Chapter Eight

Stephanie made note of the fact that the last few weeks had flown by quickly. The fact that the weeks flew, instead of trudging on, one after the other, made her feel enormously happy. As goofy as it sounded, she had a schedule she could plan her life around, and she loved it.

After the bus picked up Patrick for school, she changed into her Marta's Maids T-shirt, pulled the Olé out of the garage, and proceeded to her cleaning jobs. Marta had handed over two more clients, so she was now working Monday through Thursday.

In the evening, on Mondays, there was dance class, and on Wednesdays and Thursdays, she and Joe practiced their cha-cha routine with Ms. Rita, at the same time that Jorge and Peg were working on a rumba number. It felt unbelievably wonderful to wake up and know she had things to do and somewhere to be. And this Friday, she was going to sell her diamond rings, seeing that she didn't need them for cover anymore. God, the truth was so enriching. The freedom to sell those rings gave new meaning to the saying lying doesn't pay.

Unfortunately, she knew this was all temporary. Sort of like the perfect vacation before the Max shit hit the fan, and it would sooner or later. Eventually, and inevitably, things would come to a head. She'd get divorced, and then her life and Patrick's would be rechurned all over again. Not that she disliked change, but she had really begun to appreciate a well plotted, predictable routine.

She waved to Gloria Burnwater, who she knew was standing behind the shutters. She didn't care anymore. She had a life. Maybe not the life she thought she would have, but she had one nevertheless. Gloria should get one for herself and quit wasting her time spying on people.

Yesterday, Marta called and left a message about a temporary job close to where the doctor's condo was. She'd given it to her sister-in-law, but she couldn't take the job because her son's soccer practices had commenced. The woman, Marta told Stephanie, had stressed that the job was temporary and would end in a few months.

Right after Patrick set out for the bus stop, she was on the phone with her new client. The woman, a Mrs. Sterling, had asked if she could please start today, as in right now. While she ordinarily did the doctor's condo in the morning, she could easily switch things around and clean the condo in the early afternoon. Fantastic. This meant more cash in her pocket and a genuine plastic milk carton in the fridge to go along with the store-brand cereal. Did life get any better?

She pulled up to the security gate, punched in the numbers Mrs. Sterling had given her, and surveyed the layout of the retirement community. The patio homes were nice, one-story units surrounding a small golf course, swimming pool, and recreation center. It was like her father's place out in Mesa, only much more centrally located. This was where she would have preferred him to be, instead of way the hell out in the east valley. But it had been her father's choice, and it had been made with a great deal of thought by him.

She knocked on the door and heard movement behind it. Someone looked at her through the security peephole and then opened the door.

Mrs. Sterling smiled tentatively. "I'm so glad you could get here on such short notice. My son is coming, either at lunch or after work, I don't know which one, and I need the place clean so he knows I've done what he wanted, which was get a cleaning lady. Otherwise he'll be upset. He gets upset with me a lot. Especially since I broke my arm."

"Coming early is no problem. I'm happy to do it." She walked into the entry hall with her bucket, wipes, and mop and broom, leaving the vacuum in the truck bed.

"You don't have to bring your own things. If there's something I have a lot of, it's top-of-the-line cleaning products."

Stephanie studied the woman. She was slightly chunky and on the short side, with silver hair that was cut stylishly. Even though Mrs. Sterling had said no more to her than hello, come in, and use my cleaning supplies (with the implication that hers were better), Stephanie sensed there was something friendly and maternal about the woman. Maybe it was the eager and friendly look in her eyes that said, I really want this to work. Well, so did she.

"So you'd rather I used your products and equipment?" Stephanie asked.

"That way I know you're using the right things."

Wonderful. It was less money out of her pocket. "Is there anything you want to tell me about each room before I get started?"

Two bedrooms, two bathrooms, one sunroom, and a kitchen and living room later, Stephanie was ready to begin. "Can you show me where the cleaning supplies you want me to use are kept? I'll make sure I put them back when I'm done."

"The vacuum is in the hall closet, the mop is in the garage, and the dust rags and polish are"—she pointed to the cabinet above the sink—"up there."

"Do you have a stool?"

Mrs. Sterling pointed with her good hand toward the back corner of the kitchen.

Stephanie grabbed a red-vinyl, rickety, metal stool, an object that was past its prime in 1970. "Mrs. Sterling, I think you need a new stool." She glanced at the plaster cast on the woman's left arm. "Is that how you broke your arm? Climbing on that thing?"

"Don't tell my son, if you ever meet him. He'll make me move, and I like it here."

Make me move? What kind of a jerk had this woman spawned? "I promise I won't say a word."

"Oh, and if he asks, you've been working for the last two weeks."

My, my, she wasn't the only one who fudged the truth. The lies we tell the people we love. "Okay," Stephanie said, "but you should probably go out and buy something a little sturdier to step on, don't you think?"

"My mother bought that for me. And my son used to sit on it and watch me cook. He was such a cute little boy. I can't get rid of it."

"I understand. But maybe we could move it out to your porch and put a plant on it? Or maybe pictures of your son, or something. Then we can get one that's safer for you to use. And while we're at it, why don't we move the items that you use a lot to lower shelves, and move the things that you use less, up to the higher ones? Then you don't have to climb as much even after we get you a sturdier step stool."

"You don't mind helping?"

She looked over at two walls in the living room. Both were pasted with more pictures of family members than an oversized envelope had stamps on it. She'd always wanted to be part of a big family. Why in the hell didn't Mrs. Sterling's son, or the guy's wife, or one of the grandkids, or one of those women in the framed pictures, give her a hand? Not that she minded helping Mrs. Sterling, but her son, in particular, deserved a swift kick in the ass for not helping. "No, I like rearranging things. It's fun."

Mrs. Sterling beamed at her as though she was a genius. What a nice lady.

Stephanie motioned with her chin to the grouping of pictures on the wall. "I like your pictures. You have a large family."

"I did have a large family. On that wall is everyone who's passed away." She pointed to the wall on the right, the one with the most pictures.

Oh, god. She had a lot to learn about cleaning for the elderly. "As long as we're going to buy a new step stool, do you need a pull-up bar by the toilet? You know, to help you get up without falling? Most people do. Even me," she said, lying. "We can find someone to put those up for you."

Stephanie walked back into the bathroom, with Mrs. Sterling on her heels, and looked around. There was room for a grab bar on either side of the toilet, and Mrs. Sterling probably needed one in her bathtub shower too. "My boss probably knows of someone who could install the grab bars for you. What do you think?"

Mrs. Sterling smiled broadly. "That will make my son happy."

Just what she wanted to do, make her spoiled son happy. "Great. Now why don't I start cleaning the kitchen? That usually takes the longes—"

"I'm very clean."

Stephanie nodded patiently. "I'm sure you are. But if I'm going to do it up to your standards, I need you to check out the results when I'm done. So put your feet up in the living room, and I'll get started."

Mrs. Sterling smiled. "I like you. When my cast comes off, I'm going to make you cookies. I'll even teach you how to make them the way my son likes them."

"That'd be great."

"Oh, and after my cast comes off, I won't need you."

"That's fine. This is a transition job for me." But to what?

Helping Mrs. Sterling took Stephanie an hour longer than she had anticipated, but luckily, the doctor's condo was straight and relatively clean. Stephanie began to wonder if the guy didn't have a girlfriend. As she put the butter he'd left out away, she scanned the inside of the refrigerator. There seemed to be more fruit and vegetables on the shelves, and less takeout than before. In the back was a bag of expensive chocolates. Yep, a girlfriend. Not that this was any of her business. Per Marta's wisdom, she made a point of never snooping in the guy's personal stuff.

As usual, the money was on the kitchen table in an envelope that had the words *Marta's Maids* written on the front, and underneath that a thank-you. Sometimes the guy wrote thank you in Spanish, French, and German. It made her smile.

She hurried through the vacuuming and the kitchen and bath wipe down. Once the bedroom dusting was done, she could be on her way. The bottom drawer in the bedroom dresser was ajar, and Stephanie put down the duster to push it back in, but there was something that kept it from closing. She opened the drawer halfway to rearrange the contents, and found a stack of five, framed photographs protruding from the back, left corner of the drawer. Each one was a woman of different hair color, race, and ethnicity. Maybe with his newest girlfriend he'd probably stashed them all away. Either that or he'd gotten out the picture of the woman who was over visiting at the time. Men. They totally sucked. Even this guy. She shifted the photographs around to make the drawer close.

When she was done cleaning, she picked up her supplies, threw them in the back of the Olé, and took off for home, thinking about the guy whose condo she'd finished cleaning. Women weren't trophies, they were human beings, and she would do everything in her power to make sure Patrick didn't turn out to be that sort of man.

All the lights on Camelback were in her favor and she pulled the Olé into her driveway with five minutes to spare before Patrick got home. As usual, he slammed the front door so hard it shuddered, but she didn't care. She almost relished the fact that she could count on it. Predictability, schedules, and systems were her new loves. Yes, she was quickly becoming a top contender for the most boring person on the planet. Hopefully, the award came with a cash prize.

"Hey." Patrick let his backpack drop to the family room floor.

"Hey, yourself. Are you hungry?"

"No. You packed a big lunch, and I remembered to take it."

"I did, didn't I?" Cash, lovely, untraceable cash, and she had a pocket full of it again today, which was good, because they were one dinner short of being completely out of food. She would have to get creative tonight.

"You know, I've been thinking," Stephanie started.

Patrick's face clouded over. "Mom, whenever you say that, it involves more work for me."

"What a perceptive child you are."

"What do you want me to do now?"

"I think you should start making your own lunch."

"Fine. So now I clean my room, do my wash, and make my own lunch. What do you do?"

"I supervise you." She started laughing as he made a face of disgust. "Hey, no son of mine is going away to college without knowing how to take care of himself. I've only got three years left to whip you into shape."

"Joe's coming over."

"How's your algebra going?"

"Maybe sometime we can ask him for dinner. You know, feed him. Maybe you can teach him how to take care of himself, too?"

"I think he's pretty good at that already. How's your algebra going?"

"He doesn't have anyone."

"Oh, I don't believe that. I know his wife died, but he has family."

"One mother."

"That's all the mothers most people have."

"And he's adopted."

"I didn't know that. How's your algebra's going?"

"It's fine. Maybe you should talk to Joe more."

"Patrick. He's your math tutor, thank god, and my dance partner. Period. We dance. We don't talk. That means I don't ask him questions, and he doesn't ask me questions, and because of that it's a near-perfect relationship."

"Okay, okay."

"And, yes, asking him for dinner once or twice might be the polite thing to do. I certainly owe him something." Something other than lying to his mother about dating him when I meet her at the dance competition. "If I remember right, I offered food as payment."

"Good, because I asked him."

"You asked him what?"

"To come for dinner. Since he comes over before dance class to help me with math, I asked him to come over and have dinner with us tonight." He looked at her sheepishly. "You always say we should be nice to other people."

"You could have asked me first."

"Yeah, you're—"

The doorbell rang, followed by a knock on the door. "He's here already? When did you ask him to come?"

"When he got off work."

"Must be good to be a lawyer." She and Patrick walked to the front door, and even after her lectures to

Patrick, Stephanie opened it without looking. It was her father.

"Princess, can we talk?"

"Not if you're going to call me princess."

"Hey," Patrick said to his grandfather with a smile on his face, "you should hear what she calls me."

Bud Webloski winked at Patrick and then turned his gaze to Stephanie. "Sorry. You know, sometimes it's hard to remember not to call you that. Can I come in?"

"Sure."

He stepped in tentatively and stood in the entry hall, looking quite uncomfortable.

"Would you like to sit down?"

"On that?" Her father glanced at the beanbag chair in the living room and frowned.

"In the family room?" Stephanie clarified the offer.

"Sure. Patrick, could you give your mom and I a few minutes?"

"Go for it, Grandpa." Patrick looked from adult to adult, but moved not an inch.

"Alone?" Bud Weblowski asked.

Patrick frowned and then slinked down the hallway to his room.

"What happened to your living room and dining room furniture?" He asked Stephanie after he heard Patrick's door close.

"I got tired of it. What's up, Dad?" Stephanie sat down on the couch and motioned for her father to sit next to her.

"I haven't heard from you in well over a week, that's what's up."

She nodded. "I haven't heard from you either." It was a standoff of stubbornness. Not something she was particularly proud of.

"That's why I drove in to see you." He looked down at his snow-white athletic shoes and matching socks and then up at her. "I'm sorry. I had no business chewing you out about what you said to your cousin. It's not like you're a kid anymore, that's for sure."

"You're right. I'm not a kid anymore. But you're also right that what I said to Christie was childish, crude, and uncalled for."

Her father nodded slowly. "She had it coming. She's had it coming for years, but when Gigi called—" Her father stopped, then started again. "I don't know, Steph. It's like I went back in time to the years when you and Christie were kids, and I was the one who always had to chew you out over your behavior. The truth is, you've always been stronger than your cousin, and I don't mean your muscles. It bothered Gigi. It bothered your mother too, because you were so willful when you were little. You had your own ideas. And she ..." He stopped again. "Your mom had ideas too, and her ideas usually won out whether they fit you or not."

"Dad—"

"Let me finish. Please. I've been meaning to say this to you for a while. I don't think your mother's ideas about how you were supposed to be ever worked for you. I sat there and watched her make you do all those goddamn sit-ups, and let her shove you into her mold of what she wanted. I should have stuck up for you more. And if I would have, you wouldn't be in—" His hand swept toward the living room. "This situation."

Stephanie looked at her father. He'd never said anything like that to her, and he was obviously upset. How long had he been holding on to this?

"Dad, if you're implying that my marriage to Max was your fault because you didn't intervene when I was growing up, stop. You had nothing to do with my decision. Max was the easy way out, and I took it. The only person I should blame is myself, and if I'm half as strong as you think I am, I'll figure this one out on my own. Okay?"

"But if you need some help—"

"I don't need your help. I need your support. I need to know you like me. I know you love me because I'm your daughter, but there's a difference. I need to know that you have my back and that you respect me."

"Of course, I do."

"And I also need to know that the next time Aunt Gigi calls to complain about me, you'll tell her to stick it where the sun doesn't shine."

Her father burst out laughing. "Steph, I almost can't wait until you misbehave again and I get another phone call."

"You may be waiting for a while. For some reason, I'm feeling better. About myself. I know there's something out there for me. It's like—" She stopped and started again, trying to grab the words out of an amorphous stew in her head. "It's like I can feel myself getting closer to it, but the words aren't there."

She sighed. "And I want to resolve things with Max and get on with my life, but unfortunately, when it comes to money, he wants everything."

Her father looked at her and nodded. "Well, then he and your cousin should work nicely together."

"You know, ever since I unloaded on Christie, I've been feeling a bit sorry for her. The closer I get to figuring out what I want, the more … I don't know, the more I can forgive Christie for being a …"

"What you called her?"

"Yeah. That."

"Well, this is a first. You hated her, growing up."

"I'm not saying I like her now either." She sighed, long and hard. "Christie's still using the old operating instructions, thinking it's going to get her something. Like having more and better stuff and looking perfect are the ultimate goals in life. Somehow or another, she's going to get hurt, and Max will probably be the one who does it."

"I'd offer to beat him up for both of you, but I'm too old for that kind of stuff."

"Not to mention he'd sue your ass."

Her father nodded in agreement. "What really happened to your living room furniture?"

"I sold it, along with the dining room and the furniture in two of the bedrooms. I got a decent amount of money for it."

"Steph, if you need—"

"But I don't. I'm doing fine now."

She decided to change the subject. If her father offered to give her money again, she might fold and take it. Even with the empty bedrooms shut off, the air-conditioning bill would be astronomical in a few months' time.

Stephanie changed the subject. "Hey, did I tell you Max and Christie were trying to record me on the phone the other day? About what I said to her in front of M&N's."

She watched her father wince and try to hide it. "You should never have married that man. The only thing good that came out of that was Patrick. Be careful, okay?"

"Dad, don't worry. I know what he's capable of." She sighed and shook her head. "It's going to be a long time before I get involved with anyone ever again."

"I won't look for another date for you."

"Fantastic."

"Unless you want me to." He finished his sentence as the front doorbell rang.

Patrick came charging out of his room and ran down the hall. "I'll get it."

"Check who it is first," Stephanie yelled.

"I already know who it is," Patrick yelled back.

And then she remembered who was coming for dinner.

Joe's voice flooded the entry hall as he and Patrick said hello and immediately started talking about math. The two of them strode into the family room together.

"Thanks for the dinner invitation," Joe said. He stopped short and stared at Stephanie's father.

Bud looked from Stephanie to Joe and then back at Stephanie.

"Dad," she said, as she rose from the couch, "this is Patrick's math tutor—"

"And Mom's dance partner." Patrick beamed.

"My temporary dance partner, Joe Schmidt."

"Who is staying for dinner," Patrick added. He turned quickly to his grandfather. "Want to stay, too?"

Bud Weblowski stood and walked toward Joe with his hand out. "Nice to meet you. What was your name again?"

"Joe. Schmidt."

Stephanie's father nodded, then turned to Patrick. "Thanks for the invite, son, but I think your mother has her hands full already." He turned to Stephanie. "Dance lessons, huh? You told me about that. How's it going?"

"Fine."

"They're in a dance competition together," Patrick said. "The cha-cha."

Of all the times for Patrick to decide to get chatty, why did it have to be now? Stephanie watched a small smile flicker on her father's mouth.

Patrick kept on talking. "You're invited to the show, and so is Joe's mom."

"Well, I look forward to it. Don't worry, pri— Steph, I know my way out."

"Uh, nice to meet you." Joe called after Bud.

"And you too," Stephanie's father called back.

Chapter Nine

Dinner with Patrick and Joe was a patched-together affair, consisting of grilled cheese sandwiches, one made with two heels of bread, a couple of cans of store-brand tomato soup, and carrot sticks. There were two granola bars that Patrick pulled out of the pantry and shared with Joe for dessert. Stephanie needed to go shopping.

As they were driving to dance class, she made a mental note to remind Patrick one more time about asking her before inviting someone for dinner. There were consequences for the guest when she didn't know someone was coming. Canned tomato soup and grilled cheese sandwiches? At least Joe didn't seem to mind.

"Sorry about the slipshod dinner," she said, watching as they flew by the stores on the right side of the road.

"It's better than what I would have had at home. I keep forgetting to go shopping. If I don't go tonight, I'll being drinking orange juice for breakfast, lunch, and dinner."

She laughed. "Me too."

"My mother used to make soup like that. When I was sick."

Her mother used to have the cleaning lady pop open the can and heat it up. "Do you like to cook?" she asked.

"I never really learned. Growing up, the kitchen stove and oven were the sole property of my mother's. I used to try to learn, and she'd complain that I didn't stir something right, or I cut the onions too big, or I cut the celery too small. Truth was, she didn't want anyone in her kingdom. Besides, she is a fantastic cook."

Stephanie nodded. "I'm surprised she doesn't flood you with food."

Joe laughed, but there was a testiness to it. "Oh, she does. More than I could ever eat. I load it up and bring it into the office, which I never tell her about, of course." He stopped, then added quickly, "And when you meet her at the competition, please don't let that slip."

Stephanie laughed again. She shook her head and said, "Parents."

They were quiet for a moment, and then Joe started talking. "Lisa, she was a great cook, too. She cooked lighter and healthier. My mother uses way too much olive oil on everything. And I mean everything, including squeaky doors. But I'd never tell her that."

"And when I meet her, I won't volunteer that one either."

"Thanks. I have to keep all my lies straight."

Me too. "Patrick told me you're adopted. Do you know, was your birth mother Italian, or Greek, because you don't exactly look like a Schmidt."

"Yeah, she was Sicilian, and so is my adopted mother. They were cousins. My birth mother had me out of wedlock, and she died when I was a little kid. In a car accident. And her cousin, my mother, and her husband, my father, took me in. So as Lisa would say, I was lucky twice. Once when I was adopted and once when she agreed to marry me."

Joe's comment about Lisa put the plug in their chatter for at least one red light. It also got Stephanie thinking. She burst out her thought, only to regret it seconds later. "What's it like when someone you love leaves you?"

Joe took his eyes off the road and stared at her.

Stephanie sighed. "Can we forget I said that?"

"No. It's a good question," he said quietly. "No one ever has the guts to ask anything like that. For the last two years, everyone's been tiptoeing around me."

Stephanie stared ahead, embarrassed. "Maybe no one is that thoughtless. I'm sorry." She sighed. "When Max left me and moved in with my cousin Christie—you knew that, right?"

"No, I didn't." He thought about what Tom had told him, that Ledger lived with his office assistant. Was Stephanie's cousin the office assistant? He'd have to get some clarification on that one.

"Anyway, in addition to utter humiliation and an overwhelming fear that this would affect Patrick badly, I was relieved. I found I liked being by myself better than I liked being with Max, not to mention Max's social group. So when you said that about Lisa ... not just what you said, but how you said it, I wondered what it felt like to really lose someone you loved. And I'm sorry for blurting it out and putting you on the spot."

"Quit apologizing. Really, it's okay. I want to tell you. It's like ... it's like how they say people react to losing a limb. You still feel it, like it's there, and then you realize it's not, and it never will be again. And every time you realize you're never going to get back what you lost, you grieve, but it shocks you a little less each time.

"It never stops hurting, though. It's like someone drilled a hole in your heart, and you can't plug it up. You have to live with it leaking a little all the time. And sometimes, right before you drop off to sleep, or right before you wake up, you can almost convince yourself that you feel them, that they're there right next to you, watching you and telling you that it's all okay."

They pulled up to Let's Dance, and Joe turned off his car. He pulled the keys out of the ignition and sat there, finally turning to Stephanie, who found it easy to remain silent.

"Thanks," he said.

"For what?"

"No one ever asks about Lisa."

"No one wants to hurt you," she said.

"Yeah, but they all act like, if they don't talk about her, she never died. Or she was never there. Or something." He laughed lightly. "She told me to take dance classes. She made me promise. So here I am."

Stephanie smiled. She got out and closed the car door as softly as she could. "Ready, then?"

***

After Joe dropped off Stephanie, he took the long way home to give himself time to think. Talking about Lisa and dancing with Stephanie left him with the sensation that his top half and his bottom half weren't attached to the same person.

He'd had a good time practicing the cha-cha routine they'd worked up with Ms. Rita. It consisted of spins and turns and chases, all to the cha-cha beat of the song "Working My Way Back To You, Babe" by the Spinners. It was fun, and well, he might as well admit it, sexy. Stephanie always smiled at the end, although Ms. Rita berated them to not look down and to smile throughout the entire dance.

He felt better, more alive, and happy after every session. In fact, he had to admit that he hadn't felt this good in years. But the second he dropped Stephanie off and got back into his car, he started thinking about Lisa and how much she'd wanted him to learn to dance. Did she know this would happen?

Then he'd think about Stephanie and the fact that while she'd fessed up to him about her fibs, he was still lying to her. Correction. It was more like he wasn't telling her the whole story.

We have to keep our lies straight. That's what he told her earlier in the evening when they were talking about meeting his mother. The more he got to know Stephanie Ledger, the worst he felt about not telling her the trouble she might be in because of her husband.

He didn't want to go home and look at the refrigerator magnet of Lisa and him either. Nor did he want to look at Lisa's picture on his nightstand, or the one in the hallway, or the one in his workroom. One of those photos would certainly call out, "You like someone else." He wished Lisa would appear in his dreams and give him the thumbs-up or -down. And did it matter? If Stephanie Ledger ever found out what he did and what he knew, and why he wasn't telling her, one could only imagine the creative name-calling she would employ.

He pulled into the Bashas' grocery on the corner of Coral Reef and Sixty-Fifth, suddenly remembering that he needed milk, bread, catsup, and something else for dinner because he was still starving. A voice inside his head that sounded eerily like his wife's told him he also needed fresh fruit and vegetables. His mother's voice told him to pick up more olive oil. You could never have enough.

Thinking about olive oil made him think about the fact that he hadn't been by to see his mother in two days. Too late for a visit tonight, but he'd give her a call.

The doors to Bashas' opened, and he proceeded directly to the deli section. Next stop, the beer aisle and then some cereal, and okay, an apple or two.

***

The second after Joe drove away, Stephanie decided she'd make a run to the grocery store instead of waiting until tomorrow. If Patrick was going to learn how to make lunch, he needed something to make a lunch with. Not to mention breakfast. The last thing she wanted was to get in her car and go back out again, but after Joe and Patrick ate the granola bars, she literally had no food in the house except for a can of beef bouillon, a box of dried pasta, and some dehydrated onion flakes. But she had a wad of cash, so this would be fun, not painful.

Patrick often waited until right before bedtime to remember he needed something for school the next day, so after making a list of the things she needed, she yelled down the hallway to check before she headed out.

The night air was almost tolerable. At nine in the evening the temperature had dropped to a mere eighty degrees. Ah, Phoenix. Maybe it was hot, but then again, it was never cold. Ever. Well, maybe once.

The doors to the grocery store opened automatically, and she immediately felt the rush of cold air-conditioned air. She rounded the corner of the produce aisle only to see one of the mothers from Patrick's old school. Not one of those kids had bothered to call Patrick after he hadn't shown up for the start of school. What was this woman's name? Darcy? Maybe it was Marcy?

"Hello," she said to Darcy/Marcy. "How are you?"

Darcy/Marcy turned her enhanced breasts toward Stephanie, her professionally streaked hair pulled back in a casual yet artfully done-up ponytail that swished as she turned on the spot. "Stephanie? I almost didn't recognize you." Stephanie watched as the woman eyed her with caution and a pinch of disdain. "How is poor Patrick?"

"Poor Patrick?" Stephanie repeated. "Did something happen to him I don't know about?"

Darcy/Marcy sputtered. "Well, it is sad that he has to go to a … public school."

Stephanie felt like smothering the woman in boxes of store-brand toilet paper. "Yes. His intellect is shrinking every day. I mean, the only thing they teach at that middle school is drug use." She was almost enjoying herself. Then she remembered Christie, and the fallout with her father, and the fact that Vista Mesa Country Day school was the epicenter of Scottsdale gossip. "Really, I'm just joking. And how are you, Darcy?"

"It's Marcy."

"Right. How are you? I can see you're as perky as ever." She needed to get out of this situation fast before she dropped the B-word or an F-you bomb or something worse.

Marcy's eyes narrowed, and her stick-on smile disappeared. "And I hear you're broke and in the middle of a divorce."

"For once you heard right."

"And I heard your husband is messing around with—"

Stephanie heard a male voice behind her interrupting Marcy's commentary. "Did you get everything you needed, dear?"

She felt an arm encircle her and turned to see Joe Schmidt with a glint in his eye that said, Just go with it.

"I did. Sweetheart, this is Darcy. I mean Marcy. How could I forget again? So sorry. Anyway, her son goes to Patrick's old school."

"Oh." He leaned over and gave her a kiss, crossing the line of grocery store appropriateness by a good yard.

"Sorry," he said to Marcy. "I can't get enough of this naturally beautiful, ravishing woman. She doesn't even own a stick of makeup."

"Oh, sweetheart." Stephanie didn't have to feign embarrassment.

"Well, nice to meet you, Darcy." He gently took Stephanie's hand, and they walked down the aisle together, Joe pushing the cart.

"Thanks, and what are you doing here?" Stephanie whispered in his ear.

"Same thing you are. I was out of food, remember? Then I rounded the corner and saw the triumphant look on that woman's face, and I heard what she was saying, and I felt compelled to bail you out. I hate people like that." He looked down the aisle at Marcy and gave Stephanie another kiss.

She put her hand up like a crossing guard. "Hey. One's enough."

"Right. Okay, let's finish our shopping together in case she's watching, and get out to the parking lot where we can part company in private."

"Good idea. And Joe, I owe you big time. Seriously." She beamed at him appreciatively.

Joe rolled his eyes and smiled. "Yeah, wait till you meet my mother."

***

Joe took the last of his grocery bags inside and put the items that belonged in the refrigerator away, all the while trying like hell to avoid the magnet of Lisa and him. Done with that task, and only eyeing the magnet once, he opened a bottle of beer, took a large bite of his sub sandwich, grabbed his phone, and called his mother.

"Mom?"

"Joey? What do you have in your mouth?"

He swallowed with one chew and coughed. "Nothing. I was only calling—"

"Why are you calling so late? Are you all right? Is something wrong?"

"No, Mom. It's only half past nine, and everything's fine."

"And in thirty more minutes it'll be ten. Why aren't you in bed?"

"Because I'm not eight years old anymore." Why did he have to say something that snotty? Because she drove him nuts, that's why. "I was at dance class, and I won't call you this late again, but I wanted to know how you were. I haven't talked to you in a while."

"Oh, that's nice, Joey. I'm fine. My cleaning lady is very nice, so you don't have to worry. We're going shopping tomorrow. She's helping me buy a new step stool and handles for the toilet and the bathtub."

He'd been bugging her for an entire year to do those things. What did the cleaning lady have that he didn't? "That's great, Mom."

"So you don't need to stop by. Spend some time with your new dance-partner girlfriend. Besides, I can't really cook right now."

"But you're okay?"

"If you're okay, I'm okay. Hey, remember that book? *I'm Okay, You're Okay*?"

He had no idea what she was talking about, and he didn't want to start a ten-minute conversation about it. "Sort of."

Joe stared at his beer, knowing he would chug the entire thing the second he got off the phone. Maybe, if he'd had a sister, he would understand women a little better. Then he thought of Jorge. It hadn't helped him any.

"I might still stop by," he said, with a warning tone to his voice.

"And I might not be home. I might be out with my new cleaning-lady friend, who is right around your age. And very nice looking. But if you do come by, bring your girlfriend."

Sweet Jesus. "Mom, you'll meet her at the dance competition." And not a second before.

***

For the second day in a row, Stephanie punched in the numbers for Mrs. Sterling's security gate and pulled up in front of her patio home. What was the difference between a townhome, a patio home, and a plain old condo? She'd have to ask Peg, if she could ever tear Peg away from Jorge long enough to get her friend to finish two sentences. Even at dance class last night, Peg and Jorge had been so immersed in themselves and their rumba routine that they'd had no time to talk with her or Joe. Stephanie felt she would be hurt, if she had the time.

Technically, Jorge and Peg's rumba routine wasn't as advanced as the cha-cha number she and Joe were attempting, but Jorge and Peg made up for it in emotion, style, and sheer passion. The rumba was a dance of enticement, and the two of them oozed it when they danced together. She and Joe had the cha-cha moves down, but it was all still slightly uncomfortable, and it showed. As Ms. Rita said, the rumba is seduction; the cha-cha is merely flirtation.

Before she knocked on the door, Mrs. Sterling opened it. There she stood, ready to go, the strap of her purse on the shoulder of her un-casted arm. "This is so nice of you. I wasn't sure you'd remember."

"Of course, I remembered. We set the time and everything. Are you ready?"

The two of them walked to Stephanie's Lexus. She opened the door for Mrs. Sterling and watched as discretely as she could to make sure the woman didn't need help stepping into her car.

"Where's your truck?"

"Oh, the truck. Well, I thought this would be a smoother ride for you. The truck is for work."

Mrs. Sterling nodded thoughtfully.

"I checked before I left for your condo and—"

"Patio home."

"Right. And there's a hardware store two blocks from here that carries grab bars. And as far as a sturdy step stool, they have them as well, unless you want a more expensive, decorative type."

"Are you married?"

Stephanie wasn't expecting that one, and kept her eyes studiously on the road. "No, but technically yes."

"I thought so." Mrs. Sterling nodded in affirmation.

"Really? How could you tell?"

"Well, you're driving an expensive car today that no one drives unless they're older, not that you're old-old, and married, or have been. And yet, you don't wear a wedding band."

Wow. She was driving Sherlock Holmes to the hardware store. "That's a lot to deduce, Mrs. Sterling."

"Well, am I right?"

"Pretty much. Technically, I'm legally separated."

"Technically, that's still married," Mrs. Sterling said, matter-of-factly.

"Unfortunately, you are correct again."

"I have a son about your age."

"You've mentioned that." And he sounded like a real jerk.

"That's why I asked if you were married."

"Well, even though I'm working on not being married, it doesn't mean I'm looking to date someone. If that's where you were going with this."

"It was."

"I need to find a way to take care of myself before I even think about dating again."

"I understand. He works for the IRS, anyway. I'm sure that's a turn-off for you. It is for most women." Mrs. Sterling turned to look at her.

She laughed. "I guess it's a turn-off if you don't pay your taxes. Why should that matter to someone? It's honest work."

"You're right. It shouldn't. But he's still single. He says he has a girlfriend now anyway."

"That's good."

"It's just, you're so nice."

"Thank you."

"And we get along."

Stephanie smiled, said nothing, and kept her eyes on the traffic up ahead.

"I didn't get along very well with his first wife."

"I'm sorry."

"She thought I was pushy. And she didn't like my food. Everyone likes my food."

What was she supposed to say to that one? She hadn't exactly liked her in-laws either. Max's family was from St. Louis and made a big deal about living in the suburb of Creve Coeur. It was a French name Max's mother never pronounced correctly, but still thought she was the high cheese on the hors d'oeuvres tray, just because she lived there. The woman was a pretentious piece of puff, but who else would have raised someone like Max?

Mrs. Sterling changed the subject. "You said you wanted to do something after your divorce. What do you want to do?" She asked.

"I don't know yet. Something I'm good at, and that makes a decent living for my son and me."

"You're good at this."

"Cleaning houses?"

"No. Well, yes, but I mean helping people. Organizing things. Figuring out what people need so they don't hurt themselves. That's what you're good at."

"Thanks, Mrs. Sterling. That's so nice to hear."

"Call me Mary."

Chapter Ten

Joe stared at the pool of black coffee in his mug and shifted uncomfortably in his chair. His eyes swept the sink in the back of the IRS breakroom, and he wondered when the last time it was that he had properly washed out his cup, instead of merely rinsing it. He'd become a real slob in the last two years. Maybe he should call Jorge and get the number of his new cleaning lady. He'd told Joe she was the queen of clean.

He looked around one more time to make sure he and Tom were alone before he started talking, but Tom started in first.

"You want an update on the Ledger case, right?"

Joe nodded silently.

"Like I said a couple of weeks ago, as far as we know, and we know more now than the last time we talked, Ledger didn't start withholding income until about five years ago, and that directly coincides with the appearance of a Ms. Christine Wintershaw, his current office manager."

"Christine? Didn't you tell me he was living with his office manager?"

"Um-hmm."

"Wintershaw?" That had to be Stephanie's cousin, but he didn't know what her last name was. He'd have to work it into a conversation.

"Yeah."

"So she's involved, too?" Right now he didn't want to tell Tom that Christine Wintershaw was more than likely Stephanie's cousin. Maybe it mattered to Stephanie, but did it matter to the case?

Tom nodded. "We strongly suspect that. But it's his income we suspect he's not reporting, not hers. And unless we can directly tie her to the missing money, she won't be implicated, but we're pretty sure she's mixed up in it."

He paused for a second. "When Christine Wintershaw came to work for Ledger and Burnwater, Ledger started running a special on boob jobs. Um, I mean breast augmentation. Which is different than breast reconstruction," Tom added quickly. "I did my homework on this stuff. Anyway, you could get a break on your breasts, if you paid cash. They took money orders, too.

"Anyway, Ledger advertises this special about a week after mid-April, and they run it through May, when all the tax refunds come out. It's a pretty slick operation. Medical insurance will pay for reconstruction, but it doesn't pay for elective enhancements. So why not run boob jobs as a cash business? That's where all the money is anyway. At least in Scottsdale."

"Where do you think they stash the cash?" Joe asked.

"Wintershaw makes periodic trips to the Bahamas, sometimes Cancun. About every three months. Like clockwork. That cash never rubs up against his regular practice account."

"Hmm."

"We don't think either place is where the cash gets deposited, though. These days, the banks in both locations are under pressure to report. We think she pays cash and goes off the island, or leaves from Cancun, to somewhere else, maybe a couple of places if they're smart. But it's somewhere close to where she goes. Probably the Caymans. With all that cash, she could go anywhere for a day out of either location, then come back, have a little massage, take a dip in the ocean, get a Brazilian, and fly back to Phoenix."

"And Ledger's partner?"

"Bob Burnwater?"

"Yeah."

"I'm not sure, but I don't think he's involved in this. That's what we're waiting on to find out. That, and any involvement with the wife."

"The ex-wife," Joe corrected him.

"Well, she's not one quite yet. Anyway, Burnwater and Ledger both run specials, but the practice isn't a partnership, per se. Burnwater and Ledger are basically two separate business entities who cover call for each other and share office space. Burnwater does facelifts and injections. Ledger is the boob man, I mean breast specialist, although he does injections too. I'm sure they give a lot of referrals to one another, though. Oh, and they're both branching out into liposuction and arm sculpting."

"So Burnwater wouldn't necessarily know what's going on."

"We don't think so, but we're not sure. It's kind of like Bernie Madoff's family. How could they not have known?"

"True."

"And that goes for Stephanie Ledger as well. Both she and Burnwater might have suspected something, but they turned a blind eye. The problem lies in if they knew something, something concrete."

Tom took a sip of his coffee, and continued talking. "When the recession hit, the Phoenix plastic surgeons took a big hit. Their per capita numbers were more than the city could support, mostly because of all the business they got from Californians taking out seconds and thirds on their houses to pay for remodeling their bodies."

"Seriously?"

Tom nodded emphatically. "That's how Wintershaw, Ledger's office assistant, got started. She ran what they call a vanity concierge for Burnwater and Ledger. She'd schedule plane flights and hotel rooms for women who wanted to discretely fly in from Cali, get their work done, and then fly back after the swelling went down. To make it doubly private, she'd pick them up at the airport herself. She was rollin' in and out of Sky Harbor four times a day. And then the crash happened. I mean, recession. That's when she became their office manager."

"I had no idea."

"And Burnwater's wife? Is she in on anything?"

"No idea yet. But if she is, that probably implicates her husband too." Tom hesitated, then he leaned forward and started talking in a lower voice. "A friend of my wife's sent her kids to the same private school the Burnwater daughter went to, and I heard she had quite the run-in with Gloria Burnwater. That stuff gets around faster than pollen on a windy day. Scottsdale is a small town wrapped in a big city."

"Care to share the story?"

"According to my wife's friend, Gloria's the kind of person who freaks out if your trash can isn't pulled in ten minutes after the garbage truck comes by, which isn't all that weird for Scottsdale. But do not touch her Mercedes. That's what the fight was about. My wife's friend made the mistake of opening her door and tapping Gloria Burnwater's car in the school parking lot. Ah well, that's what keeps lawyers in business."

"She sued her over a door ding?"

"Alleged door ding. Threatened to. My wife's friend got a letter from Burnwater's lawyer with an estimate attached to buff out the alleged dent, which according to my wife's friend never existed in the first place. Mrs. Burnwater plays hardball."

"So did they end up in court?"

"No. The court costs would have been three times the cost of buffing her car out, so they paid for it."

"Man."

"Yeah. They changed schools the following year. Now my wife's friend sends her kids to some Episcopalian school in the North Central area."

"North Central?"

"Yeah, they call it Uptown now. Change the name of the neighborhood and housing prices skyrocket. Anyway, her husband drives them all the way into the city every day."

Joe nodded silently.

"See what you missed not having kids?"

       ***

After Stephanie called Marta's brother to schedule a time for him to install the grab bars in Mary Sterling's bathroom, she raced back home to change cars. She didn't want to blow her cover by pulling up to her other cleaning jobs in a Lexus. Like Marta had told her repeatedly, if they think you're poor, they tip you better. She'd been right about everything else, including Max, so Stephanie trusted her in this, too. Marta was a fighter. So was she, but up until now she'd never had anything to fight for.

She wanted Max out of her life for good, and to be independent from his skimpy monthly payments that were designed to pinch. Didn't he ever think that it left Patrick hanging, too?

Half the house and a written guarantee of tuition money for Patrick was all she had asked for. He could keep the rest of his loot and choke on it for all she cared, and she'd told him as much. Why did Max have to insist on fighting about that?

She rounded the corner to her house and glanced across the street as one of the doors in the Burnwater's four-car garage was slowly going down. Stephanie stared at the vanity plate on the white BMW. GO BIGG. What in the hell was Max up to over there this time of the day? Why was his car parked in the garage and not on the street? Did he think if she saw his car that she'd bounce right over for a talk? Sheesh. He was the last person—

And then it clicked. Her discovery made her feel the thrill she'd felt as a kid, when she and her dad would get down to the last bit of a thousand-piece jigsaw puzzle and suddenly knew where all the remaining pieces went. Gloria Burnwater hadn't been spying on her merely because she was a bored, overindulged housewife with more time on her hands than brains, nor had she been spying on her merely to report her misdeeds to Max. No, Gloria had been spying on her because she was getting it on with Max and needed to know exactly when she, Stephanie, was safely gone so Max could join her.

With all the money Max made, you'd think he could spring for a nice hotel. But Max was Max, and the one consistent thing about him in all situations was that he was a cheap bastard. He also loved the thrill of getting away with something he knew he shouldn't be doing in the first place. He was like the guy who cuts off drivers on the I-10 because he gets a kick out of the risk.

Stephanie stared at the garage and wondered how long this affair had been going on. She finally had him. All she needed was concrete proof, but how in the hell would she go about getting it? And she when did, what would she do with it?

In truth, she was counting on the fact that he loved Christie enough that when she threatened him with the evidence, he'd deal on the divorce. But what if he didn't love Christie all that much? What if moving in with her had been a convenient and financially advantageous move and nothing more? Well, there was Gloria's husband, and Max's associate, Bob Burnwater. She could threaten Max with going to him. That might work, because Max loved money more than anything else. If Bob Burnwater knew Max was doing his wife, he'd be out of that office in an anorexic second, and Max's referrals would stop along with his call coverage. In short, Dr. GO BIGG would be shopping small at Walmart.

She needed a plan, which meant she needed Peg. But before she and Peg spent any energy on putting one together, she had to be sure. She sauntered over to Gloria's and rang the bell. No one answered, so she rang it repeatedly several more times. Finally, the door opened, but no more than eight inches.

Gloria stuck her head out. "Stephanie. Why are you here?"

Why was she there? She hadn't thought this one through very well. Come on, Stephie, think fast. "Well, I've been thinking, Gloria." She frowned and hoped it look sincere. "Can I come in?"

Gloria's eye shot up like she'd been told she needed to give all her silicone back. "No. We can talk just fine out here."

There was her answer. Gloria and Max were dillydallying during the daylight.

Stephanie's idea came to her in a flash. "I wanted to apologize for the wash-on-the-line stunt." She said the words loudly. "And while I'm sorry, I'm giving you a heads-up I'm out of money again this month, and I don't know what I'm going to do."

Gloria glared at her. "Is that why you drive that noisy truck through the neighborhood?"

Ah, the Olé effect. "Yes. It's much cheaper to operate than the Lexus. And Marta," she paused and then said, "remember her? The cleaning lady you threw a bowl at, but she was nice enough not to sue you?" She watched Gloria's cheeks redden. "Well, Marta lent me the truck, since she's doing so very well in her business these days. All her clients love her. In fact, she's looking at houses for sale in the neighborhood, hoping to move closer to her clientele. You know, save on gas and all that."

Gloria stared but said nothing.

"You sure I can't come in?"

"Yes I'm sure. You can't come in."

"Okay. I just wanted you to know I was sorry. Truly. But I'm desperate, so I might have to do it again. Desperate people do desperate things, Gloria."

Mission accomplished.

She walked into her house, dropped onto the beanbag chair, and called Peg. Although she had a plan, it needed Peg's finesse. Together, they could get the job done like no one else, and she'd finally be free.

"Hey," Stephanie said, as the call picked up on Peg's end. "I have a plan. It needs you."

"When does it need me?" Peg sounded more vexed than interested.

"The sooner the better. This weekend?"

"Can I take a rain check? Jorge and I are going to Sedona."

"Oh. Well, have fun."

"What's going on?"

"Nothing. I can tell you later."

"Great. We'll catch up. Soon. Okay?"

"Sure."

"Miss you."

The phone clicked in Stephanie's ear.

***

Joe didn't have time to park his car in front of Stephanie's house before she was out the door for dance practice. He noted an extra degree of determination in her gait, which, for Stephanie, was saying something. He truly hoped that the burr that appeared to be stuck in her behind had nothing to do with him or his tax-attorney lies.

"I have a huge favor to ask, and I need your help," she told him, the second she shut the car door.

Joe pulled away from the curb and saw that the shutters in the living room across the street closed a little tighter. Gloria Burnwater. He felt like waving.

"Having trouble with algebra?" He couldn't help himself. Ever since the two of them had decided to be friends, being around her made him crack jokes. But this may not have been the best time for that, given the fact that Stephanie failed to laugh along.

"Look, this is serious," she said without the hint of a grin.

"Okay." He could do serious. He did serious day in and day out.

"I don't know if you'd be into this, and it's really a stretch even asking, but how would you feel if we switched cars for a couple of days? You'd get to drive a Lexus."

"Oh, yippee." His reward for sarcasm was a punch in the arm from Stephanie. "Ow. And may I ask why?"

She took a deep breath and began. "I need to spy on Max."

His ears perked up.

"Because I think—" She stopped, and started again. "I have a very good reason to believe he is cheating on Christie."

"You're kidding." What an idiot. He's cheating on the person who probably knows all his secrets, the ones that could get him in major deep dodo. How could someone get all the way through medical school and still be that stupid? "Christie? Your cousin? What's her last name?"

"Wintershaw. Why?"

Bingo. "Who's he having an affair with?"

"Gloria Burnwater." Stephanie shook her head. "What an idiot, huh?"

"You mean, the woman across the street in that huge pink house, staring at your every move from behind the shutters?"

"Yes. I saw his car in her garage earlier today."

"Are you serious? That's his partner's wife."

"How do you know that?"

"Uh, you told me." He really had to watch what he said.

"Oh." Stephanie cocked her head and frowned. "I did? When?"

"When we first met. Jesus, Stephanie, do you want the date and time stamped?" Uh, that was kinda mean, but he had to get her to back off. "Yeah, you can use my car, but you can just walk over and peek."

"I'm thinking that's not the only place they go, or I would have seen them before now. But I do think that's part of why Gloria's been watching me. She knows I'm gone most mornings, and I return right before Patrick gets home from school. Today, I was early."

"Where do you go?" Shit. That was way too nosey.

"Uh, to the gym. I work out religiously."

Hmmm, that didn't sound right. "You spend all day at the gym?"

"Not every day, but most days. And sometimes I … I help at Patrick's school."

Before he could comment, she started talking again, and quickly. "I'd ask Peg to borrow her car, but she has a Mini Cooper, and those things stick out like a red M&M in the candy dish. Besides, she's busy these days with your buddy.

"You, on the other hand, have a white, four-door Camry. There are at least five of them in any parking lot at any given time. I'll gas it up before I return it. I promise. If I can get something on Max, then all this finally ends, and it ends in Patrick's favor. And mine."

"And when do you intend to do this?"

"This weekend. Patrick told me Christie is going out of town, and his dad told him he was busy and couldn't have him over this weekend. Now we know with what. So Patrick's weekend with his father has been postponed until

Christie gets back from wherever it is that she goes to from time to time."

Wherever she goes. He'd have to report this. "So they spend a lot of time apart?"

"Not really. Maybe every six weeks or so, she goes someplace tropical. Usually the Caribbean. I think. That's what Patrick says, anyway. Honestly, up until now unless it involved Patrick, I tried not to know anything about what went on over at Monticello."

"Monticello?"

"Yeah. Christie's house. You'd get it, if you ever saw it."

"Look, you can use my car, but I'm going with you. And we need to plan." Why did he say that? There had to be a regulation that forbade him from doing stuff like this if the person he was doing stuff like this with was maybe, even slightly, involved in tax fraud.

"Okay. Fine. We'll plan. But I'm the one who'll take the pictures."

"Pictures?" He hadn't thought of that.

"Man, you're a novice at capers, aren't you?"

Yes, he was, but he wasn't about to tell her that. "Hey, I've caused some shit in my day."

"Really? Oh, wait. You were five minutes late for school on the last day of your senior year, right? Wow, what a bad boy you are!"

He'd never been late for anything. Well, maybe once for dance lessons, when he almost turned around in the parking lot and went home. "Funny. Real funny."

"Okay, okay." She was silent for a moment. "Hey, Joe."

"What?"

"Thanks."

They reached the Let's Dance parking lot, still working out the who, what, and where of their weekend intentions, and they continued to debate the details during their cha-cha practice, much to the consternation of Ms. Rita.

"I don't know what the two of you are talking about, but whatever it is, quit," Ms. Rita yelled.

"Okay," they said, in unison.

Ms. Rita shook her head and smiled ever so slightly. "At least your bickering is keeping both of you from looking at your feet."

"See, there's an upside to everything," Stephanie whispered.

An upside. Joe thought about it for a moment. Maybe there was an upside to helping Stephanie get the goods on her husband. If Stephanie got divorced sooner rather than later, it would dull the impact of Max's pending arrest from Patrick. And any implication of involvement in the tax fraud on Stephanie's part would be nearly negligent. I mean really, who asks for so little in a divorce settlement if they knew there was so much more stashed on some island in the Caribbean.

Ms. Rita started the music again. "Oye! You don't have much longer to practice for the competition, so I'd suggest you zip it and start paying attention. Joe, raise your arm higher when you lead Stephanie into those pivot turns. Otherwise, it looks like you're trying to shave the top of her head off.

"That's not a bad idea." He made sure Stephanie saw the grin on his face as he whispered the words. "If your head was shaved off, you wouldn't get your ass shot off taking pictures of your husband and Gloria Burnwater."

"And Stephanie," Ms. Rita called out. "It's a pivot turn. Like in the military. You turn on the spot, and you end up on the spot, not three feet from the spot. Keep doing that, and you'll yank Joe's arm off."

"Great," Stephanie whispered back. "Then you won't have an arm left to drive with. So I'll have to go alone like I'd planned from the start."

Ms. Rita cut in again, just as Joe was forming a comeback. "Okay! Forget the cha-cha. Let's have you two be the opening act as a boxing match. We can bill you as 'The Battling Bickersons.'"

"It's been done," Joe told her.

"Yeah." Stephanie chimed in. "On the radio. Decades ago."

"Really?" Ms. Rita's voice dripped with a syrupy coat of sarcasm. "I would have never known. I just made that up all by myself. Now, listen up you two. This is dance, not debate. Take your verbal tango and put it into your moves. Act it out, and for heaven's sake, shut up."

Joe looked from Ms. Rita to Stephanie, then back to Stephanie as he led her into a turn, and then another glance as he led a move that was called the cha-cha sweetheart hold. Sweetheart. Man, what was he getting himself in to? Correction. He was already there, and he had been for a while.

Chapter Eleven

Joe picked Stephanie up on Friday, and instead of going to practice their cha-cha routine, they drove straight to North Central Phoenix to stake out Christie's house.

Following the plan that the two of them had argued over for the past two and a half days, Stephanie had Joe park down the side street next to Christie's house. From where the Camry was situated, they had a good view of the garage, the back door off the kitchen, and according to Stephanie, the master-bedroom window, which faced the backyard on the ground floor. If Max left for a rendezvous, they would know and could follow him. And if he chose to entertain at home, they would also know.

An hour and a half and a fogged car window later, they were still sitting right where they'd parked. Nothing had moved, including them.

"Hey, I get why you call this place Monticello, with the domed entryway. It's a bit pretentious for Arizona, don't you think? I mean, it would fit in DC or Virginia, but here?"

"I couldn't agree with you more," Stephanie said flatly.

They continued to stare at the garage and the house for another ten minutes. Finally, Joe turned his eyes away from the house to look at Stephanie. "Maybe it's solely a daytime-fling thing."

"Maybe. Maybe I was completely wrong about my suspicions."

Joe turned his eyes back onto the house. "You know, Christie's house looks even bigger than yours. And Gloria's, too. Maybe Max is lost in there and can't find his way out."

Stephanie gave Joe a playful punch in the arm. "You used that joke on me when I first met you. It's only sort of funny."

"Sorry. I'll work on some new ones."

"But for being a stick in the mud, it wasn't bad."

"Stick in the mud? Wow. Nothing like a compliment wrapped in an insult. Only you could pull that off so perfectly."

"Thank you." She was quiet for a moment, mulling over his subtle putdown of Christie's house. Funny or not, it was an observation of her world that wasn't pretty.

"You know," she said, "when you have kids, you want a big house. You want as much space as you can get to spread out."

"Does Christie have kids?"

"No."

"Does Gloria Burnwater?"

"One. This year she goes to some boarding school in Northern California. I don't know where. Probably Napa. That way Gloria could combine parental visits with a wine tour."

"I rest my case. What's the point of having a big house if you're not going to fill it with kids?"

She was silent again, smarting on the inside from something that wasn't even directed toward her. Why did it bother her so much what this guy thought? He was just a friend. A dance partner who would be gone after the competition was over and she told his poor mother that big fat fib about the two of them.

"Maybe we shouldn't have skipped dance practice," she said, out of the blue. "We really need some work, otherwise your mother will think I'm a—how did Ms. Rita put it the other night? A clodhopper with two oversized left feet."

Joe turned his eyes away from the garage and the back door. "Let's give it a little while longer before we bag it. Then we can go to your house and practice the routine if you want. You've got the empty space for it."

"Okay." Stephanie looked at her fingernails in the evening light. Even though the car was fogged, the moon was full, and they were close to a streetlight. "I wanted to have more kids," she said quietly. "But Max didn't."

"I can understand that."

"You can?"

"Yeah. I mean, I can understand wanting more kids."

"Oh." Relief flooded her chest, and she wondered again why it even mattered. "He used to tell people that he'd fixed me up, you know, nipped and tucked me. It used to make me so mad." She shook her head. "I don't think he wanted me to have more kids for that reason. You kind of get pulled apart when you have a kid."

"Stephanie, your husband is a pig."

"Pretty much." She sighed and looked at Christie's house, remembering when she was a kid and her aunt lived there.

Sometimes their grandmother would come from Indiana and stay with Aunt Gigi, as there was more room in her aunt's house than there was at theirs. It rankled her mother, but her father always seemed to perk up when he knew his mother-in-law was staying at Aunt Gigi's instead of their house.

Joe looked at her with a twisted smile on his face. "You know, Ms. Rita was wrong. You're not a clodhopper, you're a clod smasher. Just ask my feet."

"Is that your version of a compliment wrapped in an insult?"

"Pretty much."

"Because that's really an insult wrapped in another insult, masquerading as a joke."

"I have to work on my jokes."

"Yes, you do."

They settled back into silence. It didn't look like Max was going anywhere tonight. Why? Christie was gone, and that gave Max a green light.

God, she wanted this to be over. Not just tonight, but all of it, and forever. "Sometimes I really don't know what I'm thinking," she turned to Joe and said. "I mean, I have a son and a job, and here I am spying on Captain Sleazeball."

"You have a job? I didn't know that."

Why had she opened her mouth without thinking? But why not tell him? He knew pretty much everything else, and he wasn't about to tell Max, or Christie because he didn't know them. And if she asked him not to, he wouldn't tell Jorge, or Patrick. Joe Schmidt was trustable. And honest.

"Don't tell anyone, but I clean houses. Just for now. It's strictly a cash business, so nobody knows, and Max and his lawyer won't find out, like if I had a real job. You know, a documented job. I had to do something he couldn't trace."

"You know you have to report those earnings, Stephanie, just like waiters, valets who park cars, and lawn guys. Cash is income."

"You are so buttoned up. Do you really think the IRS gives a rat's ass about the three hundred extra bucks in cash I pull in every week? I mean really, why don't they go after someone big who pulls in millions and doesn't report it?"

"Oh, they do that, too."

"Well, you should know, you're a tax attorney."

"Right."

She sighed. "It's not like this is front-page news, but I haven't told Peg I clean houses, so I'd appreciate it if you don't tell your friend Jorge, either."

"Okay. But why not?"

Good question. She cleared her thoughts before she spoke. "I don't want Peg to know, because ... well, for a bunch of reasons. Okay, maybe I am a little embarrassed, but mostly it's because she has what they'd call *loose lips*. And I don't want her to sink my ship."

She watched a question form on Joe's face.

"Don't get me wrong. I love Peg, but if she knew, she might let it slip in front of Patrick. When she gets to talking, she gets really excited sometimes, and she forgets who's around. It's happened before, and it's gotten her in a lot of trouble."

"Oh."

"And if your friend Jorge knew, he might tell Peg."

"Good point, and I completely understand."

"Good. The fewer people who know, the less likely it is that anything will get back to Max. And I don't want to ask Patrick to keep secrets from his father. That puts kids in a bad situation."

Joe nodded silently.

"And please don't report me to the IRS." She laughed.

"Wouldn't think of it."

"It feels good to tell you, though. To be straight with someone. Someone who's honest about everything."

"There's nothing to be ashamed of, especially if you report all your earnings."

"You're not going to let go of that, are you?"

"Not really. I hope you don't get audited. You know they do them randomly."

"You worry too much, Joe."

They sat in the darkened car for another thirty minutes, talking and making jokes. Finally, Stephanie yawned and said, "You know, I don't have time for this. Why can't Max misbehave on schedule? He should just give me a call and say, 'Hey, Steph, I'm boinking Gloria tonight if you want to come by and take pictures with your cell phone.' Even in his debauchery, he is the most uncooperative man I know, not to mention the king of kinky."

"Kinky?"

Why had she opened her mouth again? Did she really want to get into talking about the creepy bras with tassels and the matching postage-stamp-sized underwear? "Yeah. Max had a few uh, predilections that were a little … unique. Please don't ask me to go into details. Suffice to say that he made every plastic surgeon's convention held in Vegas, and I'm sure he was the first to register for each one."

She looked at her watch. "Thirty more minutes and we're packing it in. I should be home with Patrick this weekend making sure he's okay, not sitting in a nondescript Camry—no offense, hoping and waiting for his father to misbehave."

"Hey. I got this car in white because it reflects heat better than any other color."

"Yeah, you and half the population of Phoenix. Not that I'm complaining. Besides, I'm sure you can get used parts for it really cheap."

"You know, you just said something that made me realize something else."

"What? A Corolla has even cheaper used parts?"

Joe gave her a withering look. "No. It was when you were talking about taking pictures with your cell phone. I don't know why I didn't think of it, but I have a digital camera with a telescopic lens."

"You do?"

"Yeah, I've haven't gotten it out since Lisa passed away. We used to go hiking to try take shots of wildlife. You can be pretty far away and still zoom in. That's much safer than running up to a window with your phone."

"Or a bear." Her hand dove into the bag of trail mix Joe brought along. Better to have food in her mouth than start asking questions about Lisa.

After two handfuls, she closed the bag and handed it to Joe. "I'm going to have to do an extra fifty sit-ups to work that trail mix off."

"Why do you worry so much?" He looked at her and smiled.

Why? Because her mother hounded her from the time she hit puberty not to gain weight. You name the ab exercise, and her mother taught it to her.

Joe took her out of her thoughts when he spoke, and she was grateful. "You could gain fifty pounds and still be beautiful."

To her, those words were more precious than an out and out declaration of love. She turned and smiled at him. "Yeah, that's what you guys say—until we gain it."

"I'm not sitting here because of your looks. I'm sitting here because you're gutsy and smart and practical, and I like you even when you're making fun of me."

"I'm glad we're friends." She turned away from Joe to focus on the entrances and exits of her cousin's house.

"Hey," she said again, turning back to face him. "Seriously. We should pack it in. He's not going anywhere except the refrigerator tonight."

"I think we should stay a little longer." He leaned forward and kissed her.

She leaned in to his kiss without thinking twice, or even once. It seemed automatic to kiss him, and thinking was the last thing she wanted to do. She wanted to feel and taste, and touching his lips felt wonderful. She leaned over the console and put her arms around him as he drew her close.

Thank god, the steering wheel brought her to her senses when her right side jammed up against it. This was as far as they could go.

When they pulled themselves apart, Joe smiled and said, "We can sit here and make out in the car if you want. Like we're in high school."

Stephanie straightened up in the passenger seat. "This is wrong."

"This is right."

"This isn't like the other night at Basha's, with a million people around. We're alone."

"All the more reason."

"I can't get involved with you. I have a kid, and a divorce to finish. Heck, I'm still married."

"Legally, you're separated."

"And there's lots of things you don't know about me. And I'm sure there's lots of things I don't know about you."

"You're right, and I need to—Stephanie, look!"

She glanced out the window just in time to see Christie's silver Jaguar fly past them with Max at the wheel. "That's him. Let's go."

Joe scrambled for the keys, while Stephanie pulled her seat belt on. "I thought he drove a BMW," Joe said.

"He does. That's Christie's car, and she's out of town. He's probably trying to save on gas, the cheap bastard." Her eyes followed the car's taillights. "Hurry, or we'll miss him."

Joe pulled a quick U-turn, and put his foot to the accelerator. "Did you see which way he went after Acacia Street?"

"Turn left." Stephanie pointed. "You need to get on Central Avenue."

He turned and accelerated again, this time passing cars on the left in the hopes of spying the Jaguar.

"Hey. Be careful." Stephanie told him. "People make dead stops on this street without signaling."

He slowed down carefully, switched lanes, and ended up getting stuck between two aging Suburbans intent on going the speed limit. By the time he pulled back into the left lane, the taillights of Christie's car had long since disappeared. "How can I lose a car like that?" Joe shook his head back and forth, slowly. "I'm sorry. It was my fault."

"It was both our faults." *And it's not going to happen again.*

"We'll catch him tomorrow night." Joe turned down Camelback Road and headed for Stephanie's house.

"Of course, we will." For some reason, she thought about Peg and wondered how she was. Maybe they should talk. Maybe she should just drive over to her house, Jorge or no Jorge, but then she remembered that Peg was in Sedona. This was the first time in their entire multidecade friendship that Peg hadn't known her schemes and wasn't a part of them. She missed her.

"I can sacrifice nailing down the cha-cha for nailing your husband to the wall once and for all, so I'm happy to keep doing this." He glanced at her quickly and then turned his eyes back to the road. "If I'm being honest, I only kept going to those dance classes because you were there."

"Oh, Joe. You hated me."

"Well, at the first one, yeah. And hate's too strong of a word."

"You hated me at the second one, too."

He smiled sheepishly. "Not nearly as much."

Stephanie shook her head. "It's one thing to fake out your mother at the dance competition next month, but come on, let's not fake ourselves out. You don't want to get involved with me for real. Look at my life. It's polluted. At near toxic levels. I've been reduced to selling furniture out of my house, lying to my friends and my son, even though it's for a good cause, and cheating the IRS—according to you.

"Well, it's not a crime until you do it. Have you filed your taxes?"

"Of course not. I won't file them until one minute before April the fifteenth."

"Well, if you report the money, you'll be okay. No crime has been committed. But you have to report the money."

She rolled her eyes at him, and continue with her litany of faults. "And now I'm spying on my soon-to-be sex-husband. I mean ex-husband."

"It's not like I wanted to like you."

Sarcasm dripped from her lips. "First, thanks a lot. And second, get over it. I'm not right for you, Joe. I have a son to raise and a mean potty mouth. I don't even know what I want to be when I grow up, and I'm sort of running out of time. Besides, you're way too mature for me anyway."

"When I'm with you, I feel like I'm not so grown up."

"Oh great. So when you're with me you feel immature. I'm so glad I bring that out in people."

"No, I meant you make me feel alive."

He reached her house and pulled the Camry up beside it, putting his foot on the brake.

"Well, snap out of it," she told him. "No more kissing in the grocery store and no more kissing in the car. No more kissing under any circumstance. This is not going anywhere past a friendship."

He looked slightly put out, and she felt sort of bad about it, but this was the way it had to be. She wasn't going to fall in love with anyone until she could stand on her own two feet and had money in the bank. Money she'd earned of her own volition.

"Fine," he said. "But it wasn't like you weren't enjoying yourself."

Stephanie could feel her face turning red. Thank god, it was dark outside. "You know, neither of us has been with someone in a long time, so we're starting to look good

to each other. I only kissed you back because I was bored."
Liar. "Tomorrow night our eyes will be focused on
Christie's house. And nothing else." She got out of the car
and walked over to his side. Trying hard to channel the
sternness of her childhood piano teacher, she bent down to
glare at him in the face but found herself leaning through
the window to kiss him one more time. What was she
thinking? "And that's the very last time my lips will ever
touch yours, unless you need mouth-to-mouth. That was
my no-more-kiss kiss. Got it?"

Joe saluted.

Jeez, she wondered, letting herself in through the
front door, what had gotten into that guy? Even more
disconcerting, what had gotten into her? "Hey, Pat, I'm
home."

She could hear his feet coming from the family
room. He appeared with his arms folded across his chest.
"Are you and Joe dating?"

"Of course not." She started to walk back to her
bedroom, and he followed on her heels. "Were you looking
through the window?" she asked, suddenly uneasy.

"Where were you? Your hair's all messed up."

Stephanie's hand flew to the back of her head.
"Must be the wind." She escaped into her room with what
little composure she had left.

***

Five in the morning and Joe found himself roaming his
condo. What had he been thinking last night? His office
was investigating Stephanie's husband, and Stephanie's
cousin, and Stephanie as a possible participant, albeit on
the periphery in the offshore money scam. If Tom or Maria
found out what he had done last night, he'd get severely
reprimanded at the very least. And if Stephanie found out
that he worked for the IRS without him telling her first,
getting fired wouldn't be an issue because he'd be dead.

He had to tell her the truth. Could he trust her? He knew she detested Max, but the idiot was Patrick's father. There would inevitably be some degree of public shame that would come from his arrest. How would Patrick deal with that in a community as gossip prone as Scottsdale? And Christie was Stephanie's cousin. That reflected on Stephanie, too, even though she vehemently disliked Christie as well, he sensed there was some twisted family loyalty lurking under the surface.

What a mess.

Then there were his own feelings for Stephanie, something he should have seen coming weeks ago. She might look like a princess, but she was a fighter, determined to survive and make the best of it. He hadn't seen it coming, but he strongly suspected that he'd begun to fall in love.

The only thing he was certain of right now was that a carton of juice was sitting in his fridge, and if he was lucky, it would only be a few days past the expiration date. This had to be the first time he'd ever regretted that his mother hadn't been dumping tons of food on him. He opened the fridge, grabbed the juice, gave it a sniff, and chugged it down right out of the carton. Gently, he lifted Lisa's picture magnet off the front of the fridge, gave it a kiss, and slid it in the utensil drawer under the counter.

***

Five in the morning and there was no going back to sleep. Stephanie threw on her robe and shuffled toward the family room, thinking she could stretch out on the couch and watch the tube for an hour before she got dressed.

Maybe she would call Peg. No, it was too early. She'd tried to call her last night before she went to bed, but Peg's phone went directly to voice mail. Really, what did she expect? Peg was with Jorge in Sedona. Eventually, her friend would come up for air, and they would catch up. There was so much to tell her.

She picked up the channel changer and lay down on the couch, pulling the afghan up to her chin. For a split second, she thought about making some espresso to jolt her senses, but she remembered Max had taken the machine with him when she'd kicked him out.

Okay, so maybe she didn't have espresso whenever the mood struck her, but she had something better now. Way better. She had choices, and they were all hers and hers alone. Funny, it was the small and trivial things she delighted in choosing most, like buying store-brand mayonnaise and mustard instead of the expensive condiments Max had insisted on. Or waiting for three weeks to do a load of dark wash, or simply having peanut-butter-crunch cereal for dinner on nights when Patrick wasn't at home. She also didn't change her sheets every week and sometimes skipped an evening meal altogether— and not just for the money. These were decisions she didn't have to ask anyone about, and that felt good.

If she had one do-over in life, besides not marrying Max, it would be that she lived on her own for a while before getting married. She would encourage every woman to do the same. Maybe if she'd known herself better, she would have made wiser choices.

She thought about Peg again. When she had first been dating Max, Peg had begged her to try living alone for a while before she got serious about anyone. Unfortunately, she hadn't listened to Peg—she'd listened to her mother.

Now, she was chasing Max all over town, trying to get something on him that she could use as blackmail. She, Stephanie Ann Webloski, had been reduced to blackmail. It was disgusting.

And as for Joe, yes, she was attracted to him. Hugely attracted to him and more grateful for his help than she could express. Underneath that handsome, silent stoicism was a truly good person. Someone trustworthy. She could see him coming out of his shell bit by bit, but should it be with her? She had so much stuff to sort out, a virtual garage sale of emotional tchotchkes to purge. What was she doing falling in love?

She sat straight up on the couch, grabbed the blanket that had fallen to her lap, and pulled it back up to her chin. Had she just used the word *love*?

***

The following week, Stephanie still had no answer as to when divorce hell would end. Saturday night, she and Joe had waited down the street again, this time with Joe's fancy camera at the ready. They behaved appropriately in the car the entire time, while they hoped and prayed that Max wouldn't. Unfortunately, he was good Max, not the perpetual creep she knew him to be. What was going on? Maybe she'd jumped to the wrong conclusion. Maybe Max had been lending Gloria his car that day. But why would he do that?

The Burnwaters had plenty of money. They could rent a car on their own. Heck, they could rent a whole fleet. Besides, they had three of them, all with vanity plates. Bob Burnwater's favorite, a silver Lexus, had a plate that read FACEUP. The plate on his other car, an older-model midnight-blue BMW, spelled out, NEWFACE. That was what had spurred Max to get his, GO BIGG license.

Gloria's Mercedes simply read, BURN. Stephanie always thought that was a fitting license plate for Gloria. Did they have any idea how silly they looked to the rest of the world?

She climbed into the Olé and headed down Camelback Road toward her first cleaning job of the day, the doctor's condo in North Central Phoenix. Mary had asked her to come in the afternoon today, so she switched the cleaning schedule to accommodate her. It helped that the doctor was gone all day.

Mrs. Sterling sounded like she had something up her sleeve. What it was Stephanie hadn't a clue, but she knew she'd be finding out later in the day. Hopefully, it wasn't trying to fix Stephanie up with her son.

As she pulled into the condo parking lot, she thought about discovering those framed pictures of the five women in the guy's dresser drawer last week. She had taken to calling him, Dr. Love. Which picture would be sitting on the dresser today, or was he working on someone new to add to the collection?

She turned the key, left the cleaning supplies in the hallway, and went directly to his kitchen table where the envelope of cash was sitting, as usual. This time the words, *thank you* were written in French, below the English. Did the guy think that if the English wasn't there, she'd never have known what the French words meant?

What had started out as something she thought of as endearing had morphed into something she now considered condescending. But she was admittedly down on the guy because of the pictures. Not that any of it was her business. As Marta had warned her, you stay out of their drawers and their mail. There was a reason for that stern piece of advice, and she was learning it the hard way.

She walked back into the hallway, grabbed the rags, disinfectant spray, and vacuum cleaner, and headed toward Dr. Love's boudoir.

Her system of cleaning had become even more refined over the past few weeks. Now, instead of starting at the front of the house, she started at the back. That way, she could close the door on a wet floor, if necessary, and avoid backtracking on anything clean. Ah, systems, time management, efficiency, and ... what the hell? There, on Dr. Love's dresser was a framed picture of Peg. Her Peg. Her best friend Peg, who deserved better than a Lothario, named—holy shit! This was Jorge's condo. She'd been cleaning Jorge's condo and never known it.

Stephanie went into his home office and opened the top desk drawer, looking for confirmation. There it was, an envelope lying on top of a bunch of papers. She shut the drawer hard and quick. The envelope had been addressed to none other than, Dr. Jorge Vasquez. She was going to kill the cheating bastard.

Bigger than that, ten times more important than that, Peg was going to get hurt even worse than Christie would someday. Jorge Vasquez made Max look like a slacker in the multiple-affairs department. Peg had fallen in love with a cheater, and he would callously add her picture to the other five women in their framed photos, stuffed away in his dresser drawer.

How could Jorge do this to Peg? No one hurt Peg and lived to tell the tale, at least not without great regret and intense pain. And this guy was Joe's best friend? Surely Joe knew what he was like, and what did that say about him? Maybe he wasn't the honest person she thought he was, either.

How was she going to tell her best friend this without giving away how she'd found it out? If Jorge knew she was his cleaning lady, then Peg would know. If Peg knew, then it was probably just a matter of time before Patrick knew. And if Patrick was talking to his father, a mere slip of the tongue could make it all fall apart when she was so close to it all coming together.

She pulled out her cell phone and called Marta, who picked up on the third ring. "*Bueno, guten tag*, and hello."

"Marta, it's Stephanie."

"I know. I have caller ID."

"Listen. Quick question. You know that cleaning job you set me up with? The doctor in the condo?"

"Sure."

"Who gave you the referral?"

"Oh, your friend. The nice one. Peg. At least that's what the doctor told me when he called. She gives me many jobs with her real estate houses. I clean them when she needs me to, and my brother, the good one, not my baby brother, he does minor repairs for her when she asks. But I told you all of this. Why do you ask?"

"No reason."

"Do you need more jobs?"

"No. I'm fine. I was just curious." She started to hang up, then stopped, and asked. "Do you know a woman named Mary Sterling?"

"Yes. I know who you mean. My brother, the good one, not the rat still down in Cuernavaca, he did some work at her home a week ago. Put up some bars that he said you wanted installed."

"Right. But initially, how did you find her?"

"Oh, she called on her own. You know, word of my business is spreading. And I have a website."

"Fantastic."

177 • The Cha-Cha Affair

Chapter Twelve

The second Joe picked Stephanie up for dance class, she pounced. "How long have you known Jorge?"

Joe cocked his head, then looked in his rearview mirror before pulling away from the curb in front of her house. "I don't know. Since we were about five. Hello, by the way."

"Oh, sorry. Hi. Thanks for the ride."

Joe glanced at Stephanie and frowned. "Why do you want to know?"

"No reason. Just curious. Did you guys meet in kindergarten?"

"No. We met in adoption class."

"What?"

Stephanie watched Joe's face contort slightly, as he prepared his answer. "I'm adopted."

"Yeah. I knew that."

"And so is Jorge."

"Oh. I didn't know that."

"His mom took Jorge to the same classes my mom took me to. They were kind of like group therapy for kids who were older when they were adopted. You know, kids who remembered their biological family, and maybe had some stuff to work through because of it. Anyway, that's where we met."

"Does Jorge still have stuff to work through?"

Joe threw Stephanie another puzzled glance. "Nah. He's good. His mom and my mom became best friends, and they still are, except Jorge's mom still lives back in New Jersey, and mine, unfortunately at times but not always, moved here after my dad died. My adoptive dad."

"How did you and Jorge both end up in Phoenix?"

She watched him take a deep breath. "Jorge did his residency here at Saint Joe's. Lisa and I came out to see him in January, then flew back to New Jersey where we landed in three feet of snow. That's a whole yardstick of snow, by the way. I walked in to work on Monday and put in for a transfer to Phoenix, which finally came through. And then, like I said, my mother moved here after my father died."

"How come he never got married?" Her eyes studied his face for any clue she could pick up on.

Joe shrugged. "Jorge's been busy."

"How so?"

"First, he was in med school, then his residency, and he does a lot of volunteer work at Saint Vincent DePaul's clinic. He does have this one issue."

Ha! She knew it. "And what would that be?"

"The quest for the perfect woman."

"The perfect woman?" What a jerk. "How about trying to be the perfect man?"

"Point taken." Joe nodded. "Since Jorge hit puberty he's kept this list of attributes that the perfect woman should possess." She watched him as he laughed. "The guy's revised it several times over the years. You can use your imagination as to what a thirteen-year-old boy would come up with."

Stephanie did not laugh along with him. She watched his eyebrows shoot up as he stole a glance at her. "Sometimes, I think it was an excuse not to get involved with anyone," he said.

"Ummm-hmm. Or to get involved with everyone, and never make a commitment to anyone."

"Like I said, he started the list when we were in middle school, and he's revised it at least ten times since then. And yeah, he's dated a lot of different women." Joe shifted in his seat, turned right on Indian School Road, and headed west toward the dance studio.

"And now he's dating my friend Peg."

"Yes, but I think he really likes her. More than anyone I've ever known him to. In fact, I think it's way past the like stage."

"Well, he should. Peg is very special. But given his history, maybe she shouldn't get involved with him, if all he does is play around."

"I wouldn't say he plays around."

Of course, you wouldn't. You're a guy. "Well, you said he's dated lots of women."

"Through the years, but never at the same time."

"Are you sure about that?"

He stole a glance her way. "Pretty sure. You know, many people don't find what they're looking for right off the bat. Did you?"

She wasn't about to tell him that she'd only dated one other guy before she married Max. "No, of course not." She took a breath. "I don't want to see Peg get hurt."

"I can't speak for Jorge, and I shouldn't, but I think she may be the one."

"The one." Stephanie spoke both words with dripping derision. "Peg is a very, very ..." She paused for emphasis. "A very special person. And if someone should mess with her, or hurt her, they'd be in a lot of trouble. With me. And I mean a lot."

"Is there a message in there, blondie?"

"Did you just call me blondie?"

"Yeah."

"I can't believe you called me that."

"Well, I can't believe you called me buttoned up the other night, and a stick in the mud. So as far as I'm concerned, we're now even."

Stephanie burst out laughing. What was it about this guy that could make her bad moods dissipate like magic? "Let's get back to Jorge."

"I have no idea what toothpaste he uses. What else do you want to know?"

"Has he ever been serious about any woman he's ever dated?"

"Not that he's told me about. I think your friend Peg is smart. And likes to have fun. You know, she's willing to try new things. And she's honest. These days, I think that's Jorge's idea of the perfect woman."

"He better not hurt her."

They pulled into the parking lot of Let's Dance and got out of the car.

Joe looked at her over the hood of his Camry. "You know, Jorge's a good guy."

"Really?"

"Really. You just need to get to know him a little better. Maybe we can all go and get coffee, or ice cream, or something after dance class tonight."

"I can't. I need to get home to Patrick."

"Oh. Right."

She turned and marched into the studio for their lesson.

An hour later, after staring at Jorge and Peg nonstop and stepping on Joe's toes more than she cared to think about, Stephanie made her way out of the studio as quickly as possible. She had never wanted to be somewhere other than where she was more than right now, and when she heard footsteps behind her, she turned, hoping it was Joe. Unfortunately, it was Peg.

"What's wrong with you?" Peg grabbed Stephanie's arm.

Stephanie stopped and looked back into the studio. Joe was taking his sweet time, laughing it up with Jorge and Ms. Rita and another couple who had also signed up for the dance competition.

"Nothing's wrong with me," she said. "Should there be something wrong with me?"

"Why were you staring at Jorge all night?"

"I wasn't." She had been, and she knew it.

"You don't like the fact that we're better at the rumba than you are at the cha-cha, do you?" Peg glared at her.

"Whoa." She stared at Peg. "Are you kidding me?"

"No, I am not."

The nerve of her. "Maybe you're better with hand styling, but not footwork," Stephanie told her. "Joe and I have you beat hands down on that one." She started walking again, this time more quickly.

Peg kept up with Stephanie's pace, but barely. "You step on Joe's feet all the time. But, hey, if that's what you want to think, fine. You still need to explain why you stared at Jorge all night, because if dirty looks could kill, you'd be accused of murder."

"Has he done something bad? Something that worries him, that I might find out about? And that's if I was looking at him, and I'm not saying I was."

Peg made a face. "He doesn't have anything to feel bad about. And he didn't say a word about you shooting him dirty looks. He has manners. I'm the one who wants to know why."

Stephanie stopped on the curb to the parking lot. "Peg, are you sure he's right for you?"

Peg crossed her arms tightly right under her chest. "What the F are you talking about?"

She searched for the right words but couldn't find them. "I think you're rushing it."

"And I think you're jealous."

"You've got to be kidding me." Stephanie felt another surge of anger. Peg was her friend. Peg was like her sister. And like two sisters, they were about to go at it.

"Yes, jealous," Peg repeated. "This time someone thinks *I'm* the one. Newsflash, we're not in high school anymore, and you're not the homecoming queen."

"And you think I'm jealous of *that*?"

"Yes."

"I'm being protective. I'm looking out for you."

"You're looking out for me? Oh, that's rich. Steph, you can't even look out for yourself."

Now she'd crossed the line. "How would you know? You haven't bothered to return a phone call in the last two weeks, you're so busy with your cabana boy. How do you know he's honest?"

"Cabana boy? That's low, even for you. How do I know he's honest? His name isn't Max Ledger, that's how. And if you ever say another word about Jorge being shorter than me, I'll—" Peg stopped and looked down at her street shoes. "I don't want to talk to you again until you can promise you'll be nice to Jorge."

Stephanie couldn't believe what she was hearing. "Well, since we're not talking much anyway, that's no big deal. If that's how you want it, that's fine."

She watched Peg's face contort from anger to one of utter contempt. It was usually a look Peg reserved for her brothers. "Fine." Peg spit the word out and glared.

"Be careful who you give your heart to," Stephanie said, softly.

Peg stalked away, but not before she yelled over her shoulder loud enough for anyone within a two-block radius to hear. "Go to hell, Webloski."

It was like high school all over again. Only this time neither of them would be over it when Monday rolled around.

Stephanie called Peg several times over the weekend. She left messages on her phone, apologizing, especially for the cabana-boy comment. Peg had not returned any of her calls.

There was no reason to spy on Max over the weekend either, since Patrick spent Friday night and

Saturday with his father and Christie. If Max made a trip out, it was only for cheap takeout dinners.

She spent Saturday sulking in her too-large, nearly vacant house, borrowing Patrick's binoculars to do her own bit of snooping on Gloria Burnwater. It left her feeling small and petty. By Sunday morning, she had an overwhelming urge to run away, and she would have if it hadn't been for Patrick.

Somehow, she felt she'd ended up in the wrong novel, playing a character she neither liked nor felt had much value to the story. She desperately wanted to be the heroine, not a woman who had nothing better to do than spend her weekend spying on the queen of superficiality across the street.

She called Marta and, with as little of an explanation as possible, quit her cleaning job at Jorge's. Marta didn't question her excuse, she only asked Stephanie to clean the condo one more time so changes in her own schedule could be made for the following week, as Marta would be picking up the job.

Joe called her late Sunday morning and suggested that they practice their cha-cha routine so they didn't look like total clodhoppers at the competition. Clodhoppers. He liked that word.

The studio was closed on Sunday, so Stephanie suggested they meet at her house since, as Joe had rightly pointed out, she had plenty of empty rooms they could choose from.

She also suggested that they practice in the evening. By then Patrick would be home, and she and Joe wouldn't find themselves alone together. The irony of using her son as a pseudochaperone wasn't lost on her, although it most certainly was not an irony she would share with Joe or Patrick or her father, and sharing it with Peg was out of the question.

Once again, Patrick beat her to the door and opened it without looking through the peephole.

"When are you going to check before you open the door?" She asked Patrick.

"Mom, it's Joe."

"Yes, but you didn't know that."

"You told me he was coming."

And there he stood, grinning from ear to ear. "Are you ready?" He asked.

"Can I watch?" Patrick's grin matched Joes.

Stephanie told him no at the very same time Joe said, of course.

She flashed a look of disgust at both of them that she hoped covered her embarrassment at the thought of having Patrick watch their dance routine.

"Give us some time to practice and then you can watch. Besides, you have homework to do, and don't say you don't because you've been at your father's all weekend, and I know you didn't get it done there."

"How do you know that?"

"Patrick, I'm a mother. That's how."

It seemed to be a good enough explanation, and he wandered off down the hallway toward his bedroom.

Stephanie looked at Joe. "Ready?"

They moved into the dining room and started their routine. Joe stopped after three steps. "This isn't going to work. Like you said last week, we can't move right on this carpeting."

Her eyes brightened. "Hey, you know what's under this carpet?"

"A foam pad?"

"No. Well, yes." She stopped and then started again. "But under that is hardwood flooring. Max wanted carpeting, and he decided that after I had wood floors installed. Don't ask me why, okay?"

"Why?"

"He wanted carpeting because that's what the Burnwaters have. He picked the same stuff in a different color. Real creative, huh? It'll take us about thirty minutes to pull the stuff up and roll it back in the dining room. Are you game?"

"Sure."

It took an hour instead of thirty minutes, as Stephanie hadn't calculated the time it would take to pull up the tack bars underneath. When they finally finished, they had the perfect floor to practice on, and they practiced until sweat dripped off their foreheads.

Joe sat on the floor against the rolled-up carpeting. "Think we're ever going to get this?"

Stephanie sat next to him. Who knew dancing could wear you out this much. But the cha-cha was particularly aerobic, with all its turns and rock-step footwork. "I think we're getting better. You know, we hesitate less, and I only stepped on your foot once. And I caught you looking down only five times."

"That's five times too many," Joe said, grimacing. "Let's try it again."

They got up off the floor, and Joe turned on another song with a cha-cha beat he'd downloaded onto his phone. "We have to settle on a song, too. There's about five possibilities that Ms. Rita approved of. I'll play you bits of them on the way to class next week." He stopped talking and smiled, looking over at the archway that went from the dining room into the kitchen. "Hey Patrick. How long have you been spying on us?"

"Long enough to know you two suck pretty bad."

"Hey!" Stephanie protested.

Patrick ignored his mother and continued talking. "You want to see what you look like?" They stared at him, not quite comprehending his words. "I took a video. Just now."

They crowded around as he pushed play.

"Oh. I look down too," Stephanie said, watching the recording.

"That's not all you do, Mom. You keep pulling on Joe, like you're the one leading the dance. And you have this look on your face that makes me think you have the flu or something."

Stephanie gulped.

Patrick turned to Joe. "And your steps are way too big. That's probably why Mom lands on your feet sometimes, but not all the time. Sometimes her footwork is off, too. And when you try to turn her, I think there should be some kind of signal, you know, like your arm should arch up more."

"Did Ms. Rita pay you or something?" Joe asked. He looked at Patrick as though he'd never seen him before.

"Who's Ms. Rita?"

"Forget it. Have you been talking to Jorge?"

"Or Peg?" Stephanie volunteered.

Patrick looked at them like they were idiots. "No. I haven't seen Aunt Peg or Jorge for the last three weeks."

Joe and Stephanie stared at each other.

"Look," Patrick started in again. "All you have to do is look at the video, and it all becomes crystal clear. Anyone who's ever watched one of those dance shows on TV can see what's wrong. First off, don't look down, both of you. Mom, quit pulling on Joe. Stretch out your frame. Joe, give Mom better clues—"

"They're called leads," Joe interrupted.

"And smile, you guys, so people don't think you just flunked an algebra test. Otherwise, the only thing you two are going to win at that competition is the doofus award. Oh, and I like the wood floor, but don't pull the carpet up in the living room, okay? I like to lay on it when I play video games." He looked at them curiously. "If you don't mind, that is."

***

Today was the last time Stephanie would be cleaning Jorge's condo. As far as the loss of income went, Mary Sterling had more than made up for it with the organizing consultations she'd reeled in for Stephanie, around her retirement center. Who knew fairy godmothers came with East Coast accents?

On her way to Jorge's, the Olé backfired so much that Stephanie had to roll up the window to guard against the noise and smell. The truck sounded like she felt. If one more thing went wrong, they would probably have to tow her away, too.

Later, when she and Joe were at the dance studio, trying hard not to be clodhoppers, Peg had either scowled at her or acted as though she wasn't there. Jorge, on the other hand, had shot several apologetic looks their way. She'd suspected that Peg hadn't shared with Jorge what their fight had been about, or she'd probably be getting dirty looks from him, too.

She'd refused to talk about any of it with Joe, who more than once had prodded her to spill the beans regarding the sudden and unexplained change in her interactions with Peg.

Relief spread over her as she pulled into Jorge's parking lot, with the knowledge that this would be the last time she'd be here and that Jorge and Peg would never know she'd been his cleaning lady. From here on in, whatever happened between the two of them was none of her business, and she probably never should have made it her concern in the first place. At least that's what she told herself today and every day since her blowup with Peg had occurred. She hoped like crazy her friend would forgive her in the very near future (like tomorrow), but somehow, she suspected that Peg's anger went deeper and involved more than her warnings about Jorge.

She turned the key in the door, walked directly to the kitchen, and put the cash envelope in her bag purse. Grabbing the vacuum, she started down the hallway only to see the bedroom door open and Mary Margaret O'Malley walk out in her nightgown. Peg stood in the very hallway that she, Stephanie Ledger, was herself standing in, wearing a pair of threadbare sweats, five-year-old running shoes, and her Marta's Maids T-shirt.

Peg screamed. "What in the hell are you doing here?"

"What in the hell are you doing here?" Stephanie asked back.

"I live here."

"Since when?"

"Since … it's really none of your business, that's since when. And I have every right to be here. Why are—" Peg's eyes widened as she took in the words embossed on Stephanie's shirt. "Are you … are you a cleaning lady?"

"There's nothing wrong with that."

"Have you been cleaning Jorge's condo?"

"There's nothing wrong with that either. And this is the last time I'm doing it."

"Why didn't you let me lend you some money? I could have lent you some. I would have—"

"I'm not a charity case, Peg. I don't want to borrow money, and I don't want help. I want … nothing. But as long as we're here, I have something to show you. Then maybe you'll understand why I have my doubts about your boyfriend."

Stephanie's anger and humiliation propelled her down the hallway and into Jorge's bedroom, where she pulled open his bottom dresser drawer and hoped like hell that the photos of his girlfriends would still be nesting there. And why wouldn't they? He probably had to change the picture on his dresser top every day.

She pulled out two at a time and placed them on the floor, side by side. "Here. Look at these. And these." She reached in for two more. "And this one." Now all five were lined up.

Peg, who'd followed her into Jorge's bedroom, looked nonplussed. "And?"

Wow. Talk about denial. "Peg, wake up. You're not the only one. He has other girlfriends."

Peg's head jerked back. Finally, Stephanie thought, she's getting it. That was until Peg started laughing uncontrollably.

"Those aren't his girlfriends," Peg managed to sputter out the words between laughs.

"Then who are they?"

"They're his sisters, you idiot."

Stephanie stared at the five framed photos. "They can't be his sisters. Look at them." One of the women was African-American, two were of Asian descent, one looked like she could be Hispanic, and number five was white with hair redder than Peg's.

"He's adopted, you dodo head."

"I know that."

"He has five sisters, count 'em, one, two, three, four, five—who are also adopted."

If she could have melted through the carpeting and then dug a tunnel under Jorge's condo out to the Olé, she would have. Instead, all she managed to squeak out was, "Oh."

"Were you rifling through his dresser drawers? Is that what you've been doing here week after week? Being nosey and checking his credit card statements?"

Ouch. Now those accusations made Stephanie angry, and indignant anger felt so much better than the shame and humiliation she'd been feeling, so she waltzed with it. "Like I'd be interested in Jorge's stuff. And by the way, you get involved with this guy, you'll be doing the dishes for the rest of your life."

"We'll eat off paper plates."

"He never cleans the kitchen. Or the bathroom for that matter. And forget dusting. He obviously didn't learn that either."

Peg launched back in. "Is that why you've been acting so weird? Because you thought Jorge was cheating on me?"

"Yes." She assumed now that Peg knew why she'd reacted to Jorge the way she did, that their hurt feelings and arguments would be over, but they weren't. Instead Peg launched in from a new angle. One that, to Stephanie, came from Mars.

"Do you think I'm that stupid, that I'd go for someone like that? Oh no, I've got it. You think I'm that desperate."

"I don't think any of those things." Stephanie heard herself yell the words instead of saying them. "And it wasn't until about a week ago that I figured out this was Jorge's condo. That's when I called Marta and quit. This was going to be my last time. And I haven't looked in his drawers or anything else. Except this one, because it wouldn't shut right."

"I would have lent you some money." Peg hovered over Stephanie as she picked up the photos and put them back in the bottom drawer.

"I don't want help," she said stiffly, standing to face Peg. "I don't want anyone's help. Not even yours."

"Does Joe know this?"

"This what?"

"That you clean houses."

"Not that it matters, okay, but yes. He's not my boyfriend, he's my dance partner until this competition thing is over. Then I'll probably never see him again. What I don't want is Patrick knowing because I don't want Max and Christie knowing. It's strictly cash, Peg. I don't have to report it, and it makes ends meet. You don't know what that's like."

"What's that supposed to mean?"

"You've done something with your life. You have money. You have a career. You're someone. I'm not. You don't know how that feels."

"I know how that feels. You have a kid. You're beautiful. Everyone wants you."

"That's not true." She stared at her feet then looked at Peg. "You still don't get it, do you? None of that shit really matters. Except Patrick."

She pulled Jorge's envelope of cash out of her bag purse and pitched it onto the dresser. "Oh, and I'd say don't call me, but you won't anyway because you're so busy with your boyfriend."

Without looking back, she walked as quickly down the hallway as her shaking legs would allow, grabbed her cleaning supplies, and was out the door. Tears blocked her vision, and she stumbled as she went.

The Olé belched and then farted gray-black smoke down Camelback Road to Twenty-Fourth street, dying at the Biltmore Center in front of Saks, The Cheesecake Factory, and valet parking. Two construction workers helped Stephanie steer it into the far end of the parking lot. One of them asked her out.

She couldn't think of who to call for help. Her dad was a good forty miles away in Mesa, Marta didn't pick up, and Patrick didn't drive yet. As for calling Peg, she'd rather walk back to Scottsdale in the heat. Finally, with much hesitation and slightly more regret, she called Joe. He told her he'd be there in ten minutes.

Hoping against hope for a breeze, she sat in the driver's seat of the Olé with both windows down, texting Marta yet one more time about the truck.

A movement near the passenger-side door made her jump as a woman stuck her head through the passenger-side window.

"Where is Manny?" the woman demanded. Her face was finely chiseled and reminded Stephanie of a Frida Kahlo self-portrait, minus the mustache. She was stately looking, tall, and sleek with jet-black hair wound in a roll tighter than Ms. Rita's. How did women manage to do that? All she could ever pull off was an uneven ponytail, and even then escaped tendrils annoyingly wisped around her face.

She shoved her phone in her bag and let it drop to the floor. "Excuse me?" she said and then locked the door on the driver's side as casually as she could.

"Don't worry," the woman said. "I'm not going to kill you or take your money in that silly plastic bag you dropped to the floor. I only want to know where Manuel is."

"Who?"

"You know who. The man who owns this truck. Manuel Del Valle. My fiancée. Who are you and what are you doing with his truck?"

"Oh!" Sweet Jesus, like she needed this. "Have you talked to his sister?"

"Which one?"

Was she the only person on the planet with no siblings? For the first time in her life, she was beginning to think that being an only child had a few perks. "Marta."

"That one. Miss Bossy Pants? She is the worst of his sisters. Why would I talk to her?"

"Because you want to know where Manuel is? And Marta is a wonderful person by the way."

The woman glared at Stephanie. "She pushes Manny around. They all do, and I don't believe you don't know where he is. Why do you have his truck? He loves his truck."

Stephanie wasn't about to tell her that Manuel Del Valle was in Cuernavaca, but she was certainly going to tell Marta about this exchange.

Instead of lying, she chose to say nothing. Lying only caused more trouble, she could testify to that one.

"Look," Stephanie said, "All I'm saying is that maybe Marta knows where he is, since you're looking for him."

"Why do you have his truck?"

"Um, I'm trying to keep the battery charged. What's your name?"

"What's your name?"

"I'm Stephanie Led—, I'm Stephanie Web—. I'm Stephanie. What's yours?"

"Mariana."

"I work for Marta." She pointed to the words on her T-shirt. "And she's my friend, so don't run her down." Mariana did not look at all satisfied with this information.

"Is Manny with you now? You and your silly blond hair? I bet it's not even real. You bleach it, don't you?"

"No. No, no, no. I'm not with anyone." And her hair was real, like every other piece of her. But getting into a fight with Mariana whatever-her-last-name-was didn't seem like a good idea. This woman was ferocious and in love. Those two attributes made for a deadly combination that she had already tangled with today at Jorge's.

Out of nowhere, Joe poked his head through the driver's side window. "Hi," he said. He nodded to Mariana, then looked back at Stephanie. "Let's roll up the windows and lock this thing up. We'll drive to my townhouse and get my jumper cables. Then we'll come back and see if we can get it going again. Otherwise we'll have to have it towed."

Mariana studied Joe and Stephanie with a look that encompassed curiosity, suspicion, and disdain. After staring at them for about ten seconds too long, she abruptly turned and walked away, blending with the rest of the people walking toward the stores.

"Who was that?" Joe asked.

Stephanie rolled up the windows and got out of the truck, making sure both doors were tightly locked.

"She is the supposed fiancée of the real owner of this truck."

"She doesn't look like a happy camper." Joe looked at her disappearing figure in the parking lot.

"That's an understatement," Stephanie said.

"What are you doing with this piece of junk, anyway? When you called and told me to look for you in this, I was confused. Where's your car?"

"At home."

"So why are you driving this?"

She didn't want to tell him about Marta's theory regarding tips. "It's a long story, but essentially, I'm ... uh, Joe, can you let me go on this one? I don't want to explain another thing to anyone right now. I've had a really bad day."

"Sure."

Relieved, she got into his car. Joe smiled sympathetically as Stephanie fell into a reflective silence. She hoped against hope that Peg would keep her mouth shut about the fact that it was Jorge's condo she'd been cleaning. But since Peg had been involved with Jorge, she didn't know what her friend would volunteer or not. The winds of Peg's loyalties had shifted, and they weren't blowing in her direction.

In the silly part of her brain, in the part that was still lurking around the halls of a Scottsdale high school, she was hurt. She'd been replaced by Jorge Vasquez as Peg's go-to confidant and number-one choice for spending time with. At least Jorge wasn't the lecher she thought he was. And the more mature part of her, along with the nicer parts of her heart, was glad Peg had found someone to love.

They pulled into Joe's garage. Stephanie had never been to his condo before, and she felt distinctly uncomfortable being there. It was his space, and being in it made their relationship feel more personal, as if they were somehow more than dance partners.

Joe rustled through the neatly stacked bins in his garage, looking for his jumper cables. Stephanie's eyes took in the garage organization along with a few areas that needed tidying up and sorting out. She couldn't help it. It was how she ticked. Her eyes automatically sought out the incongruence in everything, just as her eyes had quickly found the hidden pictures in *Highlights*, the children's magazine she'd coveted when she'd been a kid. She always found them before Peg did. Wherever disorganization was hiding, she located it in under a minute.

"Hey, Joe," she asked a few minutes later. "Can I use your bathroom? Uh, may I use your bathroom?"

Joe looked up when she corrected her grammar and smiled sarcastically. "Yes, you may, and I'm sure you can. Go through the kitchen and the TV room. Turn left. It's the first door on the right."

His condo was much neater than Jorge's, and his kitchen was immaculate. There were pictures on the wall of his hallway: one of flowers and the other of succulents.

She stopped at a framed photograph next to the flowers. It was of a woman with a big smile, sitting on a boulder the size of the ones in and around the Grand Canyon. She thought it must be Lisa, his wife. The woman had an ordinary face with chin-length hair parted on the side and tucked behind her ears. Stephanie's eyes immediately leapt from the woman's rather plain facial features to a set of crooked teeth set in a genuinely friendly smile. He'd married a plain woman. A plain woman with a smile to die for. A smile that instantly told you she was someone who'd put you at ease and make you feel comfortable. Someone who would judge you based on your character, not the address of your house.

She could hear her mother's voice inside her head as she continued to stare at Lisa's picture. She needs to buy a better pair of tweezers and pluck those brows. She should have saved her babysitting money for braces. She'd look better ten pounds lighter and with a professional haircut. She could use a little makeup, don't you think?

Stephanie studied the photograph for a few more seconds. Lisa looked strangely familiar. She resembled someone she probably knew and couldn't think of right now. Someone nice.

Joe was waiting for her in the kitchen by the time Stephanie walked back toward the garage. "Found 'em," he said, smiling and holding the jumper cables up like he'd caught a five-pound fish.

"Is that a photo of your wife in the hallway?"

"That's not the best one." He walked toward the back of the house, motioning for her to follow. They entered his bedroom.

She pulled out her cell phone to call Mary Sterling and let her know she was running late because of the truck. Anything but look at the big, empty bed centered against the wall in the middle of the bedroom. Her hand shook slightly as she flipped through her contacts and pulled up Mary's number.

"Here," Joe said, picking up the framed photo off his nightstand. "This is a better one." It was a picture of Lisa standing between two tall saguaro cactuses in hiking shorts, a rolled-up shirt, boots, and a backpack.

Stephanie nodded nervously in agreement. He was right. It was nicer. Lisa's smile was even bigger, as though Joe had told her the best joke ever. He had loved her and probably still did. Not as eye candy, not as a trophy, but because of who she was as a person.

Thankfully, Mary Sterling picked up on the first ring. "Hey, it's Stephanie," she said into the phone. She smiled Joe's way, but he wasn't looking. Instead, he was staring at the photograph of his wife as he placed it back on the nightstand, while she tried not to stare at the bed.

She walked out of his bedroom and into the hallway. "I wanted to let you know I'm coming, but I'll be a good hour late. Is that a problem? Great. I'll see you then. No, I'm fine. Really. Stop worrying about me. I'll see you soon. Yes. I'll drive safely. I promise."

She waited for Joe to come out of his bedroom. Their bedroom. Their old bedroom. His and Lisa's. When he walked out a few seconds later she smiled as she put her phone back in her pocket. "That was one of my clients," she told him. "She's really nice and a bit of a worry wart."

"So's my mother." Joe nodded in agreement.

Stephanie nodded and smiled. "Once I was fifteen minutes late, and I swear she was checking the funeral homes. So I thought I'd give her a call and let her know I was running behind."

"I'm sure she appreciates that."

They stood in the hallway together, almost touching, neither of them saying anything. Part of her wanted the moment to end, part of her wanted it to lead to something more. Instead, she stared at her feet as though they were suddenly glued to the floor.

Finally, Joe spoke in a slow voice, slightly above a whisper. "You really like the people you work for, don't you?"

"Most of them. Especially the one I just called. They're all older and need a little help. You know, so they can continue to live independently. Which is very important." They continued to stand so near they would touch if one of them leaned forward an inch. "I think we should go," Stephanie said. "I need to go, really. You know, she's waiting for me. And you need to get back to work, I'm sure."

Joe let his breath out slowly. "Yeah. I do."

Without saying much of anything, the two of them drove back to the truck. The Olé was right where they'd left it, although in the last hour the back of the truck said Che Olé once again. Mariana had made quick work of the duct tape that Marta had stuck on the *C*, the *h*, and the *e*.

With the cable and a jump from Joe's battery, the truck sprang to life once again, and before Stephanie knew it, she was pulling it back into her garage while Joe sat in his car on the curb. He wasn't going to leave until he knew everything was okay.

"You still want to practice at the studio tonight?" she asked as she walked toward his car to thank him for the tenth time in thirty minutes. Hopefully, Peg wouldn't be there with Jorge.

"Absolutely," he said. "We only have a few more weeks before the competition."

"You're right. Then I get to meet your mother." She laughed. "I bet she's not nearly as bad as you make her out to be. I need to go clean a house and make some phone calls about the truck. See you tonight."

Stephanie went inside and made quick work of her phone calls, making one to Marta, for whom she left a message, and the other to her automobile association to get a quote on a new battery and installation. She glanced at the clock, grabbed her keys, and booked it to Mary Sterling's, arriving within ten minutes of her estimated time.

"Mary, where'd all your pictures go?" Stephanie asked, as she pulled the vacuum into her living room. She looked around to see that every picture in the entire room, as well as the ones in the kitchen and down the hallway, were gone, their individual nails sticking out like cactus quills on the walls. Mary had a lot of photographs.

"I'm getting the place painted starting tomorrow, so I took all the pictures down. They're stacked in the guest bedroom."

"Oh. You should have waited for me to clean after your condo got painted."

"But you clean on Wednesdays."

"But I can clean any day of the week, and today I quit the job I usually do before yours. All you have to do is ask." Stephanie narrowed her eyes. "Did you stand on the step stool with your arm still in a cast and take those pictures down?"

"I used the step stool we bought together, not the old one." Mary smiled as though she thought Stephanie would be pleased.

"When your walls get painted, make sure you get someone to put the pictures back up, okay? Don't do it alone. Or you can wait for me to do it next week. Or maybe your son could do it." He should do something, the shit.

"Oh, he's busy with his new girlfriend. I'll wait for you. We have fun together. You know, you're like the daughter I never had."

You're like the daughter I never had. Mary's comment made the rest of Stephanie's day float by. It was quite the compliment, and she allowed herself, for a fraction of a second, to consider what her life would have been like if she'd had a different mother. Would she have cared about different things? Surely. Would she have married Max? Probably not. But what was the point of thinking about what might have been? What might have been wasn't, and she had to deal with what was.

In the early evening, Marta called Stephanie about her brother's truck. It was a good time to talk, as she was waiting for Joe to give her a ride to dance practice.

"I'll bring my good brother over to change the battery," she said. "Sorry you got caught with that P-O-S breaking down on you."

"It's okay. And I do think I get better tips driving that instead of my Lexus, so thanks for letting me use it. But that's not what I wanted to tell you. When I was in the parking lot, a woman walked up to the truck. She said she was your brother's fiancée."

"What was her name?"

"Marianne? Or Mariana?"

"Her. Ha! I had no idea he proposed to her. She hates us."

"She said that you hate her, too. Anyway, she doesn't know where your brother is, and she seemed sort of desperate to find him."

"Did you tell her?"

"No. I said she needed to ask you."

"So he tells someone he'll marry them, and then he leaves without a word. What can you expect from someone who puts *Che* on their truck? He needs to grow up."

Siblings. "I wanted you to know she wasn't very happy."

"Would you be if you were in love with my brother?"

What could she say about someone she'd never met? "I'm sure, if he's your brother, he has many wonderful qualities. How could he not?"

"Good answer, my friend. And that is why I like you."

Stephanie smiled as she got off the phone. And that is why I like you, she kept repeating to herself. Well, at least someone liked her. Maybe it wasn't Peg or Mariana or Christie (like she mattered) or her Aunt Gigi. And maybe sometimes it didn't feel like her father liked her very much, but bluntly honest, enterprising Marta Del Valle did. One point for Stephanie. No, two points for Stephanie. Mary Sterling liked her, too.

The day had been too chocked full of controversy for her to ever want a do-over. In fact, if she could purge two-thirds of it, she would. But that didn't mean the evening had to be a repeat performance of the daylight hours.

Stephanie was beginning to learn that she wasn't a pawn of fate. She was an active player, and her attitude was an integral part of how her life turned out. At least that was how she felt by the time dance practice rolled around.

"Patrick, we're leaving," Stephanie yelled, when she saw Joe at the front door.

"Again? Not that I mind," Patrick's voice echoed down the hallway from his room. He was silent for a moment and then added, "Is Joe there?"

"Yes. We'll be back in—"

"Two hours. I've heard it all before."

"Hey, smarty pants, you need to finish your homework." She got no reply from the bedroom. "Did you hear me?"

"Yes, master."

She shut the front door and turned to Joe. "Okay, let's go, so I can come back and have more fun parent-child interaction."

Joe laughed. "He's really a good kid."

"Kid. That's the operative word. Hey, maybe I should take him to the cha-cha practice." She opened the front door and stuck her head in. "Patrick, do you want to come with us to dance practice? You can do your homework there."

"No!" Patrick yelled back down the hallway. "I'm fourteen and a half. I'm not going to set the house on fire, okay?"

Stephanie closed the door again and laughed. "Yeah, boy, fourteen—"

"And a half," Joe threw in.

"That's what I call a grown-up," Stephanie finished.

Tonight, they made it to the dance studio in under ten minutes. Stephanie showed Joe another shortcut, which she told him was reserved only for the offspring of people whose grandparents had been born in Phoenix, which was why this shortcut got you there even quicker than the previous one. No one had a grandparent who'd been born in Phoenix.

When Joe pulled into the parking lot, Stephanie let out a sigh of relief so loud that he turned to stare at her. Neither Jorge's nor Peg's car could be seen. Couple that with the fact that Joe hadn't persisted in asking her what she was doing driving the Che Olé around, and the day might end up being somewhat okay.

Ms. Rita pounced the minute the two of them got into the studio. "I've been wondering if you would come tonight since Peg and Jorge canceled this morning. Honestly, of all the people in this competition, you two need the most work, and now I can focus solely on you."

So Peg didn't want to see her any more than she wanted to see Peg. At least it was mutual.

"She always makes us feel so good," Joe whispered, interrupting her thoughts.

"Yeah," Stephanie whispered back, glad for something else to think about. "But it's true. We suck. Even Patrick thinks so."

Ms. Rita must have overheard them. "It's not just your steps. When you two dance, you look like you're about as comfortable with each other as two teenagers on an arranged date, with both sets of parents along for the ride.

"Pretend. Pretend that you can't wait to get your hands on each other, and you're going to have some fun flirting before you do. This is the cha-cha for cripes sake. Act like you like it and smile."

"Okay," Joe and Stephanie's voices melded into a timid, tweet-like sound.

Ms. Rita shut her eyes and shook her head as though they were the stupidest people on the planet, and the worst students she'd ever had. Before she turned on their music, she looked tersely at them both. "Every time I think you need to turn up the charm, I'm going to yell, fake it." She started the song they'd finally agreed on for their cha-cha number, the Detroit Spinners, "Working My Way Back to You Babe."

They began with three consecutive cha-cha steps in a closed dance frame, their arms around each other. Ms. Rita yelled fake it every ten seconds. The basic steps were followed by a crossover break and a walk-around-turn. During this part of their routine, Ms. Rita not only yelled out, "Fake it," but also, "Your nose follows your toes, and quit looking down. It makes you look like clodhoppers."

"Clodhoppers, again," Stephanie whispered to Joe.

At least they had yet to step on each other's feet, something Ms. Rita jubilantly announced as if they didn't already know. When they got to the finale, in which they were supposed to end with a mock kiss, Ms. Rita went off about their arm styling during the turns.

Their prize at the end of their routine was another lecture. "Do you think actors really like each other?" Ms. Rita admonished them. "No. They only like themselves. But they know how to fake it. If they can fake it for a lifetime, you can fake it for a four-minute cha-cha routine."

Stephanie burst out laughing when Joe pursed his lips and made a face. Ms. Rita laughed along with them, even though she tried not to.

The two of them got back to work, and after the fourth run-through, Ms. Rita hit the stop button on the player.

"By George, I think you've got it." Ms. Rita clapped loudly. "The last one was the best. The hand styling, the sass, and neither of you looked at your feet once. And you both faked your attraction to each other. I am so proud of you."

"Thanks, Ms. Rita," Stephanie said, beaming.

"But you still need to practice. And you may call me Rita, but not in front of the class. Now, let's run through this one more time before you go. Remember: this is the cha-cha. Shake it and fake it."

Stephanie cha-cha'd all the way through the parking lot doing her chase turns, with Joe dancing right behind her. They laughed for no reason other than it felt good.

"Why is it," she asked, "that dancing always makes me feel better? Even if I'm in a bad mood, even if I'm depressed as hell, or worried about money, or Patrick, and even if Rita tells me I'm a clodhopper, I always end up feeling better when I dance. Why do you think that is?"

She settled into Joe's Camry and snapped her seat belt together.

Joe turned his key in the car, and backed out of the parking space. "Maybe it's hanging out with me."

"Funny."

"Seriously, I don't know. It does the same for me, too. Maybe there's something about using your brain and your body together."

Stephanie nodded. "Whatever, it's nice to have fun. Who would have thought a few months back that you and I would be friends, much less have a good time together?"

Joe laughed nervously. "Well, I wouldn't have."

"And yet, here we are."

"I did like you, but I didn't want to. I told you that. In in the car, when we kissed. Remember?" He drove in silence out of the parking lot and headed back to Stephanie's house.

She'd certainly tried to forget. "You know, sometimes I think I should cave and get this nasty divorce over with. I can find a full-time job. And what I can't save for Patrick's college, he can take out loans for, and I can pay them back over time. Maybe he can get a part-time job. So what if we live in a rented apartment? It wasn't what I wanted for us, that's for sure, but other people do it all the time, and they come out just fine. And as far as Max cheating on Christie, I don't know. Maybe I jumped to the wrong conclusion. Maybe this whole thing is just a waste of time."

Joe, silent for most of the return trip, pulled up to her house and slowed his car to a stop.

"Thanks for everything." Stephanie slowly let out her breath, and then took in a deep one in preparation for what she was about to say. "Thanks for the ride, and helping Patrick, and springing for the dance competition, and everything else. But mostly for being my friend. And thanks for not asking me about the truck."

She paused to catch her breath again.

"But here's the truth. I drive the truck for the woman who got me these cleaning jobs. It's her brother's, and she doesn't want the thing parked at her house. Anyway, Marta, my friend and employer, thinks if I drive the truck to cleaning jobs, instead of my Lexus, I'll get better tips."

"She's probably right."

"Yes, but it's embarrassing to tell people. The truth is, I don't trust that many people to tell them the truth. And, well … I wanted you to know you're on the list of people I trust, so I told you. You're a good person, Joe."

She leaned over, kissed his cheek, and thought seriously about telling him she had been Jorge's cleaning lady, but decided not to. "I like you. I'm glad you're my friend."

Humming their dance song, she cha-cha'd all the way to her door and smiled at Joe one more time before she went inside.

***

Joe Schmidt was a Grade A jerk, a schmuck, a horse's ass, and every other word that nested well with liar-pants-on-fire. At least that's how he felt. He watched Stephanie dance her way to the front door with that big smile on her face, then pulled away from the curb, and felt his stomach clench. Friends? He wanted so much more.

What was he going to do? Why didn't he tell her about Max and Christie? He'd dug a hole so deep he might as well jump in and fill it up himself.

He pulled out onto Scottsdale Road and headed home, only to be cut off by yet another stupid BMW driver. Scottsdale was rife with them. Those idiots compensated for their lack of brains, and probably other things, by driving around in ginned-up luxury cars. And look at that license plate. GO BIGG. If you're going to drive like an ass, why in the hell have a vanity plate that was instantly recognizable?

Didn't Stephanie say that Max had … oh shit. That was Max Ledger's car, and he wasn't heading in the direction of North Central Phoenix. So where was he going?

Joe eased up on the gas and followed Mr. Dr. GO BIGG at a distance, so he wouldn't be detected. Why did he worry? Who would ever be able to pick a white Camry out of the identical ones more than likely in front of and behind him? He was going to nail that sucker to the wall. If he was lucky, his redemption from schmuckdom was but a few miles and a little surveillance away.

Stephanie opened the door to find Joe standing there. She was wearing a pair of worn-out sweats and a holey shirt that commemorated yet another convention of plastic surgeons. This one was had been in New Orleans three years ago. There was a big stain right in the middle of the word *plastic*, probably tomato sauce or something else that had faded into orange.

"Do you know what time it is? " Stephanie asked, staring wide-eyed at Joe. "Why are you back here so late? Oh man, did Patrick call you? Is he having problems with algebra again?"

Joe's excitement made everything he said run together. "I saw them. Your husband and Gloria. They are having an affair, and I know where they meet. Or at least where they met tonight."

"You're kidding."

"No, I'm not. All we need now is tangible proof." He took a short breath and launched in again. "Your husband—"

"Soon-to-be ex-husband."

"He pulled into an extended-stay hotel suite close to the airport."

"That doesn't sound like Max. Gloria must be springing for that one." Joe nodded. "You did tell me his license plate reads, GO BIGG, right? And that he drives a white BMW. And Gloria Burnwater's Mercedes is, BURN, right?"

Stephanie stared at him, nodding vigorously. "Pretty stupid, huh?"

"This time stupid is to our advantage. Their cars were parked right next to each other."

"Did you get a picture?"

"Shit. I was so nervous I didn't even think of it. I wanted to get the hell out of there before they came walking out."

"Come in for a second." Stephanie grabbed Joe by the arm and pulled him inside, then walked into the family room, and grabbed her cell phone off the couch. She started to punch in Max's number, then stopped, and yelled down the hallway. "Hey, Patrick. Can I use your phone?"

"Why?"

Stephanie's eyes widened. Then she said, "Because I need to."

"Why?"

"I hate lying to my kid," she whispered to Joe. "Because I ran the battery down on mine," she yelled down the hallway to Patrick. "And I can't find the charger."

"Okay," Patrick yelled back.

"I'll come and get it." She made her way down the hallway, motioning for Joe to stay where he was.

"Maybe we'll get an idea of what's going on with this call," she said when she reappeared seconds later.

After she punched in Max's number, she explained what was going on to Joe. "Max won't pick up for me anymore, but both he and Christie will answer if they see Patrick's number. Maybe I can find out if Christie and Max are together tonight. If they are, we know he's not with Gloria, and you didn't see what you thought you did."

Max's number went to voice mail. She wasn't quite sure what Christie's cell phone number was, so she scrolled through Patrick's contacts, but her name wasn't there. Then she saw a contact labeled, Ho. Christie picked up on the second ring.

"Christie, is Max there? I've been trying to reach him all week."

"Why are you calling me so late? And on Patrick's phone?" Christie asked.

Stephanie was tempted to return the volley, but if she did, she risked not getting the information they wanted.

"We switched phones because the charge went down on mine," she told Christie. It was a lie, but it was the same lie she'd told Patrick, so at least it was a consistent lie. Somehow, that made her feel better.

"I know it's late, but is Max there? I called him and it went to voice mail. It's really important." Stephanie quickly scrolled through her mind for possible topics to talk to Max about, in case Joe was wrong and Max was there with Christie. The only thing she could come up with was Patrick.

"You'll have to find him yourself," Christie said, her voice thick with theatrics. "He sent my friend and me to Coronado for a four-day weekend." Christie put extra emphasis on the word four. "Max drove us to the airport, and we're boarding any second now. We're getting the entire spa treatment at the Del. Max's treat."

The smugness in Christie's voice was so thick she could smell the vapors through the phone. But had the two of them been standing side by side, Stephanie might have hugged her obviously brain-dead cousin.

Max sent Christie to San Diego, to the Del Coronado, to get her out of the way. It was a trip he was certain Christie wouldn't hesitate to take. And to make doubly sure she'd go, he'd not only paid for her, he'd paid for her friend, too.

Spending money so someone else could have a good time was so un-Max. This could only mean one thing. The king of kinky had gotten rid of Christie so he could get it on with Gloria at Christie's. It was the very same thing she'd caught the two of them doing last year in her own house and in her own bed. Max may be sexually weird, but he was also weirdly sexually predictable. Why her cousin couldn't see through this entire scheme was beyond Stephanie.

Christie interrupted her thoughts. "I have to go. Like I said, find him on your own."

"Thanks for that, and be careful with those chemical peels. You don't want to take more than a few layers off at a time." Sometimes, she couldn't help herself.

The phone clicked off in her ear. Stephanie turned to Joe and smiled. "Are you still in for a little spying and possible blackmail?"

Chapter Thirteen

The following morning, on schedule, Max called Stephanie to tell her that he couldn't take Patrick this weekend because he had some last-minute surgery scheduled. The old Stephanie would have blurted out the fact that a boob job was seldom an emergency, but the new, wiser Stephanie got off the phone as quickly as she could. This was the weekend in which the end would finally begin, as she and Joe executed Operation Divorce Max.

Early Friday evening, the special ops commenced. Stephanie took it as a good omen that Patrick had been invited to a sleep-over at a friend's. As she paced the living room, obsessing over everything that could go wrong in the plan, Patrick busied himself packing his overnight bag.

Joe said he would bring his camera and lens, so they could take photos from a distance. They were still fighting about who would sneak around to take them and who would stay in the car with the engine running. Stephanie insisted she'd be the one to take the pictures, because, if she got caught, everyone would just think she was a loony nut job, and not over the fact that Max left her for Christie.

Max wouldn't call the cops on her, because then Patrick would have to live with him full-time. Therefore, the likelihood of her, versus Joe, getting arrested, were little to none. Joe on the other hand knew how to work the camera blindfolded. It was something he kept bringing up every time they talked.

There was a part of her that felt the further from this well thought out yet absurd plan she could get, the better she would be. What if it all went wrong? Now, besides lying to practically everyone in one way or another, and maybe cheating the IRS by not reporting her cash income, something Joe kept nagging her about, she could add stalking and blackmail to her resume. Worse yet, what if something bad happened to Joe? She couldn't even think about that one.

She jumped to another what-if. What if she got the proof they were seeking tonight, and Max didn't care enough about Christie to cave on the divorce? Could she really follow through on her threat and bust her cousin's world apart? Yes, she loathed the woman, and yes, Christie deserved it. But she was her cousin, and Aunt Gigi was her aunt, and her father, well, to say that he'd be disappointed if he ever found out what she'd done was an understatement of gargantuan proportions. No, if Max didn't cave over her threat to tell Christie, she'd threaten to tell Bob Burnwater. Hopefully, it wouldn't go that far.

She was thinking through all of this for the tenth time when Joe showed up, camera in hand. Like Stephanie, he was dressed in black from head to toe.

"Are you two going to a funeral or dance practice?" Patrick asked, as he let Joe in the front door.

"It's jazz dancing tonight," Joe told him.

Wow. Who knew Joe could lie so smoothly? She wiped the surprise off her face and turned to her son. "Patrick, text me when you get picked up. And don't open the door before looking, okay?"

"Yeah, yeah, I know."

"If you know, then why do you still open the door without—"

"Mom."

"I've got my cell phone, and it's charged."

"Okay, okay."

"And call me when you wake up tomorrow morning. I'll come and get you."

"Okay. Okay."

They left by the door to the backyard, went around the side of the house, and walked quickly down the street where Joe had parked his car. If Gloria was looking out the shutters, there would be nothing for her to see except Patrick being picked up for his overnight.

"If anybody gets caught taking pictures it should be me, not you." Stephanie started in the second the Camry was in drive.

Joe shook his head. "You're like a dog with a bone. If something happens I have size on my side."

"Size? What, now you're going to sock Max in the jaw if you get caught taking pictures?"

"If I have to. Let's hope the lens on my camera can get it all in, and fast. That way neither of us has to get too close to your cousin's house. Oh, and speaking of a dog with a bone, I even brought a dog leash." He pulled it out of his jacket pocket and held it up like a trophy. "In case I need to lie. You know, I can say I'm looking for my dog."

"Yeah, you're pretty good at lying. I can't believe how smoothly you told Patrick we were taking a jazz class tonight. You don't miss a beat, Joe."

They parked around the corner from Christie's house, the same place as last time, where they could see a large part of the circle driveway and the backyard garage.

She picked Joe's camera up from the car floor and began to look through it, focusing the lens on the garage.

"Hey. Give me that."

Damn. After she handed off the camera, she reached into her bag for Patrick's binoculars, which she'd snuck out of his room earlier today. She focused them on the garage and wondered if the Rollerblades Christie had borrowed when they were teenagers, and never returned, were in there somewhere. Probably. Christie was never held responsible for anything.

"Hey! Here comes someone," Joe said, as a pair of headlights illuminated the garage door.

A white BMW turned into the circle drive and pulled back to the side of the garage.

"That's definitely Max's Beemer," Stephanie said. "But there's only one person in the car." She felt herself drown in disappointment.

They watched as Max got out and swung open the garage doors. He moved aside as a Mercedes with the word *Burn* on the vanity plate drove up moments later and pulled all the way in next to Christie's car.

Joe started snapping pictures.

"Hot dog," Stephanie squealed. "They really are the stupid idiots we thought they were. How lucky can one girl get?"

Joe kept snapping away but said nothing.

"Try to get a shot of Gloria with part of the garage in the frame," Stephanie told Joe. "That way Christie will know it's her house."

Joe rolled down the window, leaned out, and took several more pictures of the car, and then a few more of Gloria and Max as they sprinted to the side entrance.

He turned to look at Stephanie. "I guess we should wait a few minutes. You know, let them … I don't know, have a drink or something?"

"You really don't know Max. It never takes a few minutes."

Joe opened the car door. "Okay, so he's Speedy Gonzales. Keep the car going and get ready to hit it if I come running."

He started to walk away. Stephanie rolled down the window and hissed into the night air, "I still think I should—"

Joe turned on his heels. "Shhh."

"He could get caught," Stephanie said to no one but herself. "And it would be all my fault."

She looked through the binoculars for signs of movement, and prayed that the outside lights wouldn't go on. If they did, she planned to jump out of the car and bang on the front door before Max could start looking around in the back.

Causing a scene would give Joe time to climb back into the car and take off, with or without her. Maybe she could even push her way into the house. That might give Max the automatic heart attack he so rightly deserved.

Joe moved along the side of the house toward the back-bedroom window. He disappeared into the darkness, while she watched the inside house lights go on, one after the other as Max and Gloria made their way through the house until finally, light from the bedroom glowed into the backyard. She knew Max liked the lights on, but what if the shutters were closed? They'd still have the garage pictures, and they'd have to go with them. It wasn't as incriminating as she wanted, but she'd take it.

Twenty minutes later, the front portico lights went on, quickly followed by the lights out by the garage.

"Shit!" Stephanie turned off the ignition, flew out of the car, and walked quickly around the corner to the front of Christie's house. When she reached the portico, she rang the front bell and knocked on the door.

"Max, I know you're in there. We have to talk," she yelled even louder, as she continued to pound on the door. If she was going to make a fool out of herself, she might as well go all the way. "We have to talk about Patrick." She kept beating on the door until it flew open.

"What are you doing here?" Max glared at her with his arms crossed. He was wrapped in a navy-colored plush robe tied at the waist.

Boy, she thought, he's losing his hair quicker than a dog in springtime. "We need to talk about Patrick," she said loudly, and with emotion.

"Lower your voice."

"If you're so worried about the neighbors, let me come in." Ha! It was disgusting how much she enjoyed making him squirm. She could see the panic in his eyes.

"We can talk out here. Quietly." He peered at her and cocked his head. "Sometimes I think you're really losing it, Stephanie."

She ignored his put down. "Christie needs to be a part of this, too, Max. So if I can't come in, tell her to come out here. If she's going to play a parenting role with Patrick, she needs to hear this. You are planning on her being the next Mrs. Maxwell Oscar Ledger, aren't you?"

He shut the door, and leaned against it.

"I mean, after we get our differences all worked out?" She looked at him coyly, trying hard to keep a straight face.

"Christie's not here, and I don't want you coming in." Max sighed and looked at her. "What do you really want?"

Stephanie moved so that Max was forced to turn and put his back toward the side of the house to face her. "Max, all I want is what my lawyer already listed. Half the house and enough money in an account for Patrick's first four years of college. It's not like you don't have the money. Why is that so hard for you to understand?"

Max looked visibly uncomfortable. "I don't have time for this." He turned and started to open the door.

Stephanie lurched toward him. "Have you ever thought about reconciling?"

His eyes widened to twice their size. "What?"

"Just for an evening." She swallowed and leaned in closer. Max's cologne made him smell like a cheap streetwalker. Not that she'd ever smelled a streetwalker, cheap or otherwise, but if she ever got the opportunity, she suspected they would smell like Max did right now.

"Maybe a threesome. Christie and I are related. It's the closest you'd ever get to twi—" She heard a cracking noise and looked over Max's shoulder to see Joe walking through the yard and boldly toward the portico. What was he thinking?

"Who the hell are you?" Max demanded, as he turned to look at Joe.

"Hi." Joe held up one hand like he was surrendering. The other guarded the bulge in his zipped up black hoodie. "Sorry to bother you, but I've lost my dog." He reached into the pocket of his hoodie and pulled out the dog leash.

"I was in the back of your house looking for her," he continued. "I hope I didn't scare you. I saw your lights go on, so I thought I'd better come over here and explain." He glanced at Stephanie like he'd never seen her before in his life, and said, "Hi."

Stephanie nodded to Joe but said nothing.

"Yeah, we thought we heard something." Max stared at the bulge in Joe's jacket.

"I thought you said Christie was gone," Stephanie said. She hoped it would throw Max into a defensive mode. It did.

"I meant me. It just came out as we." He turned his gaze from Joe to Stephanie.

Joe took the lead. "My dog's name is … Mary. She's a big black Rottweiler." He looked directly at Max. "Hard to see in the dark."

Max looked at Joe like he was seeing the village idiot.

"Well, if you see Mary, my dog, I live two streets over. Big pink house. I'll leave the light on. Thanks." Joe walked away quickly. Stephanie could tell he was trying hard not to run. She watched as he walked past his car and on down the street, yelling, "Mary, here Mary."

Max narrowed his eyes at Stephanie. "Where's your car?"

"Uh, it's over there." She pointed toward the Camry. "It's my dad's. We switched for a couple of days."

"Since when did your dad buy a foreign car? The last time I talked to him, he gave me shit about not buying American. And he drove a Buick."

"Well, they're assembled in the US now, and that's good enough for my dad. You haven't been around for a while, Max. This is his new, used car. They call them preowned these days." The look on his face told Stephanie he was buying her load of lies. *Thank God.* She turned to leave.

"Hey, wait a minute. About your idea."

"What idea?"

Max's eyes twinkled with childish eagerness. "You know, the threesome."

Of course, he'd fixate on that. "I don't know what I was thinking. That sort of popped out, and I didn't mean for it to. Must be your cologne. See you around." She tried not to smile too big. Max remained silent, but she could feel his eyes on her as she walked with as little shaking as possible to the car, got in, and drove off.

She made her way slowly down the street looking for Joe, finally finding him one street over still yelling for his make-believe dog. "Get in right now," she said, stopping the car.

Joe laughed and opened the door. "God, that was fantastic." He slid onto the seat and raised his hand to high five Stephanie, a gesture she ignored.

Instead, she shook her head and looked at Joe as if he was a child she wanted to ground, or lecture. One or the other. Maybe both. "What were you thinking walking up on the porch?"

"I was thinking about covering my ass—and yours. If he saw me sneaking away from the side of the house with a camera he'd get a little more than just suspicious, so I stuck it in my jacket and made up the dog lie, like we'd already talked about. Hey, I thought I did pretty good."

He had, but she didn't want to tell him that. Somehow it felt like telling Patrick he'd done a good job t-peeing the house down the street, when he shouldn't have been doing it in the first place. "Did you get pictures?" She put the car back in drive and took off for home.

"Boy, did I get pictures. Whew!"

If Joe only knew what Max was capable of, he wouldn't be so flippant. There'd be hell to pay if Max ever figured out who Joe was. But then it hit her. There would never again be hell to pay. By sneaking around with his partner's wife, Max had committed the unthinkable, and she'd caught him red-handed. Finally, she would be free—and on her terms, not his. If he ever considered coming after Joe, she'd still have the pictures.

Joe laughed again and turned toward Stephanie. "I learned a few things, too."

Again, she ignored him. This wasn't the time for jokes. "If you give me your camera tonight, I'll download these pictures onto my computer and send a few choice ones off to Max's email."

"They're all choice."

She made a mental note to herself about passwording the file to protect Patrick in the rare case that he decided to look through her photo files. "I'll bring it back to you tomorrow."

"It's late, so why don't you let me help you tonight, and we can get it done. Especially with Patrick gone. You don't want him seeing this by accident."

"Good point. You got a deal. I'll even throw in a complimentary peanut butter sandwich."

Joe snorted and shook his head.

They drove home saying very little after that, silenced and sobered from the events of the evening.

"Pull in the driveway," Stephanie said when the two of them reached her house. She laughed as she opened the car door. "One thing we know for sure, Gloria's not peeking through the shutters tonight."

They walked together to the front door, their shoulders bumping against one another. Instead of reaching for her keys, she reached her arms around his back and lifted her face up to his, feeling for his lips, which he gladly gave her.

Like two people starved for touch, their mouths and hands began a search of the other. Every part of him smelled as wonderful as his neck and chest had promised. Stephanie couldn't quit exploring him with her mouth and drinking in his scent.

His hands went up the back of her sweatshirt and then into her shirt as he undid the hooks of her bra. He slid his hands up her side and onto her breasts.

She shivered from his touch and then suddenly stiffened. "Do you want to talk about this first?" she asked.

"No. Talking is the last thing I want to do."

She breathed in and moved to find his lips once again while her hands unzipped his sweatshirt and began their climb up through his T-shirt.

He backed her against the wall as their touching grew frenetic. Stephanie undid his belt and pulled down the zipper on his jeans. "Do you want to go inside before anything else happens?" she asked him, whispering as she caught his earlobe lightly between her teeth.

"No. But we should."

She gently pushed herself away from him and searched her purse for the house keys. They stepped in to the entryway, ready to resume de-robing each other before they made their way down the hallway and into her bedroom. That was, until she heard a voice from the living room.

Chapter Fourteen

"You cheat on Manuel?"

Stephanie screamed, until Joe turned on the entry hall lights. She noted that his zipper was back up, although his belt wasn't buckled. He stood close to her and, together, they stared in unison at the woman who was struggling to get up out of the beanbag chair.

"Mariana? What in the hell are you doing in my living room?"

Mariana stood with her arms tightly crossed against her chest, making her stomach bulge slightly beneath them. "I have been waiting for you to return from your dance class."

"How did you get in my house?" Stephanie knew the answer halfway between starting to ask it and finishing her sentence.

"Your son."

Stephanie sighed. "Did he look before he opened the door?"

"No. When he opened it, I lied and told him Marta was my sister, so he let me in, and he let me stay and wait for you. He has very nice manners. You should be proud of him."

"I am proud, but he's still grounded next weekend. Now, what are you doing in my living room?"

Instead of being rude and snarky, which Stephanie strongly suspected was Mariana's default approach to life, and all things included, Mariana burst out crying. "I need to find him. Where is he?" She started to gag, then made a mad dash to the kitchen, and threw up in the sink.

Stephanie followed the retching noise. "Are you okay?"

Mariana was cupping her hands under the faucet to get a drink. "No, I am not. And I need to find him."

Stephanie reached for a glass in the cabinet and handed it to her. "Mariana, are you maybe …" She winced inside at the strong possibility that this probing question might not be taken well. "Are you pregnant? Not that you look like it or anything," she added, quickly.

"Yes." Mariana started to cry again, and cried even harder when Joe walked into the kitchen.

"Can I get you something?" Joe asked.

"My fiancée," Mariana said between sobs.

While Joe did everything he could to calm Mariana down, Stephanie grabbed her cell phone, walked into her bedroom, shut the door, and punched in Marta's number. She glanced around her room as the call rang, thinking about what she had anticipated doing in here a mere ten minutes ago. It certainly hadn't been calling Marta Del Valle.

Thankfully Marta picked up on the fourth ring. "You never call at night. Is everything okay? Do you need more jobs? Less jobs? Do you need my help? Is it Patrick?"

"No. Nothing like that. Look, I know you were going to come over tomorrow and deal with your brother's truck, but, well, Mariana is here and—"

"*Dios Mio*, what does she want now?"

"Your brother. And I don't blame her." She heard Marta snort over the phone and start to speak, but Stephanie did an end-run. "Marta, she's pregnant."

"I'll be right over."

Two hours and many tears later, Mariana and Marta, one of Marta's sisters, her other brother, and her sister-in-law all left together arm-in-arm as one loving family. Only the truck stayed behind.

As Stephanie said goodbye and closed the door on the last Del Valle, she turned to Joe and gave him a sleepy smile. "I wish all family disputes could end as happily as that one did."

"Yeah, but they still haven't contacted Manuel. God only knows what will happen then."

Stephanie nodded in agreement. "Good point. Mariana told them Manuel didn't know she was pregnant. In fact, she didn't know she was pregnant when he left. They had a bad fight, according to Mariana."

"I hope they get it worked out."

"Me too." She watched him yawn. "What time is it?"

He took his cell phone out of his back pocket and checked. "A little after midnight. I think I should probably go."

Stephanie nodded silently. She was thinking the same thing.

Joe walked to the door and Stephanie followed him to open it. He bent down and kissed her cheek gently, then kissed her on the mouth. "At least Operation Divorce Max was successful. I'm taking a rain check on the rest of our plans."

"We'll talk tomorrow."

"I … there's a few things I have to tell you."

"There's something I have to tell you, too. About Peg, and Jorge. And it involves me."

He nodded and smiled. "Okay, until later."

She closed the door and leaned against it. What a night. Max, and Mariana, and Marta's family, and Joe, and—was that the camera? She saw it out of the corner of her eye, next to Patrick's video game player.

She might as well get the pictures downloaded tonight before Patrick came home tomorrow morning. Besides, there was no way she was going to sleep much tonight anyway.

The data memory card popped right out and into her computer. She opened the file and scanned the most recent photos. Even alone by herself, in her own house with no one watching over her shoulder, her face turned a deep red when she saw them. She picked out the worst three and emailed them to Max as an attachment. If that didn't get a response by tomorrow, she'd text the photos to his phone.

She looked at more of the pictures on Joe's memory card, feeling a little bit like a voyeur, but not enough to stop. As she suspected, there were many of Lisa, some of them at Disneyland, and a few taken as she was noticeably ill. There were several of Jorge, with one or two of his now infamous sisters, and one of Jorge with a woman who she assumed was Jorge's mother. She looked familiar.

She started to click through more of Joe's photos on the memory card when her phone rang. The caller ID said *Max*. Somehow, she'd envisioned this happening tomorrow morning, after she got some much-needed sleep. But why not now? Why not get it over with?

Taking a deep breath, she straightened her back and answered her cell phone. "I thought you'd be calling."

"How could you?"

"Max, the better question is, how could you?"

"I could press charges."

She laughed. "You could press charges? For what?"

"Trespassing."

Her response was a laugh. She wasn't afraid of Max anymore.

"Okay, then, blackmail."

She laughed again. "Yes, let's take this case to court along with the receipts from your business card for an extended-stay hotel, or did Gloria spring for that? How long would it take George Burnwater to find out what's been going on under his nose while he's been in surgery fixing other people's schnozzes? And I don't even want to tell you what would happen if Christie ever found out. She'd redefine the term *hell to pay*." She paused for effect. "You cooked your goose on this one, Maxie."

Another sigh from Max's end of the phone. "What do you want?"

It was disgusting how much she loved this. "Jeeze, Max. You know what I want. Half of the house and money for Patrick's college education. And not just the promise of it on the divorce papers this time. I want money in the bank for college in an account with my name and Patrick's name on it, not yours." Having the upper hand was so much fun.

"How do I know you'll destroy those pictures? Maybe you'll keep them to get something else you want later. I need a guarantee."

"Here's your guarantee. I'm not Christie, and I'm not Gloria. I want to avoid you as much as I want to avoid the flu. Trying to wring extra money out of your greedy little soul would require more interaction with you than the money's worth. After our divorce, seeing you at Patrick's graduations and maybe his wedding, if that ever happens, is all I'm going to be able to stomach."

She paused and took a breath, thinking that for once Max was smart not to try and cut her off. "At those two future events, you will act like a grown-up with manners, and so will I."

Max snorted. "I'll have my lawyer work up some numbers for the college account."

"Max, it's in your best interest to be very generous. Think Harvard."

They paused in preparation to end the call, then Stephanie remembered what Patrick had said to her, months before. "Wait, one more thing."

"I knew it."

"After our divorce is final, Patrick gets to decide whether he wants to come over to your house on the weekends. The decision is up to him. And I want full custody."

"Fine."

It took him less than a second to agree to sign over custody of his son, yet he'd spent nearly a year arguing about money. It was an insight she'd never share with Patrick.

"I think we're done here," Stephanie said. "I expect my lawyer to be hearing from your lawyer in the next week. If not, the pictures will fly to Christie and Bob—"

"You wouldn't do that."

"Yes, I would. I really would. So you better get busy. Chop-chop, Maxie."

She heard a click in her ear, and it was all over.

Finally, she could sleep like she'd hadn't slept in over a year.

***

It was one o'clock in the morning when Joe turned the key in the door of his condo and made a beeline for his bed, kicking off his shoes, unbuckling his belt, and putting the picture of Lisa face down on his nightstand.

He'd never been bad before. In his whole life, he'd never taken a risk or intentionally broken a rule. Well, how could he?

After his birth mother died, he tried to be so good his new parents worried about him. His adopted mother would tease him in his teen years, saying things like, Joey, how many mothers worry about their children being too good? You can tell me if you don't like something. Don't be afraid to make me mad, she'd say. Whatever you do, I'll get over it. But he wouldn't tell her when he didn't like something. He couldn't.

He remembered thinking when he was little, what if his new parents decided to take him back? Where would he go? Who would he live with then?

He'd never been like the other boys, running around in high school, thinking up ways to get around the rules. Why take the chance? Even though Jorge had taken plenty of risks, he'd been the only person Joe felt understood his hesitation and anxiety. Jorge had five sisters. The guy had had to distinguish himself somehow. But not him. He'd had no one beside his parents. The fear of losing them had flooded his emotions for the first few years he lived with them. After that, he'd just buried it.

Now, by helping Stephanie nail the philanderer of Phoenix, he'd found a reason to take a risk and break the rules. It had been wickedly exhilarating. Downright exciting. He should have been bad earlier. Certainly, that's what Jorge had tried to tell him when they were teenagers. Come on, Joe, break a rule. I dare you.

After the competition, after she met his mother, he was going to tell Stephanie the truth about who he worked for and what he did. Most importantly, if she didn't put two and two together before he finished saying the words *Internal Revenue Service*, he would need to tell her about the ongoing investigation regarding her son's father. But when he introduced her to his mother, he wouldn't be lying. She really was who he'd been seeing. He really was in love with her. And he needed to come clean.

Chapter Fifteen

Since the successful execution of Operation Divorce Max, Stephanie had a renewed surge of energy. It was as though ten pounds of stress had been magically liposuctioned away. She waltzed through her cleaning jobs. Correction, she foxtrotted through them with a spring in her step. Finally, she could look forward to a future.

Although she tried not to, she kept thinking about her father. He wouldn't be proud of what she'd done, but if Max carried through with his end of the bargain, no one, including her father, would be the wiser.

And Joe? She trusted him. Now if he would call like he said he was going to, they could set up a few more practices and get their facts straight about his mother before the dance competition this Saturday. She got an email from him late on Sunday afternoon, telling her that he was busy and he'd call later in the week. Maybe then they could get their arm styling right, and if she could avoid stepping on his feet, they might not come in dead last. She would happily settle for the award of Not the World's Worst.

Where was this partnership going between the two of them? Would she see him after the dance competition? He said he had something he needed to tell her. It was probably more information about his mother, stuff that she would know if they were really a couple. But they weren't. They were just two friends who were attracted to each other, on and off.

Dancing made her feel wonderful, and whenever she danced, there was Joe. Pure and simple. She associated him with a good time. It was nothing more.

Her new life would be school, then a career, and Patrick. Not much left for anything or anyone else. Not even a dog. Not even Joe.

The shutters were closed so tightly over at the Burnwater's that Stephanie suspected they'd been superglued shut. Today, on her way out to Mary Sterling's, she glanced at Gloria's front door. A rolled-up flyer was attached to the door latch, and another one was stuck between the door and the frame. They were the same ones that had been on her front door two days ago.

She wondered if Bob Burnwater, dense as he was about everything but surgery, had found out about Max and Gloria. Or maybe Gloria, wracked with guilt, had left on a retreat to ponder the virtues of monogamy. Yeah, like that was going to happen.

She laughed out loud. A sarcastic joke and no one to share it with. Where was Joe Schmidt when she needed him?

As if the man possessed ESP, he called. Stephanie picked it up even though she was driving. "Hey."

She was tempted to ask why he hadn't called her until now. He said he wanted to tell her something. She wanted to know what it was. But asking a question like that was out of line and sort of naggish. You asked questions like that if you were involved with someone, and they were just friends. Friends who made out from time to time.

"Sorry I haven't called this week," he said. Stephanie could hear his hesitation. "So you still want to practice tonight?"

"Of course. I wouldn't miss it."

"You okay?"

"Never been better," she answered.

"Everything went the way you wanted it to?"

"Better than expected," she told him.

"Wonderful. Any word from the lawyer?"

"My lawyer got a call from his lawyer who told my lawyer that the papers will be in his office for me to sign no later than Friday morning."

"That's great. The quicker the better."

"So when I meet your mother I can honestly say I'm single. I sort of like minimizing my lies these days."

"We need to talk about that," he said.

Stephanie thought Joe's voice sounded far too serious for the joke she just cracked, but at least she finally knew what he wanted. "Sure. We can talk about your mom on our way to practice. Hey, I'm headed over to a client's. I shouldn't talk and drive, so I'll see you tonight."

"I'm glad things are going your way."

"Thanks for your help, Joe."

"And there's something else we need to talk about besides my mother. After the competition, okay?"

"Sure. Hey, don't let me forget to give you your camera back. Gotta go." There. That didn't sound naggish or clingy in the least. In fact, she was the one who'd insisted on getting off the phone.

She pulled into Mary Sterling's overflow parking lot, and cha-cha'd to her door. Max-free, life was good and should be celebrated.

Before she formed a fist to knock with, Mary opened the door, a smile on her face from one end to the other.

"Mary. How are you? When's that cast coming off?"

"Monday next week, but not soon enough for me to rehang all the pictures before I meet my son's girlfriend. She just might be coming over, you know."

Stephanie put her purse down, grabbed the step stool from Mary's kitchen and lugged it into the living room.

"I'm going to miss you, Stephanie."

She smiled. "Are you going someplace?"

"No, but I'm getting my cast off, and I know you won't be around forever. You've got too much on the ball for that. So I printed out some information about a possible career path for you, given your obvious talents. I'll just slip it into your bag."

"Uh, sure. Thanks. Now about those pictures. Do you have them all lined up?"

"No. But I remember where they go. Don't worry. I'm not that senile yet."

Stephanie laughed and shook her head. "I never thought you were. Hey, I'll grab two at a time, and you can show me where you want them."

Stephanie walked into the spare bedroom and picked up the first two photographs, checking to make sure that the hangers on the backs were still in working order. "Tell me where, Mary."

"Oh. Those are my sisters, unfortunately. Well, with one of them, it's more unfortunate. With the other … you know how older sisters can be."

Stephanie thought about Peg. "I'm an only child."

"I'm sorry."

Stephanie shrugged. "Sometimes I'm sorry, and sometimes I think life's less complicated."

"My son is an only child."

"Oh."

She went to get two more framed photos after she hung up the sisters. "Where do you want these?"

"That's my son's birth mother."

"You knew her?"

"Um-hmm. She was my cousin." She pointed with her chin to the photograph in Stephanie's other hand. "And that's my first husband, Peter. They go on the other wall."

"I didn't know you'd been married before."

"Yes. Two wonderfully happy marriages. Only I don't put my husbands next to each other. It seems indecent. I loved them both, but that doesn't mean they would have liked each other."

Stephanie laughed. "Makes total sense to me. We wouldn't want any picture fights."

"I've buried two husbands and a daughter-in-law."

"That's a lot of people to lose. I'm sorry." Stephanie went back into the bedroom and came out with two more. "Point where you want them."

"That's my second husband."

"He's handsome. And the other one? Your daughter-in-law?"

"She goes next to my second husband."

Stephanie climbed back on the step stool. She put the pictures up and then climbed back down and studied them.

"My Burt was such a nice man. I'm sorry we didn't have more time together."

Stephanie pointed to the daughter-in-law. "She looks familiar."

"Maybe you knew her. She died two years ago."

"What's her name?"

"Lisa."

Oh, god. "Lisa Schmidt?"

"No. Stevens."

"Oh." She breathed out a long sigh.

"She kept her own name when she got married," Mary continued. "Schmidt was my husband's name, and my son became a Schmidt when we adopted him. Lisa kept her own name when she married my son."

Stephanie sat down on the top of the step stool. Her legs felt like Jell-O. "But your name is Sterling."

Mary nodded in affirmation. "I took my second husband's name when I married him. You know, it's what people in my generation do. Before I was a Schmidt, I was a Leone."

"So your son's name is?"

"Joey. Joseph Peter Schmidt. His mother was my cousin, so he's really a Leone, but he goes by Schmidt like I did after I got married. And now I go by Sterling." She turned to look at Stephanie and stopped smiling. "Are you all right?"

"Mary, didn't you tell me your son worked for the IRS?"

"Um-hmm. I think it keeps him from getting dates. But now he finally has a girlfriend, and I'm going to meet her."

"When?"

"On Friday. They're in a dance competition together. That's how they met. Isn't that sweet?"

Stephanie nodded mutely.

"Joey invited me to watch the competition and then meet her after that. He's been very mysterious about this woman. I still don't even know her name, but then, I don't like to bug him about anything. And his best friend from New Jersey is in it too, with his new girlfriend. Are you sure you're feeling okay?"

"No. I don't think I am."

"Well don't go getting sick on me, Stephanie, because if it doesn't work out with his dance partner, I'd really like to introduce you to Joey."

Somehow, Stephanie made it through cleaning the rest of her day, including finishing up at Mary's. When she finally made it home and was finally alone, she didn't know whether to cry, scream, or hit something. But what she did know was that she wasn't about to go to dance practice with Joseph Peter Shit tonight, because she might kill him if she did.

After she could control herself enough to keep any hint of anger or sarcasm out of her voice, she called to cancel the practice, feigning an event at Patrick's school she'd completely forgotten about. Luckily, her call went to voice mail, and she didn't have to speak to him. Little

Joseph Peter wasn't going to have a single clue as to what would befall him Friday night.

Her thoughts scrolled back to conversations between them over the past few months. They'd talked about honesty and telling the truth and coming clean with the people they cared about. As she thought about their conversations, she realized that all those purges of conscience and declarations of honesty as the best policy had been on her part, not his. He'd never said a word, only smiled and nodded that disgustingly handsome head of his up and down. And all those fibs she'd nearly caught him in, fibs that he wiggled out of one way or the other. What an idiot she was.

Why go to all this trouble to lie to her? It didn't make sense, but she was too upset to think right now. It didn't matter anyway. What mattered was that she'd trusted him and he'd lied about who he was, and he'd kept lying when he had so many opportunities to come clean.

She sighed and shook her head. First, she was a blackmailer, and a successful one at that. Second, she was a tax cheat, and third, she would now be a revenge artist. Maybe, instead of going back to school, she could apply for a job with the mob. By the time Friday night rolled around, there would be plenty of the experience they looked for on her resume.

Joseph Peter Schmidt deserved a lesson he would never forget, and she would spend the night planning it out carefully. First, she needed to see if Patrick could spend Friday night at a friend's. He'd been trying to find a way out of going to the dance competition anyway. After that, she needed to call her father to see if he would give Mary Sterling a letter tomorrow night at the dance competition. Then it was on to revenge by cha-cha.

Chapter Sixteen

Stephanie arrived at the dance studio late on purpose, wearing a pair of shoes with stiletto heels as long and spikey as daggers. She had been up all night practicing her basic cha-cha steps in them, as well as dialing back her anger to controllable proportions while she iced her feet down in the early morning hours. At five in the morning, she decided that after tonight, all high heels should be outlawed.

Ms. Rita greeted her at the door with a face similar to the one Stephanie had seen the first time she'd slunk into dance class late. "I was afraid you'd chickened out," she told Stephanie in a terse whisper.

"I never retreat. I am woman, Ms. Rita. There is nothing I can't do that isn't doable. And like you said, if I can't do it, I'll fake it."

"I said, if you don't *feel* it, fake it."

"Whatever."

Ms. Rita's eyes widened as Stephanie strode past her into the studio, the fringe on her bright-red cha-cha skirt swishing as she stalked.

The look on Joe's face changed from worried to relieved when he spotted her as she walked toward the group of dancers in the back corner of the studio. If he only knew.

Her eyes flew over the audience looking for her father, who she located sitting next to Mary.

Peg moved through the small crowd of contestants toward her. At this point she really didn't care what Peg said or didn't say. After this evening, everything changed. She'd be starting over, and if she had to start over without

Mary Margaret O'Malley as her best friend, she would. At least that's what she told herself.

"I need to talk to you," Peg said, a fraction above a whisper. The tone of her voice wasn't one of anger, it was one of concern.

"I've been saying that for weeks," Stephanie said. Given their last interaction, she would more than likely receive a lecture from Peg, albeit probably a motherly one this time around, judging from her friend's current tone.

Fake it. She looked at Joe and smiled sweetly. She looked over at Mary, who was squinting at her, a question mark carved on her face. Mary turned to smile at her father, and he returned Mary's smile with an even bigger one. Oh god. With her luck, the two of them would end up dating. And why not? Everyone else around her was. There was Peg and Jorge, and the other contestants who all seemed disgustingly lovey-dovey.

Even Mariana and Manuel had managed to patch up their differences. Marta had called earlier today and told Stephanie the news that they were getting married, and that they'd be over to collect Manuel's truck very shortly. She'd heard that one before.

As Joe tried unsuccessfully to make eye contact with Stephanie, Peg tried whispering to her again. "We really need to talk." This time the emphasis was on really.

What was up with her? She knew she'd messed up with Jorge's false girlfriends, but, jeez, Peg, this was not the time to have a powwow.

Soft music started as Ms. Rita floated out to the middle of the studio to give her introduction. She wore a jade-colored dance costume that had rhinestones sewn into the front of the dress, and along the edge of the back, that ended in a V. She looked wonderful. It took a lot of grace to pull that look off.

After her short speech, the first couple took off doing a mean, sassy tango. They would give Jorge and Peg, who were the best beginning dancers Stephanie had seen, some real competition. After the tango, another couple performed a near-perfect bolero, followed by a duo who danced a three-step East Coast swing.

Jorge and Peg, dressed in matching costumes of black and emerald-green, performed their rumba routine. They'd only gotten better since the last time Stephanie had watched them dance. It would be a tough choice between the tango couple and them. But the best was left for last.

Joe took Stephanie's hand, and they walked out onto the floor. She made sure her fingernails dug into his palms, but not so much that he would pull his hand away. It was merely a hint of what was to come.

They began their routine in each other's arms. She smiled at him sweetly and whispered in his ears, "You're a lying son of a bitch. Your mother would be ashamed if she knew."

Joe straightened and jerked back his head. It caused him to stumble, but he regained his footing and picked the rhythm up again.

Stephanie smiled sweetly to the audience when Joe stumbled, as if to say, my partner sucks, but, hey, I can't help it. This is who I'm stuck with.

During the cha-cha turn she was again close enough to whisper, "You work for the IRS, you lying ass. What are you after?" She heard an audible sigh from Joe.

"It's not you. It's—" Joe started to mutter something else, as Stephanie moved away to do her single cha-cha breaks, then a complete turn, and finally, she cha-cha'd her way back up to him.

They moved into the finale, and she gave him a menacing smile.

"It's not about you," he said again.

"You wouldn't know honest if it stepped on your feet." And with that, she stomped quick and hard on Joe's feet, first the left one, then the right one. She left him howling on the floor, then cha-cha'd her way out of the studio without looking back.

The minute she was out the door, she kicked off her shoes and dumped them in the trash can next to the sidewalk. Good bye to those instruments of torture. She'd bought them only at Max's urging. Well, those days were gone, so the shoes could go, too.

Barefoot, she made it to her car before the studio door opened. Peg came running out as Stephanie was putting her car in reverse.

"What are you doing?" Peg shouted into Stephanie's closed window.

"I'm pulling out of the parking lot," she shouted back, then stopped and rolled down her window.

"Do you know that Joe's left foot might be broken?"

What about my heart? "He'll be fine. And if you want to know what's going on, ask your boyfriend. Ask him where Joe works."

"Steph—"

"Ask Joe why he didn't tell me. Ask him why he lied when he had every chance to be honest and truthful. I'd like to know the answer to that one." She moved the car an inch then stopped. "Please move out of the way so I don't break your foot, too."

Peg moved without saying another word. Stephanie paused to look at her in the rearview mirror before merging onto Scottsdale Road. She was still rooted to the spot, her arms crossed against her chest, her head shaking back and forth.

All she wanted was to get home, and for once she was happy to call the house she lived in just that. Home. But for how much longer would it be that? Once the divorce papers were filed, the For Sale sign would go up. In a way, the sale symbolized the fact that everything she thought about her life had been utterly false, and needed to go. Including Joe. Except Patrick.

For Sale. Time to let go. She would find something smaller and bank the rest of the money.

The garage door rolled up without hesitation, and Stephanie pulled her car in next to the Olé. She looked at the truck fondly, realizing that she would miss that wreck of a vehicle. That's probably why Marta's brother hung on to it.

Her doorbell rang the second she took off her dance skirt and pulled her sweatpants back on.

For once she looked before she opened the door. Mariana stood on her porch beaming, with an equally happy and very handsome young man by her side.

"Stephanie. This is Manuel. He's come to retrieve his truck."

Stephanie extended her hand to Marta's baby brother. In all the conversations they'd had, Marta never mentioned once how drop-dead gorgeous he was. And articulate.

"Stephanie. I cannot thank you enough for getting my family and Mariana together. Words cannot express my gratitude. We are getting married next week. At the courthouse. I will have my true love and, soon, a wonderful baby."

Although Stephanie considered Manny's speech slightly over the top, Mariana beamed. Oh, true love. A small part of her almost wished for another crisis, another revenge plot, or a nice blackmail—anything other than being smacked in the face with someone else's true love.

She sighed as she smiled faintly at them both and pushed herself to turn her small smile into a bigger one. Love worked for some people. Everyone she knew had fallen in love with someone and had been loved back—Peg, Jorge, her father and mother, Joe had loved Lisa. Bob Burnwater had loved Gloria once upon a time, and maybe still, and Mary Sterling had fallen in love not once, but twice. Maybe there was something wrong with her. Maybe she was simply unlovable.

"Come on in. Let me get you the keys." She walked back into the kitchen and turned her bag upside down. The keys to the Olé slid out along with Mary Sterling's envelope, fifty cents in change, and a coupon for fat-free powdered milk.

She handed Manuel the keys. "I'm going to miss this truck. Sort of. You know, it needs a new battery."

Manuel nodded. "I have jumper cables. May I get a charge off your Lexus? If that is too much to ask, I can pull Mariana's car up in your driveway."

"No, that's fine. Go ahead."

"He's always prepared," Mariana said, a tad officiously. "Just like your boyfriend."

Stephanie knew that Mariana had said it to be nice, to show her that she no longer held any suspicions regarding Manuel and her, but a knee-jerk reply slipped out of her mouth anyway. "He's not my boyfriend. He's not really even my friend anymore."

"Really? He looked so in love with you."

"I'll open up the garage door for you," Stephanie said, looking at Manuel. She handed him the keys to her Lexus. "If you need any help, knock."

Mariana stayed behind when Manuel walked outside. She looked at Stephanie with hesitation. "I wanted to apologize."

"It's okay. Love does strange—"

"No. I meant about calling you a fake blond. I am sorry. I knew it was not true when I said it. You have no dark line on the top of your head."

"That's okay."

"And if you want to clean houses, that's your business. But I really think you should go to college and make something of yourself."

"Uh, thanks so much for that. So when is the big date?"

"A week from today. Manny has to start his research soon, and of course"—she patted her abdomen—"there's the baby."

Stephanie smiled and nodded. "Did you say research?"

Mariana made a face. "Marta never told you? Manuel is doing his postdoc in Latin American history. I have my master's."

"Of course, she told me. I just forgot. Sorry."

The look on Mariana's face told her she wasn't buying it. "Marta thinks Manuel should work a real job," she said to Stephanie. "She doesn't consider graduate studies anything worthwhile. So they fight."

"I didn't know that. My impression is that they all love Manny ... uh, Manuel." Oh god, brothers and sisters. Marta was going to hear it from her as soon as she was capable of being miffed with anyone other than Joe. But right now, she'd had enough of emotions to last her a lifetime.

Chapter Seventeen

"Stephanie, open up."

"Aw, sweet Jesus, what now?" Stephanie struggled to stand from the god-awful beanbag chair. That was the first thing she was going to get rid of after she sold this house and moved. It was real chairs from here on in, possibly recliners.

She'd just extricated the lovebird Del Valles from her house and was settling down for a long overdue woe-is-me session when the doorbell went off and she heard someone yell through the door. Through the peephole she saw Peg and opened the door.

Her friend breezed past her and into the family room where she plopped down on the couch. Typical Peg. She was still in her black-and-emerald rumba costume, and the skirt puffed around her when she sat. She reminded Stephanie of a kid at her first dance party. It was something she quickly decided to keep to herself.

"At least now you finally look before you open the door," Peg said.

Stephanie stared at her silently and eased herself into the chair opposite the couch.

"I want to talk to you," Peg said.

"I didn't think you were here to keep quiet," Stephanie said. One look at the pinch of pain on Peg's face regarding her flaccid attempt at sarcasm, and Stephanie ceased immediately. "Are you still mad at me?" she asked.

"Hell, no." Peg shook her head for effect. "After I calmed down, I realized you were only trying to protect me. It's funny when you think about it. You know, mistaking Jorge's sisters for his girlfriends. It just took me a while to appreciate the humor, that's all. And when I finally told Jorge—"

"He knows I was cleaning his condo?"

"Yeah. I kept it a secret for over a week. Then it just slipped out. Sorry."

"It's okay." At least Peg had tried to keep quiet, and Stephanie knew she'd eventually spill the beans, anyway. Peg couldn't help herself.

"Anyway, when I told Jorge that you mistook the pictures of his sisters for girlfriends, he thought it was great that you thought he was hot enough to have that many. And his sisters thought it was hysterical."

"His sisters know, too?"

"Yeah. Sorry."

"Is that what you came to tell me?"

"No. I wanted to know if you were okay. You made quite the exit. I'm not sure Ms. Rita will ever speak to you again."

"For that I am truly sorry. Did I really break Joe's foot?"

"No. Jorge checked it out. It's okay. Both feet are just bruised. But that's not what I wanted to tell you, either. Oh, and by the way, he deserves it." Peg took a breath. "What I wanted to tell you is that I just found out this morning that Joe works for the IRS. Jorge let it slip, and then he told me Joe had asked him weeks ago not to tell me."

"You're kidding. That shithead."

Peg nodded in agreement. "I would have told you if I'd known. That's what I was trying to tell you earlier today, before the competition started." "Thanks."

Peg hesitated for a second, then she asked, "Are you okay?"

"I'm pissed as hell, and I don't want to let go of that feeling, because then I'll be left with feeling hurt. And then

I'll start crying, and I'm done with crying about men for a lifetime. I hope his mom's okay, though."

"His mom?"

"Yeah. It turned out that Joe's mom was another client."

"You're kidding."

"No. I just found out the day before yesterday that she was Joe's mom, which is how I figured all this other stuff out. You gave Jorge Marta's number when he was looking for a cleaning lady, right?"

"Right. Marta is my go-to gal."

"And, you didn't tell her that Jorge was your boyfriend."

"Well, no. I didn't know if he was back then or not. We'd just started dating."

Stephanie nodded in understanding. "I think your Jorge gave Mary, Joe's mom, Marta's number. She called him to get a cleaning lady, because Joe probably mentioned to his mother that Jorge had just hired someone. But she never mentioned that to Marta, and Marta never asked, because Marta never asks a lot of questions. And that's how I got both jobs, through Marta." She sighed and shook her head slowly. "Anyway, Joe's mom liked me just for me."

"Of course, she did. We all do, and FYI, she's inflicting more pain on little Joey than you did with those heels. When I left, she was smacking him on the head with her purse and yelling, I told you not to work for the IRS, you stupid ass. Oh, and Jorge said he can tutor Patrick anytime, seeing that you probably wouldn't want Joe to anymore."

"No shit."

Peg started laughing. "No shit, you don't want to see the Schmidt."

"Ha-ha. That's a good one." Leave it to Peg to make her start laughing.

She couldn't help herself. In a Jersey-Italian accent, she said, "I'ma going to have a fit, if I have to see da Schmidt."

Peg burst out laughing. "God, I missed you."

Stephanie wiped at her eye. "I missed you too. And I am so sorry."

"I know." Peg nodded in agreement.

"We said really nasty things to each other."

"And yet, here we are." Peg smiled at Stephanie and then asked, "Did you—do you have feelings for Joe?" Peg asked her.

"If I did, I don't now." She shook her head back and forth slowly, realizing that she was getting quite good at lying to everyone, even to herself.

"It's just one more thing to get over, and I'm getting pretty good at getting over things. So I'll get over this, too. You can count on it."

Stephanie stopped talking long enough to shake her head back and forth. "I don't get why Joe felt he needed to lie about working for the IRS. And he just kept it up. There's got to be more to it than my not reporting a few measly cash payments for cleaning houses. Maybe he's embarrassed he works for the IRS. I mean, his mother gives him trouble about it all the time."

Peg's eyes widened. She leaned forward and snapped her fingers three inches from Stephanie's nose. "Wake up! No shit there's more. Joe didn't tell you because he thought you were married, remember? Remember when you were wearing your diamonds to dance lessons as a dude deflector?"

It had been so long since that escapade, and there'd been so many others that followed so quickly. And she still hadn't sold those stupid rings. And then it hit her. "It's Max."

"Exactly. That's why he couldn't tell you when he met you, and even after that, he didn't know whether you were involved or not. Look, I'm not supposed to know any of this, and neither is Jorge. And we don't know the details, but it came out when Jorge was examining Joe's foot. His mother is furious with him. And so is your father."

"Dad's not mad at me for stepping on Joe's feet?"

"Heck no. And I would say it was more like stomping, not stepping."

"Did you find out anything else?"

"All I know is they suspect that Max isn't reporting all of his income. I'm not even supposed to know that, but I thought I'd tell you anyway. Oh, I think your cousin is involved, too, but that's just what I think. And after I told Jorge all about Christie, he thinks so too. I mean, she is the office manager."

What an idiot she'd been. "Of course. Christie does the books. How could I be so stupid not to figure all of this out?" And she knew her answer to that one. Since the minute she'd found out who Joe really was at Mary's house, she'd been focusing on emotions and revenge, not motive. There had to be a lesson in there someplace.

She remembered what Patrick told her about Christie taking minivacations to the Caribbean every few months. And all this time she thought it was just about spa-cations. "Oh, god. It makes total sense."

Stephanie stood and paced the family room. "Peg, I have to help Christie."

Peg shook her head. "Now I know you've gone bonkers. What do you owe that aging brat? Nothing. She had an affair with your husband. In your own bed, for cripes sake."

"You don't understand."

"No foolin'. I've never understood why everyone cuts her so much slack."

"Max is cheating on Christie. With Gloria Burnwater."

"Whoa."

"And if she's involved like you think, and I think you're right, she could go to jail for that womanizing, cheating jerk. What I owe her is the truth. Only I promised Max, whom I'm blackmailing by the way, that I wouldn't tell if he—"

"So you finally found a way to get Patrick's tuition out of him?

"Yep."

"Oh, Steph, you're amazing."

"Thank you," Stephanie smiled weakly again. "But keeping my promise to Max isn't worth Christie being arrested. My aunt would never recover. That changes the game."

"She's more than likely in cahoots with him up to her eyeballs."

"Only because she thinks Max is in love with her. If she provided information, the feds might go easier on her. She needs a lawyer fast."

"She also needs her head examined," Peg said.

"I bet she gets a lawyer first." Stephanie smiled sarcastically, then looked away. "Just so you know, I'm not speaking to Joe. Ever again. But can you … can you talk to him about Christie?"

"If you want me to. But only because you want me to."

"And maybe I can get Dad to talk to Aunt Gigi, and she can talk to Christie."

"That's not going to work. Your aunt is the queen of denial when it comes to her daughter. I hate to say it, but if you're duty bound to save her unworthy ass, I think she's going to have to hear it from you."

They were silent for a moment, the two of them looking as though they'd crossed the finish line of an emotional triathlon.

"He didn't trust me," Stephanie said quietly.

"Steph, he thought you were married."

"He didn't trust that I wasn't somehow involved in Max's schemes, even after he got to know me. Either that, or he didn't trust that I wouldn't go running to Max when I figured it out. Maybe both."

The tears that had been welling up behind her eyes threatened to flood her face. "All that time I was fessing up and telling him the truth about my life, he was lying to me about his. And he kept it up. He's very good at it. But don't worry, I'll get over it."

"Steph—"

But Peg didn't have time to finish her sentence before the ocean of tears that Stephanie had been sitting on since she left Mary Sterling's house two days ago, burst forth.

After the tears, both of them sat in silence, processing what each other had said.

Finally, Stephanie turned to Peg and smiled. "I do have some good news."

"What?"

"I'm divorced."

"That's great, Steph. I'm so happy for you. I have some good news, too."

"What?"

"I'm getting married."

***

Stephanie and her father took the elevator up to the fifth floor of the Desert Vista Granite Ridge Assisted Living Center. The name of the facility made her think of joking around with Joe and Patrick the evening they were making fun of the ridiculous names given to places in and around Scottsdale.

Joe. He'd tried to call her numerous times over the past three days, in addition to flooding her with texts. She'd blocked his number. After that, he'd sent her flowers with an apology letter she'd read the first sentence of and then made herself tear it up. Just to make sure she would never read it, she'd put the torn pieces through a shredder. After that, she'd burned them. No one was ever going to hurt her again.

She and her father were dressed better than their usual day-to-day attire. No sweatpants for her and no khaki shorts for her father. She had on a pair of linen pants and a cream-colored silk blouse, with a nice pair of earrings. Silver hoops, no diamonds.

Her father had a collared shirt on and a clean, pressed pair of pants, even though they were khakis as well. They both knew, without ever discussing it, that Aunt Gigi and Christie tended to listen more to people who were dressed in what they considered appropriate attire. There were many things they knew and didn't discuss about their family. They didn't need to anymore.

"Steph." Her father turned to her in the elevator. "The way I got Gigi and Christie to agree to see you is, well, I told them that you wanted to apologize in person to Christie for calling her a ... what you said."

"Lying, duplicitous, bi—"

"Yeah, that."

"So they think I'm coming to say I'm sorry? Great. Just great."

"Honey, you want to tell me how else I was going to do this? You think if I told Gigi that you suspected her daughter was involved in tax fraud, that she'd be willing to let you talk to her?"

"No."

"Okay, then. Cut me some slack here."

"You're right Dad. I'm sorry. This is just really, really hard. There's a part of me that would love to see Christie fry along with Max, but honestly, I don't think I could live with myself if I didn't try to get through to her at least once."

"You always were better than them. If it matters at all, I'm proud of you."

Yes, it mattered. It mattered more than she could ever tell him. "Thanks. You know, I have a lot of ground to make up before *I'm* proud of me."

The elevator door opened at the fifth floor. As the two of them started to get out, her father turned and gave her one more piece of advice. "Just in case I can't get your aunt out of her room as we planned, and you have to talk to both of them, do not, repeat do not call your aunt's facility *assisted living*. She only refers to this place as an *active-senior retirement center*. Our whole scheme's blown if either of us says assisted living. She'll bring out the claws and attack you with her walker."

Stephanie followed her father, because she had no idea what number her aunt's room was. She'd never been to see her. Aunt Gigi had moved out of Monticello seemingly overnight, and Max had moved right in. After that, she hadn't wanted to see her aunt or her cousin.

"Hey," he said, as he stopped in front of room 513. "I'm thinking. Maybe it would be better if you waited downstairs and gave me about five minutes to get Gigi out of her room, I mean efficiency apartment. She's sensitive about that too.

"I'll take her to the dining room to get an ice cream. She likes ice cream, especially if you tell her she's never looked slimmer. That way you don't have to tolerate the smug look on your aunt's face when she thinks you've come to apologize, and you can talk to Christie in private."

"Okay." She pivoted on the spot and made herself walk instead of breaking out in a run to the elevator as she wanted to. Right now, if she could have sprinted all the way back to the parking lot, she would have.

She gave her father six minutes instead of five, then peeked through the door of the dining room to check. There was her father with her aunt, who had aged significantly since the last time she'd seen her. It made her sad, looking at Aunt Gigi, and thinking about her mother.

She took the elevator back up and knocked gently on number five hundred thirteen, then opened the door. Christie sat on the couch, her brown hair streaked with blond, her face iced with a thick layer of foundation. She turned to Stephanie with a gloating look of expectation.

"So you've finally come to apologize," Christie said.

"Yes. Those words were beneath me. And you."

Christie's chin jerked up and jutted out in smug satisfaction. Stephanie didn't react. It was pathetic, really. The two of them never stood a chance. They had been unwittingly pitted against one another from birth in an extension of the sibling rivalry between her mother and her aunt. A rivalry that had perpetually simmered under the surface. Two sisters who were lifetime frenemies.

"There's something else I came to tell you."

"What?" Christie perked up.

She sat down on the small loveseat across from the chair that made up the entirety of Aunt Gigi's sitting space. This room, with the bed at one end and a mini-fridge at the other, was the stark opposite of the house her aunt had lived in most of her adult life.

"Christie, the IRS has been investigating Max. I think, but I don't know for sure, that they've been building a pretty strong case against him for tax evasion."

She watched Christie's chin go down and the smugness dissipate as though seconds ago it had never been there. She took it as a good sign that her cousin was listening.

"If you are involved in any way, you're going to get nailed. Christie, Max isn't worth going to jail for."

"He loves me."

Stephanie closed her eyes and shook her head. "Max loves himself. That's all he's capable of."

"He picked me over you."

She pressed her lips together and told herself that after this she no longer owed her aunt, or Christie, a minute of her life. After this, she would be her own person, set her own values, and make decisions based on her thoughts and beliefs.

She spoke gently. "Yes, he did. He picked you over me, and now I'm picking you over him, too."

"You just want more money."

"Is that what Max told you?"

"He said you want the house, the cars, the stocks, the IRAs, and three times more in alimony than you're already getting."

"Is that why you've been helping him?"

"You can't have it all."

She had hoped it wouldn't come to this. Silently, she reached into her purse and pulled out two of the pictures she'd downloaded off Joe's camera. They were the ones taken by the garage, not the ones Joe had snapped from the outside, looking in. Clipped to the pictures was Joe's office number at the IRS, which she'd gotten from Peg, who'd gotten it from Jorge. "Think about it. You might want to call this guy. He can get you in touch with the right people."

She stood and gave Christie a look that was somewhere between a grimace and a faint smile. She wasn't gloating, and it wasn't wise to express one molecule of the pity toward her cousin she surprisingly felt flooding her emotions.

"I hate you," Christie said to her as she stood and walked toward the door.

What else could her cousin have ever felt? "I know. And I'm sorry."

Sorry for all of it, but mostly for the way they'd been raised. They'd never stood a chance.

Chapter Eighteen

How had it gotten to be May already? But here they were, and there was no going back to April. The house was sold, and Stephanie was packing the last of their things. Somehow, the IRS had not seized the house as asset forfeiture when they'd come after Max, and boy, did they come after Max. That happened on the Wednesday after she spoke to Christie, and Christie had a long talk with the IRS.

She strongly suspected that her cousin had something to do with the fact that the house wasn't seized, because everything else was, and Max's name was on the title, along with hers. Perhaps someday she would know the answer, but right now she had a feeling that Christie wanted to stay as far away from her as she wanted to stay from Christie.

Aunt Gigi had put Monticello up for sale to pay for Christie's lawyer. It had sold within a week. She had no idea where Christie or Max were living, but she could bet it wasn't at the same address.

As for Patrick's college fund, that money had vaporized before her eyes. With Max's assets frozen, it would be years before anything, if ever, materialized. She had half the money from the Scottsdale house, which sold almost as quickly as her aunt's. They would be fine.

The other half of the proceeds from the sale of the house, Max's half, had gone directly to his lawyer. In fact, Max's half of the sale had gone out in a printed check addressed specifically to his lawyer. She guessed that the lawyer figured out, quicker than she ever had, what Max was all about.

A few weeks after the IRS had made their move, Bob Burnwater had made his. He'd broken up his practice with Max, and, soon after that, Stephanie had learned Bob was living in an apartment and he and Gloria were getting divorced. This had been told to her in the produce aisle of Bashas' grocery store by three different mothers on three different occasions, all of whom had children who attended Patrick's old private school. One of them was sporting breasts of such epic proportions that Stephanie tried not to look for fear of laughing. Oh, Maxie, you busy boy.

After it was certain that Stephanie would not be implicated in any of Max's money mischief, Stephanie's father produced a savings account with her name on it. He had been adding to it since the day she'd been born, and it had been his intention to give it to her when she'd gotten married, but he'd held on to it, given the fact that she'd married Max. He'd figured she'd need it later. The balance didn't amount to much by today's standards, but the savings account coupled with the sale of her diamonds, gave her enough to begin without reaching into the money from the sale of the house.

Mary Sterling's hunch had been correct. She had found the perfect career for Stephanie with the information she stuck in her bag that fateful day, when a picture really had been worth a thousand words. After Stephanie finished the required coursework this summer, she would apply to the occupational therapy program at ASU. It was her goal to specialize in geriatrics.

As for Mary and her father, Stephanie's own hunch about them had been as spot on as Mary's had been about her. Mary and her dad had hit if off like whip cream on chocolate pudding. She couldn't recall a time when she'd heard her father laugh so much, not even when her mother had been alive. That was something she didn't want to ponder in depth. Some things were best left alone. At least that's what she told herself about much of life lately.

A knock on her bedroom door told her it was time to get going. "Mom, you don't want to be late," Patrick said. "You're in the wedding, and I'm an usher. Aunt Peg is counting on us not to mess this up."

She turned to see her handsome son in his shirt and tie. It was already too hot in Phoenix for the jacket, but she knew he would put it on the moment they drove into the church parking lot. Patrick always did the right thing, eventually.

"You look great, kiddo," she said.

Patrick smiled. "You don't look bad yourself. For a maid of honor."

"Matron."

"Whatever." He looked down at his feet then back at her. "I have to ask you something."

"Shoot. Just don't kill me."

"Not funny."

"Well, we do live in Arizona."

"Really not funny, Mom."

"Okay. Just a stupid attempt at a joke." She realized that this is what she had to look forward to. They were quickly entering the my-mother-is-not-only-embarrassing-she's-also-not-too-smart stage. Oh, she would miss him, but she was sure they'd meet back up on the other end of this stage, when he turned twenty-four or so. If she was lucky.

"Look, are you going to … is it going to hurt your feelings if I talk to Joe at the wedding? If it will, I won't."

How sweet. "Of course not. Hey, he's the best man, I'm the matron of honor, and I agreed to walk down the aisle with Joe in a mature fashion." She looked at her son in earnest. "I know you like him, and I'm sure he'll want to know that you got an A in algebra."

"Um, he already knows that."

"Oh. Did Peg tell him?"

"No. I told Grandpa, and Grandpa told Mary, and Mary told Joe, and Joe emailed me, and—"

"You and Joe have been emailing each other?"

"A little bit."

She shook her head and closed her eyes.

"You know, he feels really bad."

"What, now you're his pimp?"

"What's a pimp?"

"Never mind. Have you and Joe been talking about me?"

"No. Jorge and Peg told me. And so did Mary when I was at Grandpa's."

"Well, he should feel bad. You need to be honest with people always, Patrick."

Patrick stood against the frame looking uncomfortable. "Are you going to be able to get through this?"

Note to self: do not turn your son into your therapist no matter how bad your life gets. He's your kid. You are the parent.

"If I could get through the rehearsal dinner, I can get through the wedding," she answered him. "Besides, you let me worry about me."

Stephanie straightened her back and adjusted her bridesmaid dress, pulling it down from around her waist. In the last few months she'd somehow put on ten pounds. People told her she looked wonderful. Every night she told herself she'd get back to doing sit-ups, but she never quite got around to them. Instead, she read books, ate chocolate, and fell asleep. It was heaven.

She pointed an authoritative finger at her son. "Here's the deal, Patrick. The parent worries about the child, until the parent turns eighty or so. Then, and only then, does the child get to start worrying about the parent. Got it?"

"Got it."

"I love you, P."

Patrick suddenly looked like he was trying to spit stones. "I lo ... what you said, Mom."

***

Large bouquets of pink and yellow roses mixed with off-white gardenias were placed on either side of the altar and along the aisles. Their scent filled St. Anthony's small Spanish-style chapel with a sweet aroma that had the guests commenting happily.

"May I now present to you, Dr. Jorge Vasquez, and Ms. Mary Margaret O'Malley-Vasquez."

The priest didn't yell, but the words seemed to carry effortlessly. The entire chapel burst into applause.

Couples usually waited for months to get married in St. Anthony's chapel. But somehow between Peg's mom, her brothers, all of whom were graduates of St. Anthony's High School, and both Joe and Jorge's generous donation to the scholarship fund and the newly paved faculty parking lot, an open Friday evening magically appeared.

Applause and whistles from Peg's brothers drowned out the priest's last few words, and the wedding party began to file out. The celebration was moving to a reception room at the Arizona Biltmore, three miles east of St. Anthony's.

Although Stephanie had been escorted up the aisle by Joe, and was now walking with him back down, she refused to look his way, answer his salutations, or even acknowledge his presence in any way, shape, or form. He may be walking next to her, but he was dead as a doornail as far as she was concerned.

She drove to the Biltmore by herself, as Patrick had piled into the car with his grandfather and Mary. She had no idea how Joe got to the reception, and she really didn't care. Maybe he had a date and drove with her. She didn't care, as long as he didn't die along the way and ruin Peg's one and only wedding.

The reception room brimmed with multicolored flowers of blue, red, pink, and yellow. They blended well with Stephanie's lapis blue dress and the creamy pink color of Peg's gown. Bouquets flooded the small ballroom and spilled onto the individual tables, making the entire room look elegant, comfortable, and very Southwest.

Stephanie worked her way around to the many people she knew until the last half-minute, when it was time for her to sit at the head table with Peg, Jorge, and Joe.

Joe nodded politely as she took her seat next to him, but said nothing. After trying several times to start a conversation with her at St. Anthony's, Stephanie figured he'd given up and realized she wasn't about to say a word to him. Not a single word, although she wondered throughout the dinner where his date might be—if he had one. She didn't care.

There were three women at one table up front who kept staring at him, trying to catch his attention. They most certainly weren't any of Jorge's sisters.

She watched out of the corner of her eye to see if he was focusing on one of the women, but all he did was look at his mother and her father, who were shamelessly flirting away with one another three tables away, sitting with Marta and her sister. Maybe he was as uncomfortable with that situation as she was. Something told her she'd better get used to it, because the duo of Bud Weblowski and Mary Sterling weren't going away any time soon.

The latecomers began to arrive. Ms. Rita made her way through the door with a tall, limber-looking man. Stephanie could swear he was Fred Astaire's much younger brother. She was tempted to turn to Joe and say something about it, but she didn't. She swore she'd never talk to that man again, and god dammit, she was going to be good to her word if she had to remind herself all night.

After toasts by Stephanie and Joe, separately, and many more toasts by Peg's brothers (until Peg's mother yanked them off the stage), the music began. Jorge and Peg took to the dance floor under the approving gaze of Ms. Rita. At least someone got an A in dance class.

She watched the two of them glide across the floor in each other's arms. They were so happy together. Peg leaned down when Jorge whispered something to her, and they both laughed uproariously, never missing a step.

Stephanie wrapped a defensive mitt around her heart and leaned over to Joe, the man she was never going to talk to again, right after this. "How are your feet?"

"They've recovered. The left one took a little longer than the right one."

She wasn't going to apologize. She promised herself she'd never do that, if she ever talked to him again, and she was never going to talk to him again, anyway, right after this. "I'm sorry."

"The consensus is that I deserved it."

"Did you know I'm moving soon?"

Joe turned to face her. His mouth was pencil straight. "Where to?"

"I sold the house and found an apartment to rent within walking distance of Patrick's school. He's looking at magnet high schools for the following year. The academic one is in Central Phoenix, so we might be moving there if he gets in."

He made no comment.

"It has a living room, a small kitchen, two bedrooms, and two baths, which is very important. It's enough to get us through the next year." She waited for him to say something, but when that didn't happen, she started in again. "Anyway, we should be out of the house and settled into the apartment well before school starts back up."

Joe nodded.

Stephanie watched as Peg and Jorge danced by, waving to them both.

"If your date's not here—" Stephanie began.

"I didn't bring anyone."

"Maybe you'd consider dancing with me." She finished her sentence, tapping her toes to the music.

They started out slow, but quickly got back into their usual dance mode.

"Ouch. Joe, you stepped on my foot."

"Sorry, but it shouldn't have been there. It's one-two-three, change. One-two-"

"You stepped on me again." Stephanie stopped, pulled her foot out of her shoe and rubbed it against her leg. "You're killing me here. Is this revenge?"

"No. We can do this." Joe looked down at their feet. "Work with me. We'll count together, okay?"

Stephanie put her foot back in her shoe and nodded, looking up into Joe's Sinatra blue eyes.

"We'll count out to three, then start," Joe said.

"One-two-three," they said in unison before they began the next steps.

Ms. Rita motored past them with her Fred Astaire clone. "Your steps are too big," she hissed. "Quit counting out loud, don't look down, and don't ever tell anyone you took classes from me, or I'll never get another student. Please." She winked, then smiled at Stephanie, and danced away.

"Well, I feel good," Joe said, as he watched Ms. Rita dance away. He looked down at Stephanie and smiled.

It was the smile she used to think about when she couldn't sleep. She wanted to grab his neck and kiss it furiously while breathing in the way he smelled one more time. Instead, she started crying.

"You know Rita," Joe said. "She didn't mean to hurt your feelings. She's joking half the time, anyway."

What an idiot. She wasn't crying about Rita. She leaned into him, took a whiff, and brushed her cheek against his suit. Then she cried some more.

Joe maneuvered the two of them over to the side of the reception room, and through a door to the hallway. By this time her tears had become sobs.

He bent down and peered into her face, then grabbed a handkerchief from the pocket of his tux and dabbed at the tears gushing down her cheeks. "You okay?"

"You think I cry for fun? No, I am not okay." She took the handkerchief from him and sniffed. Why did everything have to smell like him?

"Blow your nose," he said.

"I'm not talking to you, much less doing what you want."

"You're talking to me right now." He looked away and sighed.

"I don't have to blow my nose just because you tell me to."

"I'm sorry. I should have told you I worked for the IRS. I should have trusted you. I was in this quasi-legal corner because of your husband's case. I wanted to tell you the second I knew you weren't involved, and I should have."

"Yes, you should have." She blew loud and hard, then wadded the handkerchief up in her hands. "I tried not to like you, but obviously it didn't work. And I hate you for that."

Joe pulled her close and patted her back as her sobs increased.

After a few minutes, she stopped, sniffed, and smiled weakly. "Would you like to be my date for the wedding?"

"Not if you hate me."

"But I hate you because I like you."

"Well, I think I love you, and I don't hate you for that. So there." He bent down, kissed her gently on the lips, and then pulled away to look at her.

She dabbed her eyes with the already wet handkerchief. "You know what the problem is? You're the right guy at the wrong time. Why couldn't you wait until I was completely independent, and then show up? I would have dated you then, even if you do work for the IRS."

"Here. Give me that." He took the wet, wadded-up handkerchief from her and gave her a clean one out of his back pocket.

"I can't believe you had two of these."

"I come prepared," he said, as he handed it to her.

Just then their parents danced past the open door in each other's arms.

"What are we going to do about that?" she asked him. "Are you okay with them?"

"Let me put it this way, if you and I ever get together, we won't have to worry about which side of the family we spend Thanksgiving and Christmas with."

Stephanie laughed so loud that several people turned to look toward the hallway door.

"After Lisa died, I never thought I'd fall in love again. Then you showed up, and thinking about you was all I did."

Stephanie nodded in agreement. "It really gets in the way of getting anything done, doesn't it?"

He wrapped his arms around her, pulled her to a stand, and then kissed the top of her head. The two of them stood there silently for a few minutes, holding each other, swaying to the music from the reception room.

"Stephanie, I know you're scared. But I'm not going to ask you to do or be anything you don't want to. Deal?"

"Deal." She nodded nervously.

"It's like dancing. Eventually, if we try, we'll get it right."

She looked at him in all earnestness. "Can we just date for a while? You know, like normal people?"

"We are normal people."

"Not really. You work for the IRS, and I'm a complete nutjob. Just ask anyone here." She took her shoes off. God, she hated heels. They danced out in the corridor alone by themselves while inside the party continued. Stephanie heard Jorge singing something in Spanish that everyone wildly applauded when he finished.

A few minutes later, she could tell by the sound of Peg's brothers yelling and laughing that they'd managed to pull off some gag. Hopefully, it hadn't embarrassed Peg, and it hadn't involved Patrick. But between Mary and her father, and Peg and Jorge, she knew things wouldn't get too out of hand. It felt good to know there were people in the world who looked out for him. She breathed a sigh of relief.

"Happy?" he whispered into her ear and then buried his nose in her hair.

"Absolutely. Hey," she said as she looked up at him. "Do you think if your mother really does marry my father she'll give me her recipes?"

Joe laughed. "That only happens if you marry me and there's a ring on your finger to prove it."

"Not a big ring, okay? Just a band. A plain, simple, gold band. No diamonds. And maybe someday, but not right now."

"I'm not going anywhere."

"Joe, neither am I."

The End

About Lynne E. Marino

Lynne E. Marino was born and grew up in St. Louis, Missouri, where she was always the first in line for the Bookmobile. She has spent most of her adult life in the Southwest, still reading away. Now she writes her own stories. She currently resides in Tucson, Arizona.

Social Media

Website:
https://lynnemarinoauthor.wordpress.com/2018/01/02/lynne-marino-author/

Facebook: https://www.facebook.com/lynnemarinoauthor/

Acknowledgements

A big thank you to my critique partners Kerry Morgan, Jill Hannah Anderson, Ann Markow, Judy Grout, and Sylvia Wright. I would also like to thank my dance instructors, Danielle Beaulieu and Elizabeth Keyes who are in no way as strict as the dance instructor in this novel. You all inspire me.

www.ingramcontent.com/pod-product-compliance
Lightning Source LLC
Chambersburg PA
CBHW051523050726
47503CB00014B/1118